DA MICK

To Kenny:
Thanks so much for you and your mom's support! Have the happiest of Birthday's. Always remember, there are no accidents.

Billy O

BILLY O'CONNOR

ALSO BY BILLY O'CONNOR

Confessions of a Bronx Bookie

Da Mick
Published by Poets Press
20050 N Cave Creek Rd
Phoenix, AZ 85024

This book is a work of fiction. Names, characters, locations and events are either a product of the author's imagination, fictitious or used fictitiously. Any resemblance to any event, locale or person, living or dead, is purely coincidental.

Editors: Jennifer Beale and Laura Beth Walker
Cover Design: Adam Scott Waddle and Tom Brock
Cover Photograph: © Tom Brock
Back Cover: Tom Brock
Cover Layout: Kästle Olson
Interior Design and Formatting: Deborah J Ledford

BronxBilly.com website by Jessie Kilker

Funding and editing assistance through Rivista productions,
CEO Tom Brock

Issued in print and electronic forms
Trade Paperback ISBN: 978-1-9853261-6-3
Electronic Book ASIN: B07CF7XB4V

Manufactured in the United States of America

AUTHOR BIO

BILLY O'CONNOR was born in County Cork Ireland and grew up in the Bronx. After Vietnam, Billy was an illegal bookie, a Teamster, a pub owner, and a New York City firefighter.

More importantly, he was also an alcoholic.

The tragedy of 9/11, and the loss of 343 of his brother firefighters brought with it an epiphany. Billy sobered up and attended the University of Florida. At the age of 62, he earned his journalism degree and began to write.

O'Connor has written two highly praised weekly columns, two screenplays and numerous political pieces. His second book, *Da Mick*, follows his award-winning first novel, *Confessions of a Bronx Bookie*.

For the past seven years, Billy's acerbic wit as a stand-up comic has also entertained audiences throughout, California, Florida, New York, Nevada, and Arizona. He has shared the stage with great comedic talents such as Jim Florentine, Orny Adams, Todd Berry, Jon Lovitz, Paul Virzi, Julian McCullough and Finesse Mitchell.

His inspirational story reminds us that with the proper attitude, life begins at 60.

Billy can be reached at Oconnor.williamp@gmail.com or at BronxBilly.com.

"Every saint has a past, and every sinner has a future."

– Oscar Wilde

PROLOGUE

THE FIRST RULE of writing is: write what you know. Consequently, every work of fiction has more than a small piece of the author in it. The stories and anecdotes in this novel are based on my twenty years with the FDNY. As a first responder at 9/11, my tale is about men I knew, acts that I have personally witnessed, or stories that I was told by my brother firefighters.

In no way do I attempt to glorify or hyperbolize my former profession. There's no need. As you'll find out, firefighters are ordinary men who are anything but ordinary. Their dedication to service speaks for itself.

ONE

HE REACHED FOR her warm body but touched only a cold, empty space. For those first conscious, motionless moments, he thought about the softness of her mouth, the tenderness of her touch, her smile. Eileen had been one of a kind, so bright, so lovely to look at, so particularly exceptional that she would have driven both the celibate and the happily married man to question their vows.

Shattering the morning silence, a shrill sound pried open his eyes. He dwelled on his late wife's memory a little too long before punching the clock and scanning the room.

Where da hell am I? Why'd I set the alarm?

His head crashed back to the pillow.

No use, Mick. I can't remember shit, might as well crawl to the bathroom and chase the bats out of my dome.

He rolled over a bulge the size of a swollen fire hose.

What da hell?

He tossed the covers and couldn't quite process what he was seeing . . . a prosthetic leg?

What da fuck?

His trembling hands shot below his waist before the cold fear faded.

Thank Christ, still two.

His heart kept racing.

How in the hell did I end up with a prosthetic leg in my bed? Think, Mick, for Chrissakes, think.

Three fingers of his right hand scratched a slow, confused circle on his chest. Ridges creased his forehead.

Surely to God if I had slept with a one-legged woman, I'd have noticed. It's not like a mole or a stutter.

His eyes rescanned the room for a clue, still nothing.

How drunk must this chick have been to come home with a guy who doesn't even remember her? Then another thought. *Good God, what in Christ's name have I done now? What kind of a monster must I have been that this chick would actually hop out of here rather than risk waking me up to get back her fucken leg?*

His hands splayed the floor and slowly peeked under the bed, nothing.

The bathroom?

He stumbled in and splashed water on his face, still no sign of her. He trudged to the phone to dial the front desk.

"Good morning. This is Mr. Mick Mullan. Could you check on what room I'm in, and send up a pot of coffee with two Bloody Marys and some scrambled eggs?"

He glanced at the three crumbled up singles next to the phone.

Wonder how much I spent?

His idle hand lifted the wallet beside the lamp. The billfold was empty, but at least his credit cards were intact.

"Rye toast will be fine, thanks. Wait. Wait. Don't hang up. What day is it . . . Friday? Thanks."

He cradled the phone.

When did this load start, Monday? Christ, that's four missing days. Think, Mick, think. I remember those two English gals, the booze, and the Percocets. Am I still in Melbourne? Where's Shifty?

The stationery pad next to the phone read Dorchester Hotel, Cairns. He was still in Australia, albeit a different city but still in country anyway.

How da hell did I get to Cairns, and how in da fuck did this leg get in my bed?

A SMIDGEN LESS than six-foot, blond, and blue-eyed, Mick Mullan had passed his third decade but seldom passed a saloon. When done properly alcoholism doesn't leave much time for anything else, which wasn't Mullan's problem. He was both a successful bar owner and a Bronx firefighter.

He had yearned to see Australia all his life. The Irish songs of the Clancy Brothers, the Dubliners, and the Wolfe Tones, which he had sung in Bronx and Yonkers bars, had whistled through his ears for years. And now that he was finally here, like a schmuck, he'd gone and lost four days.

But Mick's tale begins in New York, not Australia, and starts the year that he first met Erin. That was the year that Mick Mullan won and lost everything.

TWO

DRIZZLE FELL THROUGH the streetlamps, and Northern Boulevard's streets had the odor of a damp cave. The air outside Mick's nightclub was wet, cold, and gray. From the doorway's shelter, he watched the strong, winter wind bend and tilt the branches of the huge oak tree draping the corner hardware store.

He blew warm air on the hand holding his scotch while the other lifted a joint. The smoke flooded his lungs as his eyes scrutinized the sky.

"Just our luck, we've got a full moon tonight." His gaze shifted to Buffalo. "That means the whack jobs will be out in strength."

The 320-pound gentle giant, who every club owner longed for, worked his entrance, and no one was better at it. Buffalo had a face as round as a pie plate and fists as big as buckets, but a born diplomat, he seldom used them. Mick was one of the few who knew first-hand that beneath Buffalo's silk veneer lay cold hard steel. When he bought his club, Buffalo had come with the deal, and for that Mick counted his blessings.

The two stood under a 50-foot, neon sign that glittered, Nobody's. He hadn't even thought about what to call his new place until he was open a week. When packs of salesmen blew in every five minutes preventing him from getting any work done,

Mullan had an epiphany. He'd call his place Nobody's. That way when the parasites asked, "Who's the owner?" Mick would deadpan, "Like the sign says, nobody."

He passed the reefer to his bouncer.

"I hate fucken New Year's Eve, a real amateur night. It gives us professional drunks a bad name. You better be on the ball tonight. Be extra tough at the gate. If there's trouble, we gotta stop it there. We're gonna be packed, and you know a brawl will empty the place." Mick took a sip from his scotch and had an afterthought. "Remember, no hats. I don't know what the hell it is with guys who wear hats, but they always start trouble."

Buffalo was athletic and deceptively fast. Blessed with broad powerful shoulders, a dancer's dexterity, and cantaloupes for calves, he was a Bronx legend. Above a veined nose, swollen jowls and cheeks, his bloodshot eyes brightened.

"I can always take their $15 and then toss them later . . . with or without their hats."

Mick's eyes found his and gave a half smile. "Always thinking, ya cocksucka."

NOBODY'S FAÇADE WAS white brick and beige clap-oard topped by a flat green parapet. The Christmas lights stapled around the window frames and the bright-green awning made it stand out from the other dreary, dull, commercial buildings along the block. Mick grabbed the handle of one of its huge, hinged, wooden doors.

"Toss that roach, and let's go inside, might as well face the night." As an afterthought, he spun and said, "You wanna go bar hopping after we close?"

Buffalo took the last pull off the joint. His cheeks had the hue of ripe plums. An alcoholic benevolence shone through his veined eyes. He swirled his drink, drained what was left, and crunched the ice between his molars. His smile widened. "You buying or crying?"

"I said after we close, ya fuck. You're drinking on my dime now. I gotta pay for your booze after work too? And not for nothing, but if you gotta guzzle my scotch, why do you have to drink the Johnny Walker Black? Drink the cheap shit."

Buffalo swallowed the ice, flicked the roach, and smirked. "I have refined taste."

"Refined taste my ass. Ya fat prick, you'd drink kerosene out of a urinal. You never even heard of Johnny Black until you started working for me." Mick brightened. "We can't stay out too late, though. I'm working a day shift at the firehouse. Maybe when we leave the after-hour's joint, I'll just go straight to work and grab an hour or two in the bunkroom. Of course, I'll have to stop at home to walk and feed Oliver. Poor little tyrant is getting old."

"You and I ain't?"

As they entered his nightclub, Mick shouted over his shoulder, "I'm gonna shoot down the cellar and bring up another $500 in fives and singles. Take it easy on that scotch, will ya? I need you sharp tonight."

When Mick disappeared, Buffalo skipped three quick steps to the bar, told the bartender to fill his empty glass with Johnny Black and grinned like a gorilla that had just seen his reflection in the mirror.

WHEN MICK RESURFACED, Nobody's was half-full. At the door, the Big Man was grabbing cover money and checking driver's licenses. An hour later the 60-foot pine bar was four-deep with revelers, and three bartenders furiously pumped drinks.

Balloons, hats, and horns saturated the smoky room. A 30-foot stage in the corner held a hot rhythm and blues band, which played to a packed dance floor. Above the band, a rectangular-white banner read, HAPPY NEW YEAR 2001.

Mullan sat close to the back-door sipping scotch on the rocks and scanning the crowd. Despite Jamie Rowinski's small talk, Mick was preoccupied, eyes rotating, never fastening, like a driver in moving traffic. Always on red alert, his eyes still hadn't settled on his childhood buddy when he said, "Don't get me wrong. I'm thrilled when guys from the old neighborhood make good. I love success stories, Jamie. Fair play to ya."

A young 36, Jamie wore his blond hair cropped like a drill sergeant and shared both Buffalo's broad shoulders and enormous capacity for alcohol.

"Thanks, man. Lord knows I worked hard enough for it. I'm just sorry my mom's not around to see it. She always told me that just because I grew up poor didn't mean I had to stay poor. But enough about me, I ain't seen you in days. What's going on with my favorite, misguided socialist?"

Mick faked a broad smile.

"No small talk tonight, huh, cocksucka, right to the ball breaking? Because I'm a Democrat, I'm a socialist? Come on, your Party has gone nuts. Republicans wanted to crucify Clinton over a stinking blowjob?"

He shot Jamie a look of disgust.

"Christian fundamentalists have hijacked the Republican Party, impeachment over a fucken blowjob? They're laughing at us all over Europe."

Jamie's eyes turned to ice.

"It's not just the sex. He used the Oval Office like a whorehouse and lied to the American people. And what the hell have you got against Christians? You're Catholic. I vote Republican because Democrats want to tax and regulate Wall Street too much. Besides, I'm against abortion."

"You're against abortion for the poor, you mean." White lines threaded the corners of Mick's eyes. "If Paris Hilton wants an abortion, she gets on a plane to Europe and gets one." Mick's voice had a knife in it. "And how does the party of smaller government get to decide whether a woman has a baby or not, or whether two people in love can get married? There's nothing Christian about you fuckers. Christian my ass, next Republicans will be selling indulgences."

"C'mon, Mick, Democrats are even bigger hypocrites."

Mick didn't respond, instead he eyeballed a redhead who approached the bar wearing a short, white cotton dress that barely covered her thighs. His eyes harpooned her ass as he spoke.

"We Democrats aren't nearly as bad as your so-called party of Christian family values." His eyelids dropped to his drink. "Screw you phonies; the only time your God ever answered my prayers was when I prayed for Eileen's death. That was when the Big Bwana came across. He answered my prayers then all right and took His own sweet, bloody time about it too while she suffered in immeasurable pain, God of benevolence, my ass."

Mick stopped his rant long enough for his gaze to fasten again on the redhead's tiny frame. Her legs looked so fine in beige six-inch pumps that he thought it a pity she only had two. He hinged his chin toward the stunner.

"Hey, you got one vote. I got one vote. Enough of this shit, man, concentrate on that. We're all here for a short run, and I aim to go out with a smile on my face."

The doll called for a drink from one of Mick's bartenders, Dewey.

Mick had grown to depend on his well-toned, irreverent buddy and not only to pour drinks. Dewey fought fires with Mick at 60-Truck and was also from the old neighborhood, which gave him liberty to make cracks his other bartenders couldn't.

While Dewey polished the space in front of the redhead with a bar rag, she flashed a flirtatious smile. "Can I get," she purred . . . "a slow comfortable screw?"

Dewey's smile broadened to a grin. His hazel eyes sparkled

so bright they glared. He leaned forward and whispered, "Too busy right now for anything slow or comfortable. How about a quick blowjob in the kitchen?"

The redhead laughed. Mick did too and turned to Jamie.

"Some old lines never lose their zing."

But the smile fled his face. A fight had broken out in the middle of the bar. His legs turned to springs with Jamie close at his heels. After four swift strides, he left his feet and hurled all his weight into the calves of a bulky man wearing a Giant's hat. Both flattened to the floor in a resounding thud.

Two other men started trading punches. Jamie spun and clasped his enormous arms around one. A bouncer grabbed the other. The brawl spread. Two more went at it. Buffalo shoved two guys toward the exit. Innocent customers shuffled to safety. All three bartenders hurdled the bar, and finally another bouncer joined the fray before the staff finally got it under control.

When Mick regained his feet, two of his bouncers had a grip on the wide man he had tackled. He glared at Mick, cheeks raging with color, white nostrils flaring like an angry bull. Struggling a few more seconds before calculating his odds, he finally submitted. The guys with him swore their innocence.

Jaw clenched, face drawn and taut, Mick's head went back and forth from one face to another. The glittering points of light in his blue eyes dulled a moment. His neck bulged before barking, "I don't want to hear it. I don't give a shit. Innocent or not, every one of you pricks are out of here. I ain't running a gymnasium. If you got a problem in my joint, you tell a bouncer. Once you start throwing punches, you've disrespected both me and my club."

Mick waved his index finger. "You three are done for the evening. Keep bitching and you'll be barred for life." He pointed to the guy wearing the Giant's hat. "Take Spartacus here with you, and hit the bricks."

In mild protest, one agitator toppled a stool, but the other two meekly pocketed their change before parading into the cold night air. Mick returned to the end of the bar.

"You handled that as smoothly as possible," Jamie said.

"Thanks for bear-hugging that guy, man. I appreciate the back up, but no matter how quickly I get it under control, it still costs me fucken money. Even if the rest of the night goes fine, all anyone will be talking about is the brawl. Ya can't win with a fight. A lot of women are already heading for the door."

Mick downed his drink and pointed to his empty glass in disgust.

"This would be a nice place to open a bar, Dewey. You working or not? Give me another belt, and take the air out of Jamie's glass too."

"Sorry, Mick, I didn't see that coming." Dewey reached for the top-shelf scotch. "The jerk you tackled just flat out cold-cocked the guy in the brown leather jacket. It happened too quickly to stop it. Shit, I was only a few feet away."

"What started the fight?"

"What do ya think, Mick?" He turned his palms up. "Alcohol."

Mick knew that Dewey always had his back, wouldn't take a penny from a dead man's eyes, and wouldn't have to. Dewey could buy and sell Mick financially and had little in the way of bad habits. Mick couldn't say the same about himself. He had a well-deserved reputation for get rich quick schemes, gambling, and bad investments. When Mick went bankrupt a few years back, Dewey's mischievous eyes had sparkled.

"At your age isn't it gratifying to be all the way back to even, hooknose?"

"You'll never have to worry about that, ya cheap prick," Mick said. "You still got your Communion money. But when you're right, you're right. If I bought a fucken cemetery, people would stop dying."

He ran a loose ship at Nobody's, and let his staff do their

jobs in their own way. But when the chips were down, they delivered, aces up. Mick would trust his life to Dewey and had. All of Mick's workers were characters, but all of them, firefighters or not . . . had character as well.

He spoke over the rim of his rocks glass.

"What the fuck, we ain't serving holy water. It's all part of the game. Let's pray we didn't scare that redhead out of here. Man, was she hot. I bet there are at least a dozen guys in here trying to swallow enough liquid courage to chat her up, including me."

"Oh, yeah, like you need the booze," Jamie said. "You've always been lucky with women, you bastard. They know that you're gonna be fun because of that ridiculous laugh."

Jamie stirred his martini with a tooth-picked olive. When he lifted it to his mouth, he tossed the used toothpick into the ashtray and pointed a thumb to his chest.

"With me, women sense security and boredom. That's not what I want to project, but that's me . . . I'd love to find a woman with a great sense of humor to compensate for my shortcomings, one who thinks like me. I'm getting up there. I want to start a family. I gotta find a gal with a brain though. I can't do stupid."

"Oh, you can do stupid. We all do stupid. We just can't do it very long." He lifted his drink. "And what's with the pity train? Shortcomings? C'mon man. You've got the world by the balls. What did Tom Wolfe call you cocksuckers on Wall Street, Masters of the Universe? Level headed, nothing wrong with that. I wish I were more like you." As he swallowed his scotch, his eyes watered and brightened at the same time. Mullan's body responded to alcohol the way plants did water.

"And now, you're looking to get married? Knock yourself out. I just don't think I could put myself through that again." His neck tightened as his voice rose. "And another thing, being good with women doesn't mean a damn thing, if she ain't the right woman."

Although he drank too much and slept around even more, the unalterable reality that governed every moment of Mick Mullan's waking life was simple. The love of his life was dead, and no one would ever replace her. His features softened.

"There was and always will be only one Eileen. God, I miss her every day."

"I know how much you miss her, man." Jamie said. "But you gotta move on. You gotta stop with this shit. It's killing ya. You gotta forget her."

"Forget her?" Mick's jaw hardened. "I don't want to forget one little thing, or one little moment that I was blessed to share with her. If her memory has to hurt, so be it. That's the breaks." Mick slid slowly from his stool. "After we close the joint, I'm going bar hopping with Buffalo. Ya wanna come out for a few pops? Just for a few hours though, I gotta work a 24-hour shift in the firehouse tomorrow."

Cracking the cap off a Budweiser, Dewey overheard him. He snatched $20 bill from a short, bald man's hand, poked the register's keys, slipped the change back on the bar, and then fixed his eyes on Mick.

"If you're gonna go to Tom Thumbs with the Big Man, you better hope the firehouse is slow tomorrow, Mick. The only thing that Buffalo punishes worse than whiskey are the morons who try to keep up with him."

"You're telling Mick about Buffalo? Buffalo doesn't know how to bounce a little. It'll turn into an all-nighter." Jamie tilted his head. "You think he doesn't know that?"

Yeah, Mick knew that all right. But what he didn't know was that although the night would be long, the following day would be longer still . . . and almost his last.

THREE

UNDER THE LAST stop of Jerome Avenue's rumbling elevator train, Tom Thumbs was the perfect location for an after-hours club. Because of the train's clanging and banging, no residential buildings were nearby, and the joint was perfectly sandwiched between Moshulu Golf Course and the entrance to Woodlawn Cemetery. Golfers don't play at night, and the dead never complain. The noise made by crowds coming and going well past sunrise was never a problem.

A cute blonde tended bar. She was short, savvy, and as fast and fluid behind the bar as any man. Her name was Geri Ann, but everyone just called her "Toots."

Although a lot of cops were regulars, a blackjack game flowed full tilt in the back room, and the bony, bald man who shuffled cards out of the shoe was another popular Bronx bartender named Pete Watson. Every bar owner, bartender, and waitress in the North Bronx hung out there, and Pete and Toots knew them all. The patrons were the kind of hardcore drinkers one would expect to find in a watering hole only open weekends after three a.m.

Mick ordered a Heineken from Toots and headed straight for the back room. He bought $500 worth of chips and sat at "third base." He bet the $10 minimum and started to count the cards that Watson shuffled across the felt. After twenty minutes of boredom and monotony, the picture card count was low and the percentages high, so he began to bet $100 a hand. A few minutes later, Pete reshuffled. Mick did a quick count, realized that he was up $500 and cashed in.

Might as well have a few pops at the bar with Toots.

No clocks were in Tom Thumbs by design, so one squirt led to another, and when Mick's phone read 7:30, Buffalo was deep in conversation with an overweight brunette. Mick could have pressed him to leave, but the big man was catnip for full-sized women.

Once Buffalo entered a room, he sucked the air out of it. Not only because of his prodigious physique, but because of his hunger for life. His appetite required alcohol and laughter in massive amounts, and what he didn't gobble up splattered over an eager entourage of hangers on and bottom feeders who figured 50 percent of Buffalo was better than 100 percent of anybody else.

Two decades older than Mick and indispensable, his blotchy-faced buddy had the remarkable gift of making everyone around him feel more alive. Mick knew that there was no sense in arguing. Buffalo wasn't going anywhere until he closed the deal, so half stewed, he told Buffalo he was splitting for the firehouse.

WHEN HE LEFT Tom Thumbs, dense clouds hid the sunrise. Above the gray elevator-train platform, the dawn barely broke through the bitter, bleak sky. Gusts of wind whipped piles of leaves along tires of the parked cars lining both sides of Jerome Avenue. When the low moan from the south side of the tracks turned his ear, he looked up to see the train's single eye pick out the last station before coming to a screeching halt.

Well familiar with the racket, Mick continued to trudge his tired legs down the long block toward his Honda. He turned the ignition, heard the engine bark to life, and headed for his apartment to walk and feed his constant companion, his Jack Russell terrier, Oliver.

His chore complete, he grabbed a container of coffee at the local bakery, and darted down the Major Deegan. Once off the highway, cheerless streets littered with beer cans and broken glass sped past his car windows.

At each corner, mountains of large, black-plastic garbage bags awaited pick-up.

A hand-drawn cardboard sign advertising "very cold cuts" rushed past his windshield. Mick always grinned when passing that delicatessen window. In the South Bronx, English was a second language, and the next store he passed usually spurred another smirk. A painted cardboard sign promised Chinese food "to go or take out," but Mick wasn't smiling today.

He hadn't slept a wink, and his mouth felt like the Turkish Army had marched through it barefoot. He prayed for a slow New Year's Day, so he could grab some shuteye; but the odds weren't good. In poor neighborhoods, winter shifts were usually busy.

In half abandoned buildings without heat, desperate tenants plugged illegal space heaters into overloaded sockets. Mick figured that he would be hopping all day and night, yet he was praying for a miracle, a couple of hours sleep in one of New York's busiest stations.

He parked in front of a windowless, blue Buick with milk crates for wheels. Imagining some poor bastard trying to start it, he said to himself.

It'd probably just groan.

He hiked the firehouse stairs to change into his uniform. Rummaging through the back corner of his locker, he spotted the amber glass vial that he was looking for and began a familiar ritual. With a rolled up five-dollar bill, he snorted two lines of white powder off a mirror, rose to his feet, closed each nostril with his finger, sniffed, blinked, and widened his eyes. Then he licked his finger, wiped the residue off the mirror, and rubbed it on his gums. Well fortified, he went downstairs to guzzle caffeine.

Over a dozen firefighters sat around the two, long, thickly laminated dining tables that dominated the dayroom. Mick said a casual good morning, reached over Pete, grabbed a bagel, and began slathering it with a quarter inch of cream cheese. Sipping his coffee, he was just about to sink his teeth in when three air-horn blasts shattered the silence.

The house-watchman's voice thundered over the intercom, "Everybody goes, truck, engine, and chief. Everybody goes. Get out. Get out. Get out." This refrain was followed by three more deafening air-horn blasts.

The two giant apparatus doors lifted, and the Brothers scrambled to don their turnout gear and boots. They leapt on the two weathered, red rigs and their sirens roared into the sleepy streets of the South Bronx. While tearing through the second intersection, the dispatcher reported possible children trapped.

In the distance, thick, ugly smoke painted the cloudy morning sky with black ink. The Brothers rounded the corner minutes later to flames roaring from a ground floor window.

"We have a 10-75, working fire," The Lieutenant transmitted to the dispatcher.

"Ten-four, Ladder 60," dispatcher 330 responded. "Alert all incoming units. We have a 10-75 in the Borough of the Bronx."

The officer replaced the voice piece, rotated his body, and hammered his fist on the Plexiglas separating him from his crew.

"We've got a job."

Mick slipped his arms through the straps of his Self Contained Breathing Apparatus, fastened the harness to his waist, and although he wasn't green enough to turn his air on, last minute nerves drove three fingers to routinely tap his air valve.

The ritual completed, he clutched his tools, sprang from the truck, and raced toward the involved apartment. A roaring tongue of flame from the first-floor window painted the second-floor's brick edifice a coal black. Despite the danger, Mick's eyes sparked a gleam of recognition, and a slight grin teased his face.

My parents lived in an apartment just like this. I can find my way around in there blindfolded.

By the time a line was stretched and the front door forced, he calculated any possible survivors would be lost. He also knew that he couldn't start a search through the window next to the flames. If he broke that glass, the fire would chase the oxygen and fill that void as well cutting off any chance he had of escape.

If he leapt directly through the fire window and hugged the wall, the fire would seek its least resistance, which would be the open window above him. Remembering the dispatcher's warning that children might be trapped, Mick had an edge and decided to use it. He vaulted the sill and vanished into the flames.

"Holy shit, Lieu. Get water on that fire fast," Pete screamed, his face reflecting red from the blaze. "Mick just jumped through the fire window."

The Engine Lieutenant cursed from the cab. "Jesus Christ, even a fucken Probie knows better than to start a search without a charged line in place." He yelled at his crew. "Stretch a hose. Get me water, fast."

Snaking hose lengths toward the building's entrance, Engine 17 flew into action. The chauffeur hooked the Pumper up to the nearest hydrant while his boss screamed, "Come on. Come on. Move it. We have a fireman in trouble."

NOT AT DEATH'S door, but hardly safe, Mick had rolled below the window, and the flames hungering for oxygen were licking, and bellowing skyward above him. A blast of radiant heat burnt his ears, driving his chin even farther to the floorboards. He had gambled that his turnout coat would protect him from the intense heat, but he had forgotten to pull down the earflaps lining his helmet.

Crawl left or right? A closet or a bathroom where a child might hide should be opposite the window.

The flashlight attached to his helmet speared a dull beam through the thick smoke. Mick slithered slowly and sightlessly to his right, his gloved hand tapping the wall for guidance. He crawled away from the fire-breathing window, past the closed window, and into the heart of the darkness.

His heart was pounding so hard in his chest that he thought his ribs would break. His eyes were pressed shut, maybe because they were useless, or maybe, like the metaphorical atheist in a foxhole, he was praying. One thing was certain, he had better make a quick search and get the hell out of there fast. If radiant heat blew out that second window, he was screwed.

Raining down on him, plaster, shards, and burning hot embers forced his nose ever closer to the floor. Whatever little visibility he had was at ground level, yet through the blinding smoke, he could still see the hungry orange rivulets of fire glowing along the ceiling's length.

Groping slowly, he could almost taste the acrid, black gas though his mask. When the wall made a left angle, he gained a splinter of hope and quickened his pace.

I've got to glue the pattern of the wood planks to my brain. If I get disoriented, at least I'll know if I'm crawling parallel or perpendicular to that window.

The flashlight lit a foggy soft glow into the shadows. His left hand dragged the wooden hook and the heavy, steel Halligan tool, right hand splaying the floor for balance, elbows inching ahead of his knees, the little muscles in his hands and thighs twitching and dripping sweat.

His stomach seemed to be jarred loose, his heart rattling inside his ribs. It was so quiet that he thought his ears had failed him, until he listened to the measured sounds of his own breathing, but then out of the tomb like silence came a voice almost like an open-mouthed statue laughing at his recklessness. No sound, just a voice taunting him how he had overplayed his hand.

He inched farther and farther, absolutely convinced he was about to die until he stumbled upon a miracle. The tip of his nose almost smacked into a small, metal wheel. A wooden leg seemed to climb from it. Was he lucky enough to have found a crib?

Shimmying the wood, his gloved hand probed between the slats, and felt a bump in the bedding. He stood, held his breath, and lifted his face-piece.

Holy shit an infant.

He let his tools slide to the floor, unclipped his turnout coat, and wrapped the baby inside. Any minute now, the engine company would burst through the front door, open their hose, and turn the living room into white-hot punishing steam. The silent voice from the darkness reminded him that if the blistering heat blew out that second window, both he and the child would be memories.

It's gonna be a crapshoot to get out of here. Stay calm, Mick.

The atmosphere had become so toxic that his eyes were useless, but he knew that if he cut vertically across the horizontal pattern of the wood floor, he should find his way out.

Waving like a blind man, Mick could hear the crackling and slavering of the hungry flames devouring what was left of the room's oxygen. With his left forearm cradling the baby, his fingers clutching his tools, he probed the darkness with his right hand and tiptoed gingerly, almost glacially until a shrill alarm shattered the silence. His heart rose to his mouth, a throbbing pulse pounding at his throat.

Shit, only a few minutes of air left. You got this, Mick. Don't panic. Slow your breathing. Drop back to the floor. Tap above your head at window level.

He let his knees collapse, hugged the limp baby tighter to

his chest, and began crawling and tapping, crawling and tapping.

If I don't find this window fast, we're screwed. Is this poor little thing dead already? Should I risk a few precious seconds to stick my mouth over its face?

He kept inching and feeling, scrabbling, and sensing.

Fuck it. Maybe I should just stand, make a run for it, and just pray that I don't trip over the furniture. If that window breaks, I'm dead anyway.

When the wall turned again, he chanced it. He thumped the corner and sprang, his gait morphing into long quick strides. After three of them, his gloved hand struck gold.

Thank God, the windowsill.

Even though the glass was black, soft, and weak, Mick was left-handed and wasn't sure his right hand had the strength to take out the entire pane. With fire still roaring from the adjacent window, he had to bail out fast but couldn't expose the child to more gases.

His right hand weakly swung the steel Halligan-bar, nothing.

I might have to risk placing the baby on the ground.

Summoning strength he didn't know he had, on his second swing the glass burst mercifully into the street. He ignored the pain of his singed ears and frantically pushed and pulled the heavy crowbar like tool, knocking large shards of glass from the corners of the window frame.

A firefighter in the street ran to the hail of broken glass, his six-foot hook gripping the casement, the iron tip yanking again and again until the entire frame blew outwards. As dense smoke poured from the room, the yellow stars and blue circles of a child's wallpaper materialized by the baseboard. He reached under his turnout coat and gently placed its precious contents into his comrade's eager hands.

Garbled voices from the doorway caught his ear. The Truck had forced the door, and the Engine's inch-and-three-quarter canvas line would soon advance down the hallway, its heavy bolt of water ripping and churning into the guts of the fire, crashing, splashing, and carving a path through the thick smoke, pushing the boiling steam out of the living room and into the crisp Bronx morning.

Mick leapt the sill and hit the pavement just in time. He ripped off the face piece of his spent air tank, collapsed onto the concrete, and hurled black phlegm from his mouth. Spread on all fours, the sidewalk a foot from his face, his heaving chest felt like chards of glass had punctured his lungs. He puked the tar-colored poison into a pool of his own spittle.

Minutes later, his chin rose to the sound of the chauffeur's voice.

"Nice grab, Mick. That kid's gonna make it."

His blood raced to Jack's sweet words and a warm ripple, as invigorating and intoxicating as a powerful drug, surged through his veins. The fast charge of adrenalin flew through him like an electric shock, sweeter than any rush he had ever felt from gambling or any sport that he had ever played.

Mick wouldn't have traded the thrill of that rescue, that one single moment, to be the CEO of Goldman Sachs. In that one jubilant instant, he understood why men chose this profession. Even if he never got to feel this thrill again, he would chase this powerful, addictive dragon the rest of his career.

THE BLAZE EXTINGUISHED, the apartment gutted and overhauled, char-faced firemen methodically repacked multiple lengths of lines on the engine hose bed, some sipping water, many hacking and spitting coffee-colored saliva into the gutter. With a cup of water in one hand and a Marlboro Light in the other, Mick sat on a nearby curb, dry heaving and coughing the corruption from his lungs. The Safety Chief approached.

"Didn't you get enough smoke inside that apartment?"

He poured water from the Styrofoam cup over his singed ears, studied the frail man's bent body a moment, and smiled.

"Funny Chief, it seems like the only thing that gets that harsh taste out of my mouth is more smoke."

The Chief's jaw stiffened, his face shining like a red lamp under his white helmet.

"I don't know whether to recommend you for a medal or department charges, Mullan. You should know better than to start a search before a protective line's in place."

"It was instinct, Chief. The dispatcher said kids might be trapped. My parents lived in a building just like this, so I knew the apartment layout. I figured if I stayed low enough and hugged the bedroom wall, I just might make a grab."

"Taking the rescue into consideration, I'll overlook the breach of regulations. That was one hell of a move, but I won't stand for any more insubordination. You're only on the job a few years, Mullan. Learn it first. Then play hero. This is not the first time I've warned you about safety issues. Do it again, and I'll send you down for psychiatric observation."

"Sorry, Chief. I guess I screwed up. Every firefighter has a reverence for life, me more than most." Mick took a long drag on his cigarette before he spoke again. "Thanks for the break. I know I was a bit reckless, but the kid's gonna make it, and that's why I came on the job. If it were your kid . . . well, you know."

"Yeah, I know. I get it," the Chief said. "His parents weren't so lucky. God rest their souls. We found them in the bedroom dead from smoke inhalation."

Mick stood, took one last drag of his butt, flicked it into a pool of water and joined his brothers loading wet, dirty hose back on the engine bed. He had beaten the Grim Reaper temporarily, but death plays hard every day.

FOUR

MICK'S MOM, MONICA, was stocky, solid and stern, with chocolate eyes, warm and lustrous, yet charged with energy at the same time. Monica was a no-nonsense, God-fearing, Irish immigrant who left her family and friends as a teenager to brazen a flight to a new world.

She was a caregiver with a huge heart, a woman who had sacrificed her whole life and would have forfeited every treasure on earth to give Mick an ounce of joy.

Despite her seven decades plus, Monica had come from a family of butchers in the old country and was full sure that she was still able to slaughter and split a cow into shanks and steaks. His mother had left Cork City when it was practically prehistoric, and the ever-changing chameleon of steel and stone that Monica had raised her son in was very different from the Big Apple of today.

When Mick was a child, the Bronx was a simpler place.

He had slept in the back bedroom of a ground floor apartment but spent as little time inside that five-story tenement as possible. Home meant grief and supervision while the streets offered freedom and excitement. Only a few of his buddies played organized sports, but they used a rubber ball in every way imaginable, bouncing that Spaldeen off walls, caroming it off curbs, or belting the air out of it with broomsticks all day and into the night.

There was no Internet.

Instead of writing checks to TV evangelists, his parents actually got out of bed every Sunday and stuffed the scam-artists' collection baskets at church proper. But Mick didn't need some gold-covered, silk-slippered, slick-talking, hypocritical, pulpit-proselytizer to tell him what to believe. He saw his mother as a living saint and knew well what was right or wrong.

MONICA KNELT ALONGSIDE her bed beneath a picture of the Sacred Heart, her gray hair pushed neatly under a black-wool knit beret, ebony rosary beads slipped slowly through her thumb and index finger.

"Although you've tested me more than once Lord, you've yet to give me a trial that I couldn't burden." She stared up at the compassionate image. "I pray today, not for myself, but for my only son who lost his way when he lost his wife. Mickey's all I have left Lord, and before I die, if he would find his way back into your grace, I'd be at great peace."

Lowering her forehead into two calloused, veined hands, her features were striking, not pretty; a chiseled nose, long and bent, and firm determined eyes that glistened with her lilting laugh. Monica blessed herself, stood, threw on her coat and made a last-minute inspection of the kitchen stove. The gas safely off, she tossed an oversized leather bag over her sturdy left shoulder and headed out.

She started to tumble the lock when she paused and reopened the door. A plastic figure of the Virgin Mary nailed to the hallway wall held her holy water. She dipped in four stubby fingers, blessed herself and said another quick prayer.

"Bless us Our Lord."

SHE NAVIGATED THE last step of the building's gray cracked stoop, turned right, and went off to her job as a meat wrapper in the local supermarket, all the while thinking about this coming Sunday. After Mass was when she'd subway out to Queens to see the light of her life, her only son, Mick.

FIVE

NEW YORK CITY is not a national or state capital, but as the capital of finance and culture, it is considered by many to be the capital of the world. In this melting pot of all people and all lands, this complement to entrepreneurship ever evolves. No structure is sacred, neither Yankee Stadium nor Penn Station. Its constant evolution once inspired O'Henry to write, *"New York would be a great place if they ever finished it."*

Within one of seven buildings that comprised the World Trade Center, Jamie Rowinski's firm had an office as big as an airplane hanger. High in the second tower of this city's great tribute to free enterprise, in the heart of 16 acres of the most expensive real estate on the planet, the phones in his cubicle rang furiously. Jamie barked into one of them.

"I'm telling you, Mrs. Corsairs, this can't miss. Sure, that's smart. You have to diversify. If you have all blue chips, you're not maximizing your profit-to-risk ratio."

Mick's best friend, Jamie Rowinski, wore a three-piece tweed suit over a white button-down shirt and a yellow tie with red stripes. Jamie waved to a co-worker passing by, winked, and pointed his index finger to the phone. He shook his extended thumb and pinky up and down rapidly to signal "a live prospect."

"Of course, you don't understand the complexities of your

portfolio. That's why you hired us."

As his co-worker smiled, Jamie grinned like a satyr. He scissored his fingers and thumb like a sock puppet to mimic the elderly widow's babbling.

"Don't worry. I'll take care of it. Believe you me. You've made a smart move hiring our company. Just leave it to us." Jamie slapped the phone back onto the receiver.

"She seems like a live wire," his co-worker said.

He slid his swivel chair from the cubicle and glared out the clear glass wall and watched the orange sun start to sink in the west. Gazing reflectively out at the magnificent skyline of lower Manhattan, his prestigious view was one only a man who had attained a certain level of success could hope to have.

"It's almost too easy," he sighed. "I'll do the best I can for her, but even if she loses, I win."

When he spun around again, the lines around his eyes had hardened.

"But have ya ever wondered what it would be like to make a living doing something that you were really, really proud of, or is that just me?"

His cell phone interrupted him. He looked at the caller I.D. and pressed accept.

"Hey, Mick, my man. What's up?"

"Getting off in two hours, wanna grab a beer?"

"Perfect. I'll pick you up," Jamie said grinning. "Gotta go, busy."

UNLIKE JAMIE'S MODERN office, the ancient firehouse where Mick worked was entrenched in tradition. The dayroom's tattered walls were peppered with plaques and awards won by 60 Truck and 17 Engine. Covering a gray, drab stone floor, three couches, and two easy chairs surrounded two laminated dining tables, which dominated the dayroom.

The paneled walls rose to meet a ceiling that supported two

wood-bladed fans, and four long fluorescent lights, which shone brightly on pictures of proud men in dress-blue uniforms marching in parades or saluting at memorials.

While waiting for Mick to change clothes, Jamie was reading the names off the bottom of a Paddy's Day parade shot. Mick entered the dayroom and dented the photograph with his index finger.

"A lot of those guys are still here, older and grayer, but loaded with wisdom," Mick said.

"You're lucky. I never met a fireman who didn't love his job," Jamie said.

"It's the camaraderie," Mick said. "Every man has a position, and if one guy screws up, the whole plan goes out the window. Watching the team work go down is better than watching a well-executed football play. Only the stakes are higher, and firefighters don't have the luxury of chalkboards and erasers. No shit, man. It's amazing to be a part of."

THEY HAD DECIDED to tip a few in a neighborhood joint a few blocks from where Mick's mother lived. Madden's had the coldest draft beer in the Bronx. The bartender placed two perfect pilsner glasses on coasters in front of them, their heads white and foamy.

"Yeah, no one gives a shit what's said in the firehouse," Mick said. "We're taught in Probie School that personality conflicts can't interfere with the job. It's just common sense. A good fire operation depends on complete co-operation and precise execution. One mistake and people die, firefighters, civilians, maybe both."

"What kid didn't want be a firefighter at one time or another? I get that you love your job," Jamie said. "You should be proud of what you do. I am too, despite what you may think."

"No, of course, you should be proud, man. Look at what

the fuck you've accomplished. You make a boatload of money for your clients as well as yourself, but firefighters are different animals. We don't go too far down a hallway, or put our ass on the line for money, accolades, or even for medals. We do it for the guys next to us. I'd go to hell and back for them just as they would for me. No way I'd abandon a Brother. No matter how bad it gets."

He drained half his glass and placed it back on the damp coaster.

"But what's funny is when we get together off the job, no one talks about heroism or rescues. All we talk about are the laughs. When my career ends, it won't be fires, heroics, or funerals that I'll remember. It'll always be the men, the ball breaking, and the laughs."

SIX

EVERY FIREHOUSE HAS a few treasured wiseasses, but once in a generation, a genuine Picasso comes along, a virtuoso, someone who can take practical jokes to an art form. Mick was lucky enough to share many of his shifts with one supreme shit-stirrer, Joe McLaughlin, whom the men had affectionately christened "Joe Da Mutt."

"Da Mutt" was a twisted laureate who did all he could to earn the nickname and exponentially more again to spread it. He would do anything for a laugh, no matter how irreverent. Everyone in the division had heard stories about Joe Da Mutt, but he wasn't just a live wire. Joe excelled at his job as well.

Mick's first time on the nozzle, his company caught a mattress fire in a city housing project. Mick had been nervous, not about dying, but just like every other rookie before him, he was afraid that he'd let the other men down or make a fool of himself.

Heat and smoke banked down from the ceiling of the three-bedroom apartment. Just as he was taught in Probie School, Mullan knee-inched the floor ready to sweep the water's stream clockwise along the ceiling the second he saw an orange glow. Mick towed the nozzle slowly while sucking air from his Scott-pack in long hard gulps. Probie Mullan didn't know that smoldering mattresses push loads of smoke but produce little fire.

A gloved hand gripped his collar. "This way, the fire's in the back bedroom," Mutt's unmasked, unimpeded voice said.

After Mick squelched the smoldering bedding, Mutt pulled his shoulder.

"You're not done yet. We've got a closet fire in the next bedroom. This might be arson."

The alligator stains on Mutt's battered helmet testified to his experience. Like a World War II aviator's "Fifty-mission crush," a firefighter's beat-up helmet was a source of pride, and Joe's helmet looked as if someone had baked it in a pizza oven.

Mick dragged the hose to the back bedroom and whipped the nozzle clockwise, up and down, then back and forth across the rows and rows of burning clothes and shoes.

Mick felt Mutt's hand again.

"We've got a separate fire in the front bedroom, definitely arson."

Mutt had led Mick to fires in three different rooms and acted like he was buying a newspaper. Probationary firefighter Mick Mullan was in awe of veteran Joe McLaughlin, but the Brothers called him Da Mutt for a reason.

"HEY GUYS, COME out and see my new car."

Tommy was understandably proud. He had just bought a Volkswagen Super Beetle, no small purchase on a firefighter's salary. A couple of guys left the dayroom and went outside to the small, gated parking lot adjoining the firehouse to admire the source of Tommy's pride.

"What a ride. I can't believe the gas mileage. From my house upstate to the firehouse, the gauge hardly moves. I must be getting 35 miles a gallon. It'll pay for itself on what I save commuting."

Everyone who took the trouble to walk the 90 feet congratulated him and went back inside.

Firefighters have the same tragic flaw as many civilians. They never know when to give it a rest. Tommy, a short, slender, almost sinewy man with a cream white face around dark eyes and a tiny black mustache was no exception.

"You know even though the parking lot is fenced in, somebody might break in or steal it. You know how the South Bronx is."

That was true enough and why most firefighters drove "ghetto cars" to work, old bombs that barely stood up to the wear and tear.

"I wonder if the chauffeurs would pull the rigs out, so I can park inside the garage?"

Although a bit unprecedented, the guys understood, and the two chauffeurs involved were willing, but once the Beetle was inside quarters, it became a focal point. Every time Tommy worked, his car was all he talked about. My Beetle did this. My Beetle did that. He never gave it a rest.

Finally, the inevitable, "I'm getting a little fucking tired of hearing about Tommy's car," Kingsley said. Kingsley was a few inches past medium height, a bit overweight, his black skin smooth and unwrinkled like coal-burnt tallow.

"Yeah," Dewey said, followed by a chorus of "me too's."

"I got an idea. He's always boasting about his gas mileage." Kingsley was unanimated as if his mouth were painted on his skin. "Every time he drives to work, let's siphon some gas out of his car. He'll figure something's wrong with it."

"Fuck that," Mutt said. "That's amateur stuff. Instead, we'll add five gallons for a couple of weeks. Once he gets used to the extra mileage, then we'll start siphoning it."

A good practical joke, like a good con, needs the perfect mark. Tommy was the complete opposite of Mutt, tacit, practical, and gullible, so after adding gas for two weeks, Tommy was insufferable.

"What a car, I can't believe it. I'm getting sixty miles a

gallon."

He wore his black hair long, and if it weren't for the solemn thin lips that showed a missing front tooth, his face would have been about as memorable as a grocery bagger's.

"You can't be getting that," Kingsley egged him on.

"I swear to God. I clock it every trip. You guys have to get one of these Beetles. Incredible, I'm saving a fortune."

ONE WEEK LATER, the start of the dayshift found Tommy screaming into the firehouse pay phone. Both shifts bolted from the dayroom to find out what the hell all the commotion was about.

He was banging his palm against the inside wall of the phone booth. His neck veins throbbed, his face flushed, his mouth hung open, and his eyes rolled halfway up into their sockets. He appeared to be having a stroke.

"Don't fucking tell me I couldn't have been getting sixty-miles a gallon. I clocked every trip I fucken made since I bought this car from you two months ago. I'm telling you, something is wrong with this fucking car. I'm only getting twenty-five-miles per gallon. You guys are going to fix it, or you're taking it back."

A few nods sufficed. The "Brothers" had played this game before, and were too experienced to laugh out loud and spoil Mutt's gag. They'd no longer be subjected to Tommy's disgusting display of affluence. Soon, he'd be driving a ghetto heap and parking in the lot like the rest of them. Everyone couldn't wait to tell Mutt's how his gag went down.

MICK AND THE boys were high in Madison Square Garden's blue seats among the Ranger fanatics. All of the firefighters had guzzled a few beers, but "The Big Duff" was out of control, which was hardly rare.

At one time or another, the Duff had been bounced out of every bar in the Bronx. It wasn't by coincidence that the

Brothers had bought him a green T-shirt that read "Instant asshole—just add alcohol." He was powerful and stubborn, and a dangerous combination that all bartenders dread—someone who likes to fight and can. The seats weren't warm yet when he set the table for a brawl.

"Let's go Winnipeg. Let's go Winnipeg."

At Duff's vile epithet, a herd of Ranger fans turned in rage. Mick's face screwed with contempt.

"Come on, Duff, don't start with that shit."

"What, what, what?" He planted his battered mug inches from Mick's face. "I can't root for my team? I've been a Winnipeg fan all my life."

The Duff wouldn't know Winnipeg from Wisconsin.

In his late thirties, Duff was average height, hard, and deceptively strong with a square head that gave the impression a cinder block had landed atop his sloping shoulders. The Brothers affectionately nicknamed him "cement head."

ONE MORNING, DUFF stormed into the firehouse howling.

"That's it. The fucking mailman is dead. That's it."

All conversation stopped. The Brothers' heads turned and wondered what could have wound his clock so tight so early. Stubbornness and relentless determination made him a fine firefighter, but a short fuse made him the perfect dupe.

"I ain't taking this shit no more. I'm going to kick his ass." Duff slammed eight inches of mail down on the laminated surface. Pedophile pamphlets, and magazines skidded across the table, spilling coffee, and knocking donuts and bagels to the floor. "That son of a bitch keeps putting all this homo shit in my mail box. Look at this stuff, all old men and young boys."

Of course, the Brothers sympathized.

"You know what homoeroticism is?" Paul said. "Guys who aren't quite gay but have a tingling deep inside them that they can't come to grips with?"

"Yeah Paul's right," Patty said through tears of laughter. "You could be a sleepwalking salami smuggler."

"Yeah, you might be sending away for this shit without knowing it," Kingsley chimed in grinning. "They call it latent tendencies."

"Fuck you guys. It's that fucking mailman," Duff screamed. "I'm going to kill that cocksucker."

Mick eyed the end of the table where Mutt clutched his stomach in a silent laugh. After Duff went into the kitchen, a corner of Mick's mouth lifted into a grin.

"What did you do to "The Duff," ya prick?"

Mutt could barely talk through his tears.

"The Duff's mailman thinks he's a sexual predator. He lives alone, so I sign him up for all this pedophile shit." His hands held his stomach with suppressed laughter. "I just got my hands on a NAMBLA application. I'm sending away for everything they got. Don't tell him shit."

Now Duff was a fifteen-year veteran, and somebody was breaking his balls. You would think that the last place that he'd come for sympathy would be the firehouse?

SEVEN

IT WAS A clear Sunday afternoon in late January when Mick's mother hiked the steps of the Queens' subway. An effulgent Monica bounced up Northern Boulevard and smiled at the soft, white clouds streaking the sky.

When she reached her son's bar, she slipped onto a stool by the front entrance, ordered a vodka and soda, and, despite the bartender's reluctance, insisted that Butch let her pay for her drink. Butch was 28, short but powerful, and wore his brown hair long. A Fu Manchu mustache and long sideburns helped camouflage a coarse complexion.

When Mick surfaced from his office downstairs, he gave his mom a warm salute and hustled to the stool next to her. He attended to Monica's every whim like the dutiful son he was, but whenever they talked at length, the conversation inevitably turned to Monica's youth, her relationship with Big Tom, or even worse, religion.

I DON'T UNDERSTAND, Mom. How could you marry an alcoholic?"

"Shush, Mick, that's an awful thing to say. Your father wasn't an alcoholic. He never missed a day's work, a heavy drinker, yes, but not an alcoholic. Sure, you didn't know him at all. When he was younger, if he had a pint of Guinness a week, it was a lot. I blame this country and the big money he started to make working construction."

Monica avoided Mick's eyes and spoke dreamily of the world of her past.

"He was a fine, handsome man, your father. He could do anything, fix anything, and was one of the finest athletes in the whole of Muenster County. It was this bloody country that ruined him."

Mick would nod agreement, but in reality, he didn't believe a word of it. The old man had a genetic disorder, plain and simple, and his disease had progressed rapidly. His mom would call him a good, solid man, up to, and including, the day that E.M.S. workers dragged him from his easy chair to St. Vincent's Hospital for the last time where he would die of cirrhosis.

Given his own shortcomings, Mick was hardly one to judge. If his old man were cursed with a chemical brain deficiency leading to alcoholism, how in the hell would he have known?

Big Tom had come from a simpler, far-away place, in a harder era, where each day was a struggle to survive and support his family, a place with little room for pharmaceuticals or psychiatrists. It's a long way from modern science that Mick's parents were born.

If a shrink had recommended therapy for Big Tom, he would either have laughed aloud, or would have broken the doctor's jaw. Chemical deficiency? He'd have put no credence in that bullshit. With Tom, life was simple and empirical. A day's pay for a day's work, food on the table was a victory, and enough for a few shots and beers a miracle.

The magical "Old Country" his parents reminisced about was 3,000 miles away. Mick knew little of it and wondered how a place could be so perfect. Years later, he'd realize that his parent's memories were fantasies, which all of us blessed to live long enough take refuge in. Adolescence sketches a future filled with hope, unlimited achievement, and limitless vision, fonder recollections than the broken dreams and disappointments that come with age.

His parents' stories of their youth in the Emerald Isle seemed whimsical, supernatural, a place filled with saints, superstition, and banshees.

"Don't ever cross two knives on the table," Tom would scream and turn his head quickly from death's omen. "Uncross them, quick, quick," he'd cower, and Monica was worse. She would tell young Mick stories about banshees.

"I'm not telling you a word of a lie now, Mickey. Wasn't your aunt Nora on her deathbed in Riverdale from the breast cancer when I heard the banshee's wail as plain as I hear your voice. It would have made your marrow quiver. And the stench, sweet Jesus, it would fill your nostrils with the breath of the grave."

Ever on guard for the devil's attacks on her son's idle mind, Monica was an uncanonized saint who upheld a stern religious environment and did all she could to raise Mick in an orthodox Catholic home.

"Here, bless yourself," she would say.

By the door, a small plastic image of the Blessed Virgin held holy water. After his mother sprinkled four fingers of it through the air, Mick would dutifully make the familiar sign of the cross. This ritual was repeated whenever he left the house.

Despite his mother's diligence, religious conviction dissipated with puberty. For young Mick, sexual experimentation made faith a massive inconvenience. Once he began exploring his own body, he decided Catholicism was a philosophy for the young, who did as they were told, and the old who needed faith to prepare for the inevitable.

As a child though, he believed. Mick carefully fingered the decades of his rosary praying to be someday in the presence of the resurrection and the light. But merciful God didn't live in

Mick's apartment, Big Tom did—and didn't vaguely resemble the perfect fathers portrayed on pleasant TV sitcoms.

As Tom's disease progressed, instead of receiving God's benevolence, both Mick and his mother suffered steady escalating doses of his father's temper. His voice grew proportionately louder with the amount of whiskey consumed.

"What's this shit?"

"It's your supper," Monica said meekly eyeing her shoes. Constant verbal abuse had left her with a nervous tic, blinking like a prisoner of war sending a coded message.

"Dinner? You call this shit dinner? How many times must I tell you that I don't like bread? How many Goddamn times?" Mick watched his father fling the plate out the window shattering it in the courtyard.

In Big Tom's day, alcoholism wasn't a widespread alarming issue in Ireland. Self-medication was a way of life, the disease barely acknowledged. Most alcoholics were simply labeled heavy drinkers. If A.A. existed in the Old Country, it was truly anonymous.

The insanity and instability weren't lost on Mick. He was afraid even to say the word alcoholic aloud. Awash in the scrum of adolescent turbulence, some mornings he'd awake to a wet bed, a pattern in his teenage years, which became a source of constant suppressed humiliation and shame.

"Never bring dishonor upon the house, and never, ever mention anything you witness at home to anyone," Monica said.

And Mick never did.

He never spoke about what happened at home to anyone except his best pal, Eddie. He and Eddie had always shared everything until that terrible day that young Mick first began to question his faith.

TOWARD EVENING, MONICA was saying goodbye to the bartender when Mick plopped back onto the stool beside her. "It was great spending some time with you, Mom. Now ya can go home and complain on the phone to me all week about your head splitting open because of those few lousy high balls."

Monica jabbed him with her elbow and laughed.

"Two. Two was all I had. My head is fine. It's your bloody head that needs watching."

"You had four, but who's counting," Mick teased.

She shoved his shoulder lightly with her arm, a huge grin across her glowing face.

"Why must you be so bloody stubborn? There's no sense in spending money on a cab. Why won't you let me take the train? Sure, I'll be alright."

"Ya will in the pig's ass. I had Butch call a cab." After spending time with her, he'd sometimes subconsciously lapse into a bit of a brogue. He rarely drank liquor around his mom, so he lifted his club soda, and clinked her glass before saying, "No way you're walking home from a subway station in the Bronx at night. I'd run you across the bridge myself, but we're starting to get busy. I wish you'd call me when you want to come out. I'd drive in and get you."

He placed his seltzer back on the bar and smirked.

"And no wonder I'm stubborn. I'm your son. I come by it genetically. You'll take the cab and like it."

"Stubborn, am I? You better watch yourself," Monica said only half-joking, "You're not too big to get a bloody fine clout of my pocketbook."

"And that thing is big enough to do some serious damage," Mick teased. "It looks like a footlocker. Maybe I should let you take the train. God help the mugger who stumbles upon you."

Monica's eyes crinkled. She reached for her vodka, took a small sip, placed it back on the bar, and turned deadly serious.

"Come here, when was the last time that you were at Mass?"

"Aw, Mom, don't start with that stuff again. Will ya?"

"You're only hurting yourself, Mick. If you don't have God in your life, you have nothing."

"I know, Mom. I'll start going back to church again. I swear."

Mick glanced at the clock above the bar and wondered why the conversation always had to drift back to this. She came from a land of fairies and leprechauns and had been brainwashed by the Church since childhood. Of course, Monica believed that a man was born of a virgin, crucified, and then resurrected.

Interrupting their conversation, Butch walked the length of the bar and tilted his head toward the front door.

"Hey boss, the cab's out front."

Mick kissed his mother, placed her safely in the cab, and promised to stop by for dinner Wednesday night.

THE SUN DISAPPEARED in soft pastels, and the bar soon filled. Jamie and Mick sipped pints on their usual stools.

"Hey, I saw that new BMW you're driving. Nice, ya Polish prick. You've become the merry little capitalist," Mick said.

"If you weren't such a Donkey lush, I'd let you take it for a spin."

"Easy, I've told you a dozen times. When you're Irish, drinking's an ethnic responsibility."

Jamie was the kind of guy who probably shined the soles of his shoes. Always impeccably dressed, he wore a charcoal suit over a blue silk-shirt, and dark tie with red flowers on it. Three years older than Mick, his flawless manners compensated for a sullen mouth, thick nose, and thin chin. Jamie was what women referred to charitably as not bad looking.

"What about the Peruvian marching powder?" He looked hard. "How much of that shit are you shoveling up your nose? Be careful, Mick. You're on dangerous ground. I've seen guys screw up their whole careers over cocaine. It's all over Wall Street."

"Not my drug of choice, coke just helps me drink more."

"Yeah, I've heard that shit before. Do you have a package with you now?" Jamie asked.

"No. I can get one if I want it. It's everywhere, but I do have two eight balls stashed at home. I'm flying to Australia at the end of the week for the trip of a lifetime. I'm going all in on this one. I ain't holding nothing back, so I'm gonna need all the help I can get." He paused and his eyes narrowed. "Although I've got one huge concern. Oliver has been sick. He's acting so pitiful that it's breaking my fucken heart. I've already paid for the trip, but I'm not even sure that I can leave him right now."

"Ahhhh, you've had Ollie what, thirteen years now? If you're stuck, I can stop by a few nights a week and walk him."

"Thanks, Jamie, I appreciate that, man. He likes you. With you watching him, I feel a little better about going. Butch and Dewey said they'd help out too. I don't wanna put him in a kennel."

"Jesus, you and Australia?" Jamie shot him a sarcastic grin. "Still in search of that elusive happy place, huh? It ain't out there, Mick. Happiness starts on the inside."

"Maybe so, but there's no downside to having a few laughs. One more tour tomorrow night, and I'm bound for South Australia."

EIGHT

IT WAS A slow night in the firehouse. Mick dealt five-card draw in the basement. He usually bluffed early while it was cheap. He'd advertise that he was a loose player now before the pots got steeper and then play tighter than a crab's ass. He spread his cards and read a scrambled hand, crap.

The firefighter on Mick's left, Ray, opened for $5. Two players folded. Mutt called. When it came to Mick, he called the $5 and raised $30. Ray called. Mutt folded. Ray drew three cards to two kings. Mick scanned his cards, and nothing had changed—garbage—yet, "I'll play these."

After the draw, Ray didn't improve on his two kings, so he checked. Mick bet $60. Ray deliberated a few moments and folded. Mick dragged in the small pot to add to his chips, but before he could stop him, Ray reached across the table, and flipped Mick's cards.

When he saw that he had been bluffed, Ray's eyes poisoned.

"You didn't have anything. You bought me out."

"Where do you get off doing that, man?" Mick asked. "You've been playing poker long enough to know ya gotta pay to see the cards."

"Bullshit, man. We're in the firehouse. We're supposed to be friends," Ray roared.

"Hey, man, poker is poker. We are friends, but one thing

ain't got nothing to do with the other."

Ray stood to his full height, his face flushed with anger.

"One thing has everything to do with the other. What if your coked-up ass gets one of us killed?"

Mick sprang from his chair. The two stood nose to nose.

"So, this ain't about the card game. Say the fuck what you really want to say, ya miserable prick."

Before it could escalate, Pete separated them, and no one was going to argue with Pete.

"Easy boys, easy. Let's not say shit that we'll regret later."

Probie School teaches wanna-be firefighters that anger in the firehouse is absolutely taboo. You can't throw a punch at one of the Brothers. Politically correct is out the window. Anything can be said, but no matter how malicious the words, no fights, and no exceptions. For a few moments, the two glared like gunfighters but remembering where they were sat back down.

"Deal the cards, Mutt," Pete barked.

Mutt had no sooner dealt the hand and placed the deck back on the felt when three loud blasts of an air-horn, followed by a frenetic voice over the intercom, interrupted him.

"Get out. Get out. Everybody goes. Everybody out."

"The hand's dead," Mutt said.

The men leapt from the table and scrambled to the rigs.

Minutes later, both companies pulled up to the city project building listed on the computer printout. Awaiting the elevator, the engine company burdened heavy rolled-up hose lengths over their shoulders.

"Who's the roofman?" the truck lieutenant asked

"I am, Lieu," Mick said. "What's the apartment number?"

"The call came from 20B. Start up. The elevators could be broken."

Mick ran to the stairwell and started the slow ascent to the top floor. Carrying his mask, his tools, and breathing heavily, he paused on floor 16 and barked through his handi-talkie's voice piece.

"Almost there, Lieu."

Mick vaulted the last four flights and pounded on the apartment door. A woman's voice lilted, "Who is it?"

"Fire department. Open up."

A 300-pound woman opened the door smoking a cigarette.

"You call the fire department lady?"

"Yes, I did," she sang.

"What's the problem?"

"I heard a loud smell."

"You heard a loud smell?" Mick asked incredulously.

Still breathing heavy, Mick laughingly squawked through his handi-talki, "Hey, Lieu, we got a loud smell coming from 20B."

"A loud smell . . . lovely, just fucken lovely . . . get a name. Then take a look around. I'll transmit the false alarm."

Although Mick knew that the alarm was bogus, he spent an extra few minutes dutifully sniffing the other apartment doors on the floor.

IN THE ENCLOSED rig on the way back to the firehouse, Ray leaned over his jump seat and said quietly, "Sorry, Mick. I was hot and way out of line with that drug crack. Sometimes I got a big mouth."

Mick held an index finger to his lips and leaned forward.

"Forget it, Ray. I know you were pissed off," he whispered. "You didn't mean nothing by it."

He whipped his eyes across the rig's back enclosure at the two firefighters seated on the chauffeur's side and was relieved that they hadn't heard. It was bad enough that the guys in the basement knew. He leaned forward and said, "Do me a favor. Be careful what you say. Will you, Ray? You never know who's listening."

"But Mick," Ray leaned even closer. "Legit, a lot of guys are talking. Watch yourself."

Mick nodded and whispered back, "I know, man. I gotcha. But now's not the time, okay?"

To Mick's mind, coke wasn't his problem, alcohol was. The powder just enabled him to drink more, and anything that helped him keep drinking couldn't be bad.

When the rig pulled into quarters, a few men glided into the dayroom. Some hiked up to the bunkroom, but Mick and the card players hustled back to the basement.

"You believe this shit? I had to throw in three tens for a loud smell?" Booze and fires had weathered Mutt's once athletic build, and Irish good looks, but the sparkle in his eye, and his passion for life made him appear years younger.

"I had a job last week. Fire was blowing out three windows," Pete said. "I'm running up the stairs, and a guy comes running down carrying a television on his shoulders screaming, 'Hurry up, man. Kids are trapped up there.' "

Everyone laughed.

"A real citizen, huh, a regular fucken hero," Mutt said. "Last month I had a coronary victim. I'm getting ready to do mouth to mouth, so I yell out, 'Does anybody know if he has HIV?' A guy in the crowd said, 'No, I think he has Blue Cross.'"

When Mutt laughed, which was often, his two hands clutched his stomach, and his body trembled like a palsy victim at the epicenter of an earthquake. But not a yelp popped out. He just shook and shook until gasps for breath gave way to tears and finally long, loud, infectious sighs. It was a joy to behold.

The men continued jabbering until a gray-haired man with a square jaw sitting on the pool table put down his magazine and spoke softly, "As bad as the neighborhood is now, you guys have no idea how bad it was during the late seventies." Jack Ryan was the senior man, so when Jack spoke, everybody listened.

"One freezing cold night around Christmas, fire was

blowing out four windows, and I had to take a nine-year-old boy down an aerial ladder. I couldn't believe it. He was almost as calm as me. Turns out, the kid tells me that he's been evacuated like this three times."

"Are you kidding me?" Pete said. "Nine-years old and he had been bailed out three times?"

"That's fucken wild, Jack. Wow, the war years," Ray said. "You know what cracks me up. If there's a dumpster fire in Manhattan, crowds stop and gawk. In the Bronx, there could be a raging inferno and people are so conditioned to seeing that shit that they barely look up."

"Ray's right. I had a third alarm last week," Mutt said. "The only people watching were a few Fire Buffs with cameras. When I see television coverage of Manhattan firefighters putting out car fires, I wanna scream."

Mick shuffled the cards. "I can't say I'm not looking forward to flushing this toilet for a while. Tonight's my last tour before vacation." He placed the deck on the felt. His left palm smacked his extended right forearm in that familiar Italian gesture before laughing. "Screw you mooks."

He was about to spread his hand when he had another thought. "Shit, I meant to ask. I was on the phone earlier when you guys were talking about Paul. How's he doing?"

"It doesn't look good, Mick. Without a thumb, he'll have to leave the job," Pete said.

"That's a tough break. That could've happened to any of us. I've had that partner-saw slip on me a few times. That fucken tool's no joke," Mutt said.

"It's not just losing the job. His hand will be useless without a thumb," Pete said. "Two years ago, he saved my ass. We're losing one hell of a firefighter."

NINE

THE FOLLOWING MORNING, Mick trudged from the firehouse to his battered Honda. Thirty minutes later, he parked in front of a spotless, brick-surfaced building surrounded by shrubs where he had his two-bedroom apartment.

He sprinted up the stairs, opened his apartment door, and entered a clean but modest living room. Pictures of Eileen crowded every flat surface. Mick picked up a picture of his beloved wife and stared at it before putting it back on the coffee table. He knelt down to where his Jack Russell loafed on a dog cushion. Tying a red kerchief around Oliver's neck, he said, "You miss her too. Don't you, boy?"

The brown and white terrier's ears stood attentively to the sound of his master's voice, but Oliver's eyes were wide and intense as if it were he in charge, not Mick.

"I know it isn't fair, Ollie. Life's not fair. But she was in fierce pain towards the end. Even I was praying for it to be over."

Mick reached into an apothecary jar for a dog biscuit and caved back to his knees.

"Listen, cocksucker. I'm gonna be gone three weeks. I don't want you in a kennel. Jamie, Dewey, and Butch will be here every day to take care of you. Don't break their balls the way you do mine."

Mick hooked a black leash to his dog's red collar and led him to the door. "Come on Ollie. Off we go." With Oliver's jaws sandwiching the biscuit, Mick watched his tail wag as he led him down the three flights of stairs.

AN HOUR LATER, Mick poured his third coffee and carried the cup into the bedroom. He filled a large suitcase with clothes and then went back to change Oliver's water, and fill his empty bowl with kibble. When he bent down to pet his old buddy, Oliver placed his paw on Mick's hand and then swiveled his head away as if embarrassed.

"Awww, are you kidding? You just went down, ya fuck. You've got me running up and down these three flights of stairs every minute. You don't even wanna look at me. You're only supposed to go out three times a day. Go back to sleep."

Persistent, Oliver patted his paw on Mick's hand.

"Ahhh, Oliver, did you just fart?" Mick wrinkled his nose and curled his lip. "I can't believe you, man. You just took a shit on your last walk, you little tyrant."

Mick rubbed both hands back and forth along his terrier's mouth slowly and affectionately.

"You're lucky that I've got a new rug. You use that paw the way a gangster uses a gun. Don't you? Don't you?" Mick kept rubbing Oliver's cheeks with his palms. "That's what you are, you little bastard, a Jack Russell terrorist. Aren't you, huh? Aren't you?"

His hands moved higher to Oliver's neck where he quickened and deepened the massage. Mick reconnected the leash, grabbed his old Navy pea coat, and repeated the outside ritual.

After walking him a second time, Mick scrambled six eggs, fried a tomato with a slab of ham, wolfed it down, checked the time, and headed out to his Queens nightclub.

TEN

BEHIND AN OLD wobbly table in Nobody's cellar, Mick studied a ledger and punched the keys of an ancient adding machine. On a small mirror atop the laminated table sat two rows of neatly chopped white powder. A figure wearing black chinos, a white collared shirt open at the neck, and a black vest framed his office doorway.

"Hey, boss, there's a girl upstairs looking for a job," his bartender said.

Mick snorted the two lines and shook his head like a man awakening from a coma.

"Another one? Continuously running that help-wanted ad was the best move I ever made. For $15 a week, I have a conga line of girls looking for positions. What is this one, a barmaid or a cocktail waitress?"

Butch ignored the question and drew his eyebrows together. His gaze flitted the room before lasering back on the coke.

"None of my business, but you're hitting that stuff a little early, ain't ya, boss?"

"I had this stashed from Saturday night. I had no sleep at the firehouse last night, just need a line or two to get shaking." Mick pointed to the ledger. "What's this shit? Buffalo borrowed another $100 last night? I told everybody no more money for Buff. He treats debt like job security. If he owes me money, the cocksucka knows that I can't fire him."

"Yeah, like you'd ever fire Buffalo. You'd sooner stick needles in your dick. What do you want me to do about this chick?"

"Tell her that she'll have to pass an oral exam," Mick said with a mischievous smile, then wiped the glass with his index finger, and licked it. "Just kidding, have her fill out an application."

"Not this one, boss. This one's different. This one you should see."

"Why?"

"I don't know boss. I can't tell ya. She's just different, and I guarantee ya, she ain't taking no oral exam."

"This better be good."

Mick closed the ledger, and the two climbed the steep wooden stairs to the main floor where sitting at the bar was a green-eyed gypsy beauty, straight from the mists of Irish mythology.

Taken aback, Mick measured his words.

"Hi, you here about the barmaid position?"

"Yes, I filled out an application." She offered a lithe hand. "I'm Erin Callahan. Are you the owner?"

Her lips were pale and full, her skin delicate like perfect white porcelain, not a hint of red, not even in her cheeks. She appeared to have more hair than she needed, and it was arranged in an elaborate coil atop her head. A long auburn curl fell across just the right amount of forehead, accentuating an elegant composure.

"Would you like something to drink while we talk, a coffee?" Mick asked in a flat, business tone.

"No, no thanks. I won't be that long. You are the owner then?"

He took her hand and asked Butch for a coffee.

"Yes, I'm Mick. Nice to meet you, Erin."

"I saw your ad in the paper. I have my resume' right here." When she lifted her handbag off the bar, he turned around to straighten a plaque on the wall behind him. Adjusting it, he glanced over his shoulder.

"Ever do any prison time?"

"Excuse me?"

"You know prison time, a bit, a stretch?" Mick did an about face and stared directly into her mesmerizing but confused emerald eyes.

"Of course not!" She put aside her resume' and stroked long, lean delicate fingers slowly across her arm. "Are you serious?"

"I'll take that as a definite no?" he shrugged. "Okay, you're hired."

"I got the job. Just like that." A slight snigger slipped her lips. "You didn't even glance at my resume.' What if I would have answered yes to the prison question?"

"You would have gotten the job, and I would have thrown in health benefits and a pension."

"I already have those. I'm an assistant professor at Iona College, but I'm delighted that I don't have to be an ex-con to work in your fine establishment."

Mick grabbed his coffee and pointed to her violin case on the floor.

"What's with the Tommy gun?"

"I play Irish fiddle."

Wow, a professor, beautiful, and a musician?

"Really? I love Irish music," he said. "I'm first generation, both parents born in Cork . . . and a fiddle . . . no shit? You can have all the guitars and horns you want, but a fiddle . . . a fiddle touches the heart. It has everything in it, tears, laughter, the sun, everything."

When Mick lilted about her passion, a beautiful smile full of mischief, joy, and promise broke above Erin Callahan's lovely chin.

"Oh boy, I've got a feeling that I'm in for a wild ride, aren't I?"

"One of us is," his eyes flashed. "Do you know any tunes by the Dubliners?"

"I can play just about anything Irish."

"Play your cards right. You'll be running the joint in a month."

He drank half his coffee in a single gulp and sauntered away beaming.

I played that perfect, just perfect.

ERIN LEFT THE club optimistic about the job yet a bit unsettled by the variables of Mick's considerable presence. He seemed personable enough but erratic. She shoved it to the back of her mind as she drove. She had a few errands to run and time would deliver its own verdict.

Later that afternoon, she returned to her parent's Woodlawn home where all the surfaces were uncluttered and freshly waxed. The couch and chair were still wrapped in the store's protective plastic. When Erin entered, her mom was pushing a vacuum across an unsoiled rug. Nora pulled the plug.

"I got a job tending bar, Mom," Erin said.

Nora Callahan seemed neat and tidy rather than attractive, a petite, impeccably groomed woman with no excess pounds.

"Tending bar, is it?" Her mouth changed from a straight line to a sour scowl. "Wasn't it enough bars that you idled in while you were wasting your time playing that blasted fiddle?"

Beige curtains with tiny green flowers on them rose from the breeze that blew through the old oak in the side yard overhanging the property. The cold air distracted Erin a moment. "It'll help me pay back the loans from graduate school."

"Barmaid? Is that what you plan on doing with all the

education and talent, a barmaid? Sure, any eedgit could do that," Nora reached for the vacuum's plug. "But there's no sense of talking to you. Thick like your father, you know it all."

"No, you're right, mom, no sense in talking to me, none at all."

When Erin fled the room, Nora harrumphed and resumed her housework. Neither of the two knew it then, but by tending bar for Mick Mullan, Erin would further her education alright and learn lessons not taught in any university.

ELEVEN

JUST THE THOUGHT of Australia made Mick salivate. A country the size of the United States with the population of New York State was almost too good to believe. Tales of the outback and the riotous pubs had long piqued his curiosity, and because the patriotic Aussies had sacrificed so many soldiers in the Great Wars, Mick had been told wild, exaggerated stories about seven women to every man.

The World Fire-Police Olympics gave him the perfect excuse to finally see the Pacific. He was no athlete, but as a compulsive gambler, he shot a reasonable game of pool. What difference did it make? All he really wanted to do was dive the Great Barrier Reef, see the country, and sample those Sheilas he had heard so much about.

Before heading to Kennedy Airport, he decided to make the obligatory stop at his local pub, The Jolly Tinker. The sun had barely broken in the Eastern sky, yet Webster Avenue was already congested with drivers rushing to work. When he pulled open the metal door, the bar was empty, but the cellar's trapdoor was tied open. He leaned over the weathered mahogany bar and yelled into the basement's darkness, "Mike, is that you down there? Come join me for a pint of Guinness before I head out to Melbourne."

Minutes later, a short, chuckling man climbed the cellar

stairs carrying a small metal box. The "Tinker" had mischievous eyes that sparkled when he talked.

"What? You're having a pint this early in the morning?" His pupils danced when he sang the next sentence. "Jesus, it didn't take you long to get back in the groove after your short sabbatical."

Mick had plunged back into the sauce after being on the wagon five-long years. Now back on mother's milk a year, the scotch and Guinness were as he remembered, brilliant.

"Why kid myself, Mike? C'mon, it's Australia. I'm gonna make the most of it. Besides, I gotta keep up with a bunch of screwballs for three weeks. How in da hell could I make this trip sober?"

The Tinker was the owner of the oldest bar in the Borough for over 35 years, a Bronx legend, and one of only two men Mick had ever met who had no enemies.

"Yeah, but Jesus, Mickey look how far you've come. What has it been, five or six years? The way you were punishing the drink after Eileen died, none of us thought that you'd ever comb gray hair. How old are ya now, thirty-four?"

Mick wore blue dungarees, work boots, and a navy-blue pea coat over a thick black sweater. He stood behind the bar next to Mike, pulled the tap's tall wooden handle, and watched the porter paint the sides of the glass. After waiting the necessary few seconds to let the foam settle, he topped off the masterpiece.

"Yep, on the job five years. If the neighborhood guys hadn't persuaded me to take the test, my tired ass would have been too old."

"But if it weren't for the promise of that job, you mightn't have straightened out to begin with. I remember all too well you puffing in here after your daily jog through Botanical Gardens and refusing to touch even a drop of beer. This from a man who after his wife died was so mad for whiskey that once a bottle was opened, he wouldn't rest until it was empty."

Unbeknownst to the Tinker, nothing he could say would convince Mick to change his plans. He had a quarter ounce of cocaine and twenty-five Percocets tucked away neatly in a shaving kit buried in his suitcase. Mick wasn't planning a breakout. He was planning full-scale chaos.

"You should think about this a bit more, Mick. You know yourself, you can't drink like a normal man." Mike had known Mick all his life, was fifteen years older, and knew both his parents as well. "You let that genie out of the bottle now, and it'll affect your job, your health, and everything that you've worked for."

As Mick's eyes hungered for that poisonous pint, he thought a brief second about what Mike was saying, and flashed back to all the sacrifices, the abstinence, and training he endured to pass that FDNY physical.

"I don't want to lecture you, but you know bloody well that your genetics don't support the luxury of a few pints." Mike tried again. "I've been watching you the last year. You're drinking as heavy now as you were before you quit."

The cloud finally disappeared from Mick's glass, and in flawless contrast to the blackness beneath it, the head turned creamy white. Mullan stared at that tantalizing pint a moment and reflected. He had always dabbled in what he considered light drugs: coke, weed, magic mushrooms, and such, but he knew that once he was loaded, he was up for anything.

There would be no restraint or moderation on this jaunt, not a chance. He'd hoist the Jolly Roger, chart his course, and sail for the wonderfully familiar, turbulent waters of insanity. He'd be on a glorious three-week vacation that would probably be superb without alcohol and drugs, but screw that. Why take chances?

Mick lifted his glass in a wordless toast to Mike. His tongue made a swipe at his lips, and with a quick motion of his hand, he emptied half of it. As soon as the Guinness hit his belly, an energy bolt exploded, struck every nerve ending in his body, and sparked a smile.

"Look Mike. You know, I love you, but I didn't come in for a lecture or to drink alone. Are ya gonna share a pint or not?" He emptied the glass and savored the violent, powerful impact as it hit its mark. "Besides, I quit before. After my vacation, I'll quit again. A few pints of Guinness never killed anybody."

The corners of Mike's mouth moved downwards. He shrugged and lifted the black pint Mick had built him.

"I hope for your sake that it's as easy you think, but I've got more than a few years on you. I've seen what havoc drink can wreck, and if you can shut it on and off like a light switch, fair play to ya. But I doubt it."

TWELVE

MICK SETTLED INTO the jet's seat glowing from his morning pints. When the cocktail cart came by, he ordered a double scotch, and braced himself for the six-hour flight to Los Angeles. It was cold and miserable in NY but summer in Australia. Grinning, he pictured himself scuba diving beneath the Reef's crystal-clear waters.

After landing at LAX, the connecting jumbo jet to Melbourne was packed, not one seat empty. Hoping for an aisle or a window, Mick was disappointed to find himself in the middle of a row of five. The stewardess made her usual announcements about safety and said they'd be showing three films before landing in New Zealand to refuel.

He started reading *The Last Lion*, William Manchester's biography of Winston Churchill and was just past the first chapter when the elderly man seated next to him noticed the book and introduced himself. Despite the lack of elbow space, Mick was delighted to hear that the avuncular gentleman was a professor of Western Civilization, from "Plato to NATO," he punned.

As the crew prepared for liftoff, the old man lectured about the causes of the Great War and how its unfair peace had led to World War II. An eager Mick was captivated and grateful for his good fortune. The professor would make the long trip blow by, but then the smell of a child's soiled diaper soured his breathing, engulfing him in a suffocating stench. He looked for an infant but not a baby in sight.

Suffering Jesus someone shit their pants.

The meek academic, who wore a heavy sweater with a large red scarf wrapped twice around his scrawny neck, turned and said, "You'll have to excuse me. I have an uncontrollable flatulence problem."

He was bald and short with a hawkish nose, a small mouth, and a thin gray mustache. Mick turned, stared compassionately into his saddened eyes, smiled, and said, "No problem, professor."

Fucking lovely. I'm a seventeen-hour prisoner in a Saturday Night Live skit.

Mick nodded at the old man again, secured a Percocet from the money pocket of his jeans, and switched plans, no conversation. He ordered another double scotch, chased the pill, and decided to hit Australia running.

The stewardess didn't even bother to wake him to eat.

When the 747 landed to refuel in Auckland, the other passengers looked like survivors of the Bataan Death March. Grateful for modern chemistry, Mick awoke refreshed, buoyant, and as exuberant as a child at the gates of Disneyland. Only five hours left to Melbourne. The Irish ballad, "We're Bound for South Australia" echoed in his brain.

Just wait until these Sheilas get a load of my act.

WHEN HIS FLIGHT landed, the weather was hot, not humid, and Melbourne both historic and modern. The Rendezvous Hotel was reasonably priced and screamed character. Mick checked in at the lobby's oak, and marble counter with his roommate, Gary Shiffle, a tall and toned, prematurely bald probationary firefighter, whom the Brothers had christened Shifty.

Once inside their room, Mick stripped off his black sweater, blue T-shirt, jeans and work boots. Leaping onto the queen bed in his boxer shorts, he immediately sifted through the local phonebook where scores of escort services lined page after page. He lifted the phone to punch the front desk and yelled to Shifty, "Holy shit. I can't believe all these ads. There should be a separate phonebook just for the hookers."

"Front desk, Henry. How can I help you?"

"Hey, Henry. I'm with the cops and firemen up in room 802. While thumbing through your phone book, I couldn't help but notice the incredible number of call girls listed."

"Oh, prostitution is legal in Australia, mate," he said.

"Legal?" Mick tried not to seem overenthusiastic. "Legal? No shit? What's the going rate?"

"Usually $100."

"Australian or American?"

"Australian."

Mick did the fourth-grade math quickly, *$80 American.*

"What about tips, or carfare?"

"No," he said, "all inclusive."

"Really, $80 includes everything? Are they attractive?"

Henry told Mick to just specify what type he preferred. It was that easy. Before hanging up, Mick asked him to recommend the name of a service.

Leave it to the Irish. What a country, the guy at the front desk doubles as a pimp, and even gambling is legal, civilization at last.

Mick dialed the number that Henry suggested.

"Hello, I'm at the Rendezvous Hotel, room 802. I need two girls."

"Certainly sir," the professional voice said. "What types of girls are you interested in?"

Cheap, enthusiastic girls who refuse to testify?

But instead of breaking balls, he played it straight and answered with the only attractive Australian name he could conjure.

"Well send me one who looks like Elle McPherson and another blonde as well."

"Very good, no problem. It will be about an hour. Will that be cash or credit?"

Credit cards? Is he kidding?

"Okay if I use American Express?"

"Certainly sir. The girls will run your card when they arrive."

Mick hung up.

What a fucking country. I'm getting laid and getting frequent-flyer miles besides. Australia and I are going to get along like gin and tonic.

His roommate had studied the negotiations through a gimlet eye.

"I'm out," Shifty said. "I didn't come 12,000 miles to pay for pussy besides I don't get any kick outta prostitutes. With me, it's always about the chase, the conquest."

"So, once the enemy's taken, the battle won, and the puzzle cracked, your interest wanes? Screw that." Mick laughed. "I hoard the memories of every woman that I've ever slept with the way a pirate enjoys his booty. The memories mean as much to me as the sex."

WITHIN THE HOUR, a series of thumps pounded the door.

The taller one was almost six-feet and, astonishingly enough, a dead ringer for Elle McPherson. The petite one's tongue sported a small dazzling diamond stud, her confident cobalt eyes, and blonde spiked hair as brazen as a slap in the face.

Before she crossed the threshold into Mick's room, the blonde whipped open her long, tan Macintosh to reveal white nylons, red garter belt, panties, and bra. Her astounding legs ended in six-inch crimson heels.

Mick thought all of his Christmases had come at once. The two hookers were so extraordinarily perfect that he got giddy.

"Wow, that's some calling card, nice lingerie. No small talk, huh? You must be the life of the family picnics."

Her butch hair was wild, streaked, and bleached at the tips from the sun, her skin tanned almost olive. She was narrow at the hips, flat in the stomach, and her generous breasts jutted from the red bra.

"I'm definitely in on this," Shifty screamed from the bed.

Mick looked over his shoulder and shot his roommate a suave smile implying,

Leave this to me, kid. I got this.

In reality, he was as shocked and surprised as Shifty. The shorter, brazen blonde, Grace, wasn't as classically beautiful as the Macpherson doppelganger, Norma, but she definitely had more of what Mick looked for in a working girl. She was confidant, poised, and wild, more the Hollywood central-casting type. All that was missing was a long run in her nylons and smeared red lipstick.

"You take Norma. I'll take this screwball then we'll switch."

Champagne on ice, two bottles of wine, and a bottle of vodka crowded the dresser. Norma waved a cautious backhand across the dresser's edge to make room for her purse. As she did, her lovely face raised and fixed on Mick.

"Come ere, mate, you sound like a gangster."

"That's what I do for a living."

"What do you mean? 'That's what you do for a living?'"

"I gangst," Mick grinned.

He bussed his lips across Norma's cheek before inching her aside to build the two girls cocktails. When Norma removed her short, white-fur coat, a white peasant blouse revealed a lean muscular stomach, and her black leather pants emphasized the considerable distance from her ankles to her ass.

Mick swigged from a green bottle of Heineken, handed

Norma a vodka and cranberry juice, and asked the girls if they would mind if he smoked a joint.

"Roll a fat one, Yank. Don't be scrimpy," Norma said.

At that, Grace smiled, nodded her head in agreement and strutted to the closet to hang up her beige raincoat. As she removed it, Mick's eyes devoured her. She caught his leer, spun quickly and said, "We got lucky, Norma, two, good looking, young Yanks. This will be a party, not work."

Grace played the same game every smart hooker does. She made her John's feel like she was only after a good time. The standard rhetoric goes something like this, "Shit, if it wasn't business honey, I wouldn't even take the money. I'm having too much fun."

Mick knew that a good pro plays to a man's fantasies. Sex happens between the ears, not the legs. Grace pitched, but Mick had played this game before and wasn't swinging.

Yeah, right! She must think that I just fell off a pumpkin truck.

And as sure as night follows day, once the festivities were in full swing, and just before Mick was about to climax, Grace got cute. She held off, slowed up, tortured and teased him, trying to shake him down for an extra $80, which he agreed to with little debate.

"Don't worry about the extra money honey. Do what you gotta do," he whimpered. At that point Mick would have promised her a townhouse on Central Park West, but after the deed was done, and he'd climaxed with a wild howl, he stewed.

Does this chick think that I'm a rube? I'll nip this little game in the bud.

Mick asked Grace if she'd be interested in something a little stronger than the weed. When she asked what he had in mind, he reached into the dresser drawer and whipped out the twisted Baggie tied above the cocaine.

She glanced at the eight ball with thinly disguised hunger and then turned her gaze deliberately to Mick's hardening cock.

She let her eyes linger there, licked her lips, and with a lascivious look doubled down.

"Will the drugs let you stay hard enough to stick it all the way down my throat, honey? I want to make it nice and slippery." Grace's voice was low and throaty, her words soft and inviting. "That's how I like it best."

HE HELD UP the yellow-tinted vial that held the Percocets and flashed an even broader grin when he spilled one into his hand.

"If you really want to have a few laughs, I have these too."

"I'll do a few sniffs of the cocaine, but I'll just try a half of that pill. I like to keep my wits about me to ensure my customers the ultimate experience," she said sarcastically.

But Mick wasn't listening. All he had heard was what she had said about his slippery dick. Mick knew it was theatre, but he was starting to admire Grace's cold efficiency. She was smart, a real pro, and he was willing to wager that she was as monetary as an investment banker and twice as cagey.

Lest you think Mick was naive, philanthropic, or under the illusion that these girls would perform better if they liked him, or got free drugs, get it out of your head. Mick was a conniver.

He figured if Grace rapped him $160 for the first hour instead of the agreed upon $80, he had better knock her off the meter. He didn't want the clock to keep ticking, but he also didn't want the party to end.

Once that Percocet and the booze kicked in, Grace wouldn't want to go anywhere, never mind ripping him off by renegotiating the price after he had already bought the merchandise. She'd need more coke to function, and where was she going to go that was more fun or safer than where she was?

Paid for or not, Mick always made damn sure any gal with him had a good time because if they weren't enjoying themselves, how the hell could he?

LATER THAT NIGHT, Grace cuddled on Mick's chest, her breaths even, her hair perfumed, their legs entwined.

Man, this chick's something else. What is it about her that makes the synergism so perfect? Unless she's the greatest actress since Meryl Streep, we seem to connect.

Mick had never had bad sex but often wondered what made for a really great romp in the hay. Years ago, he thought that he had it figured out. If a woman acted like Mick was driving her nuts that did it for him. If a woman screamed, moaned, and gyrated, well, it was only natural that he was going to feel relaxed and perform like a porn star. Hookers know the quicker they can get a guy off the faster they can turn a buck, so prostitutes pretend for a living. That was fine with him.

Just as fascinating banter makes books sing, good dialogue catapults sex to higher dimensions. Lovemaking involved all the senses, and enthusiasm was key. He assumed it had to be the same for women. Consequently, when he made love, he held nothing back, screeching constant praise, cheering them on.

When the intensity of the experience peaked, he usually finished with a loud howl, and immediately followed that with a fit of wild laughter. His cackles and gasps sounded like a jackal in heat. Mick's fire department buddies and close friends who had heard tales of his "expressive orgasms," or had heard them first hand through hotel walls on trips like this one, labeled the explosion "Mullan's mating call."

Even for a pro, Grace was unusually uninhibited. Aggressive and stunning, she knew her way around the rack like no woman Mick had ever met, and he wasn't starved for comparison. She appeared immune from the misfortunate dissipation, and riotous living normally accompanying her occupation.

Her body was framed in lingerie, her face dark in shadow, and her short-cropped hair dripped with light. She stirred, rolled over, and touched his face with her hand, kissing him on the mouth, lightly at first, then her mouth opened, and her wet tongue excited him.

Grace threw her body against his, and Mick lost himself in her again. He had already climaxed earlier, so it was inevitable that the build up and release would take longer. When she opened to him this time, hypnotic heat rippled through his skin, a tingling sensation ran up his arms and through his loins, building up more, and more, and more pressure, longer and longer, and longer, until the volcanic release that followed, then the screams, and then, and then . . .

When the laughter began, Grace retreated to the foot of the bed in fright but soon relaxed and giggled while muffling Mick's mouth with a pillow.

"Quiet, quiet, please, Yank, quiet. You'll wake the whole hotel."

But he could no more stop the involuntary reaction than he could stop his eyes from closing when he sneezed.

A heavy hand pounded the door.

"Oh shit, the cops." Mick said. "Hide the drugs."

Then he remembered that in Australia, prostitution was legal.

The knock quickened, became more urgent. He wrapped a towel around his waist and cracked the door cautiously. From the hallway, a young concerned face peered through the door.

"Is everything all right in there? I'm a firefighter in the room next door. I thought I heard someone having a heart attack. If you need help, I know CPR."

Loaded from the booze and drugs, Mick's mating call kicked back in. He bent, grabbed his knees, and cawed like a crow. When he regained his composure, he widened the door and startled his misguided savior with a scrumptious view of the naked knockouts.

"No. No heart attack yet, but check back in an hour."

Seeing that the girls showed no sense of modesty, the firefighter's eyes got as big and round as the wheels of a child's bicycle.

"Are they prostitutes?" he whispered.

"No, Australian girl scouts." Mick howled. "I bought two hundred boxes of thin mints."

He had been "in country" less than six hours.

THIRTEEN

THAT JANUARY WAS bitter cold, so Nobody's thermostat was set high. Friends clustered in small groups, and the jukebox blasted Marvin Gaye's "Sexual Healing." Behind the bar, Erin glided like an ice skater, filling glasses, empting ashtrays, and slinging one-liners to keep the customers smiling.

Jamie pulled open the back door, tossed $20 bill on the laminated-pine bar, and yelled, "Hey, beautiful. Who do I have to screw to get a drink around here?"

Erin's head whipped to his voice. One eye narrowed.

"Act like a gentleman, or you'll die of thirst."

Ignoring Jamie, she served two young girls instead.

"Let me have a vodka and orange juice and a screwdriver," the shorter one said.

"A screwdriver, and a vodka and orange juice are the same drink." Erin said. "Do you girls have I.D.?"

After both girls flashed driver's licenses, Erin built their cocktails.

"I put two stirrers in the screwdriver," she teased. "That way you won't confuse your order."

As she punched the register's keys, Buffalo entered the back door, slammed his unopened wallet next to Jamie, and sang, "Give me a triple Johnny Walker Black on the rocks in a pint glass, and get Jamie a belt on me." Buffalo's eyes were full of scotch and mischief. "While you're at it, you might as well give the whole bar a drink."

Erin's head pivoted to the sound of the thunderous roar, then the hard line of her mouth loosened into a slow delighted smile. She raced to that end of the bar and flung a coaster alongside the gentle giant's wallet.

"Get the bar a drink, is it? Thanks, Buff, you're always a sport." Her eyes slid. "So, it's Jamie, is it? I didn't know that you were a friend of Buff's. I was still debating about whether to serve you or not. I wasn't crazy about your opening line, or the way you've been staring at my ass."

"I had hoped you were too busy to notice," Jamie smirked.

"When it involves my keister, I multi-task."

"Don't kid yourself." Buffalo said. "She doesn't miss much."

"Sorry." Jamie offered his hand. "I'm one of Mick's best friends. I was just kidding around. When you have a chance, I'll have a bottle of Heineken."

Her hand was warm and soft, about half the size of his. He held it for only a second, but it was long enough to get that jolt that goes through your body when you touch someone who matters.

She placed a green bottle in front of Jamie, a pint glass holding scotch in front of Buff, and hustled up the bar to fill the rest of his order. She filled the empty glasses and pitched coasters in front of the full ones to indicate which customers had rounds coming.

"That's on Buff, on Buff, on Buff," she repeated. After pouring the round, she wheeled back to where she had started. "Mick's best friend, huh? He's an odd duck. Isn't he?"

"When he gets back from Australia, you'll find out, guaranteed," Jamie said. "You're right up his alley."

"I don't spend much time in alleys," she said. "And I don't know much about him except what the customers say, but from the general scuttlebutt, he certainly seems like a lively act."

"Don't believe everything you hear," Jamie said. "Most people don't know him the way Buff and I do. He's a bit self-destructive but a paradox of sorts, a solid dude."

"Dead right." Buff's face was ruddy and cheerful. "Even though he's a whack job, you could drop a stone in his heart and never hear it hit bottom." He slugged his scotch, took a sleeve to his lips and said, "Don't get me wrong. He also has a well-deserved rep for sticking his swizzle stick in anything that moves." The color bloomed in Buff's cheeks. His eyes took on a warm shine. "He's got enough demons to intimidate an exorcist, but at least, he always plays by the rules."

"Oh, most of the customers say he's a good guy but then artfully add that he's a lunatic," Erin said.

"Most of them would be right," Jamie laughed. "Like all of us, he has many sides. Only with Mick, the only time those sides seem to converge are when his fingers are wrapped around a whiskey bottle." He lifted the Heineken from the coaster. "You're different than the girls Mick usually hires. You're bright, witty, and talented, but not unlike the others, light on the eyes."

Erin's lower lip rose to meet the upper.

"Thanks for the compliments, but how did you know I had talent?"

"Mick told me that you play fiddle."

"So you've discussed me, have you? I'm not sure how I feel about that. Are you an Irish music fan?"

"Nah, I'm a jazz guy, but if I'm at a wedding, I'll make a fool of myself with a good Polish Polka," he said.

"Jazz? Polka? A band without a fiddle isn't music; it's just noise." Erin grinned before turning to Buff, "That's $64 big fella."

"No problem," Buff smiled. "Give me a $100 out of the register. Put $20 in your tip cup, and tell Mickey I was in."

Erin's jaw fell.

"Aww, you gotta be kidding me? The first thing that the boss told me was not to give you money under any circumstances. You're gonna get me in trouble."

"Okay, can't have that," Buffalo's tongue was thick and pink on his teeth. His eyes filled with merriment. He gulped his scotch before smiling at Jamie and said, "Put all the drinks back in the bottles."

Erin's eyes bore directly into Buff's but were impossible to read. Finally, she shook her head, laughed, and with a demeanor both ambiguous and impish almost jigged to the register.

FOURTEEN

MICK SAT AT the hotel's marble bar in khaki shorts with flap pockets, brown Birkenstocks, no socks, and a crisp tan shirt with the sleeves folded back over his forearms. After a long night with Grace, he wanted to knock back a hair of the dog. A Bloody Mary or two should get him right.

Recapping last night's festivities to a group of laughing firefighters, Mick's hands flew in all directions. He tried to gulp his Bloody Mary and almost poked his eye out with the celery stalk. Shifty was grinning like a Lotto winner as Mick spoke softly.

"I don't care that I paid for it. She was unbelievable. If there's any better gift than waking up with a beautiful woman in the morning, I don't know what it is."

Mick paused to bite the celery, glanced around to see if any women were listening, and lowered his voice yet again.

"She told me that if I wanted a really perfect blowjob, I'd have to jam it all the way to the back of her throat to get it slipperier, and she was a bombshell, a knockout."

Mick knew better than to kiss and tell and never did. It was boorish and a sure way to ensure no repeat action, but with professionals, all bets were off. He was spreading the word about this wonderful service to help the single Brothers enjoy their Australian vacation.

Mick and Shifty had a lot of fun in that hotel room. The tale bore repeating over a few pints. In Mick's mind, it was always about the laughs, and the advertising certainly wouldn't hurt the escort service.

"I've been with hookers, lots of them, but this chick was unreal. Not only was the sex unbelievable, but she was smart and funny. All she wanted to do was laugh, drink, and screw." Mick carefully skipped any mention of drugs. "She hung around the rest of the night for free and only left about an hour ago."

Shifty slugged half his pint and placed it back in the wet circle on the bar. Mick could almost hear Shifty glowing.

"I thought Mick was fucken nuts. He didn't even wanna switch, and the gal I was with looked like a supermodel."

"Screw looks. Good looking girls are a dime a dozen," Mick said. "I need a chick with some moxie, a gal with smarts who's great between the sheets and can make me laugh."

"How smart could she have been?" someone asked. "She's a hooker."

"She speaks five languages and works for the Australian consulate. She only sells her ass part-time. I get that she's a pro. It's her job to bullshit me, but it's like a chick with fake tits."

"Fake tits?"

"Even though I know they're phony, I still wanna play with them," Mick grinned. "I haven't had that much fun with a woman in a long time, and that's an area I try to keep current."

THE NEXT MORNING, he went to represent the FDNY at "The Games." The stadium held 20,000, and at the astonishing opening ceremony, each country marched under their flags and circled the huge track. The crowd response was both thunderous and embarrassing. He harbored no illusions about his athletic ability and was acutely aware that he was only here to drink the country arid, screw as many Australian women as possible, and dive the reef.

He hadn't stroked a cue stick in four years but later that afternoon cabbed it to the other side of Melbourne. His plan was to lose gracefully, enjoy the rest of the week, and head to the reef, but he played a Russian and astonishingly enough won two straight games. While awaiting his next opponent, he spied a cute Australian. Having disposed of the inept Ivan, his jingoism in full display, Mick felt obligated to impart a little billiard advice and strike up a conversation.

Dianne's brownish-red hair was tucked under a blue beret. Her lipstick was bright burgundy, and she wore too much of it. But when she parted her mouth and looked into his eyes, she gave Mick the kind of jolt that he usually felt after a morning eye opener. They hit it off, so he asked Dianne to the "Rock the Dock" party later that evening.

In the spirit of international friendship, the locals had arranged a series of parties supplying the visitors with alcohol, DJs, and huge buffets. Needing civil service escorts to enter, droves of Australian women loitered outside of each venue, more gifts from Mick's Australian Brothers.

UNDER A YELLOW moon, perched in a black velvet sky, bursting with stars, they left the party hand-in-hand. Her body was petite and covered in pastel cotton from throat to feet, but the sleeveless dress left her bronzed arms bare. Dianne's turquoise eyes and seductive mouth glowed under her beautiful, long russet hair, which she had brushed out over her shoulders.

She was striking, smart, and captivating, a keeper. Day turned into night, then another, and another, but Mick had played this pipe and slippers game before. She was classy, different, and dangerous—and not in his plans.

"Baby, you've been amazing, but I'm leaving town, tonight," he lied. "I have to shove off for the reef, but if it's cool, I'd love to see you again."

"Mick, I'm a cop, and you're a firefighter. We're separated

by over 10,000 miles. We both knew that this was only for a few giggles. Call me if you want, but let's not kid ourselves."

He hadn't given her enough credit and never dreamt she'd be this cool. He would have loved to see her again, but she was right. The logistics were insane. He went back to the hotel alone regretting his lie. He and Dianne would have had a lot of fun.

To mollify his mistake, he decided that before he left Melbourne another bout with Grace wouldn't go astray. He was about to punch her number when he thought better of it and cradled the receiver. Propped up on three pillows, he wondered what the hell it was about this prostitute that had him so captivated. Sure, Grace was stunning and loads of laughs, but she'd cost $200 a night, and that was a bargain considering that she usually commanded $80 an hour.

Why pay for sex when he could have it for free? Australian women were beautiful, wonderful company, and cost nothing. He juggled those thoughts a while and came to what he thought was a logical conclusion. He couldn't fall for a hooker, so he was paying Grace to leave, not show up.

All he knew was that he wanted her, and so what if she cost $200? He had paid that much in juice for betting on a football or basketball game. He was vacationing in paradise on his way to fulfilling his childhood dream of diving the Great Barrier Reef. Money wasn't an issue. After tonight, he'd never see her again, so what was the harm?

He leaned back in his comfortable king-size bed, picked up the phone, and dialed Grace's number. Mick was creating memories, and anyone with a thread of sense never puts a price on memories.

FIFTEEN

LIGHT SNOW HAD fallen sporadically throughout the day, and Northern Boulevard was slick and wet. Jamie avoided the fender bender at the stoplight by turning left into Nobody's rear parking lot. He slogged through the back door wearing a blue shirt with matching tie and charcoal slacks. When Erin tossed a coaster in front of him, he hung his long wool overcoat over the top of the high-backed stool, ordered a much-needed Heineken, and asked her what he had been thinking about for days.

"Hey, you wanna grab some dinner later?"

Erin's eyes were green, warm, lustrous, and charged with energy all at the same time.

"I don't think so Jamie but thanks."

"You're not seeing anybody, are you?"

"No, not at the moment, but I don't think it's a good idea to date the customers. I've seen too many barmaids screw up their business like that. A lot of guys come in to shoot the breeze, have a few laughs, and tell me their problems. They're not necessarily hitting on me, but I can tell it's somewhere in the back of their minds just the same."

Erin slid the cover off a stainless-steel cooler, popped the cap off a green bottle, and planted it atop Jamie's coaster.

"Relax, I simply thought it might be nice to grab a bite to eat." Jamie said. "I'm not proposing marriage here."

"No, I understand," Erin's eyes left Jamie's and followed a straight line to the wet spill next to the bottle. She patted a bar towel inches from his beer. "I just don't want to create any ill feelings. I like you. I appreciate your conversation and company, but right now, I'm not looking for a relationship."

He pulled his beer halfway down the sweating bottle and parked it back on his coaster.

"Relationship? Jeez, I just asked you to dinner."

"Sorry, Jamie. I didn't mean to act like a jerk. Sure, why not? A gal's gotta eat. Two conditions, I can't make it a long night, and don't take me anyplace too expensive. I wouldn't feel right about it. Deal?"

"Fair enough."

THE WAITER BROUGHT Erin white wine and poured Jaime's Heineken into a pilsner glass. "I'll be back in a few moments when you're ready to order."

"Floessel's is a College Point Landmark." Jamie said. "The food is great and the price is right. Try the beef strudel soup. It's amazing."

The smell of strong German beer hung over the dining area like a blanket. Erin studied the red and white checked tablecloths, the spidered hutches, the dented tin ceiling, the ancient mahogany bar weathered with dents and scars.

"I like this place already, great ambiance, and I love German food, especially the potatoes. One of my Italian friends, Maria, always teases me about having bland taste, 'You freaking Donkeys boil roast beef.'" She made an involuntary shrug and laughed. "She wasn't far from wrong. In my house, we only have two spices, salt and pepper. That's it, and it isn't even black pepper. It's white."

"I'm not a heavy spice guy either, not big on Thai, or Indian food."

The waiter appeared and penciled loin of pork and Wiener

schnitzel on a pad. After he left with the menus, Jamie found himself rubbing the back of his neck and over-thinking what to say next.

Erin broke the silence.

"How long do you go back with Mick?"

"Since I can remember. We were so young that we used to walk each other to the soda fountain for egg creams. We're two different people, Mickey and me, but I think he'd take a bullet for me."

He sipped his Heineken and leaned back in his chair.

"He's a strange guy. After his wife died, he built an armadillo's skin around a huge heart. He feels like God has kicked him in the balls, yet he's the first one to put his hand in his pocket for a charitable cause. You'd never hear it from him though. He hides his good deeds the way others hide their sins, but enough about him. What about you? I know you're an English teacher. How are you on economics? Do you follow the markets?"

"No, but I know they interest you, and I like to learn, especially from someone who knows what they're talking about. I'm curious about most everything." She lifted her wine. "As long as you don't start talking sports, have at it."

"I gamble on a world stage. That's why I'm always trying to convince Mick to stop betting on things he can't win at like casinos and sports. My job lets me follow perceived trends and give advice to people without business acumen. It's a great feeling to make investors successful. For the next decade or so, oil will boom, and my clients will be all over it. I've been killing it on the Street lately. If this keeps up, I'll walk away a rich man at an early age."

Using esoteric language, Jamie rambled on about puts and calls to an apparently fascinated Erin. In reality, she was thinking about her last time in a German restaurant when Gene had told her their engagement was off.

Gene was everything that Jamie wasn't, charming, funny, and a habitual liar. She had wasted two years of her life with that two-timing bastard, and she'd never make that mistake again. Jamie didn't have Gene's confidence or good looks, but maybe that was a good thing. He didn't seem to have that bum's wandering eye either.

Jamie was smart, and with intelligence came depth. She'd endure this monologue, and his best qualities would surface soon enough.

When the waiter returned with their order, Jamie was still talking futures, and Erin began to wonder if he'd ever switch the subject. Some dates go fast. This wasn't one of them. She raised her right palm to her mouth to smother a yawn and wondered why all solid, reliable men bored her to tears.

SIXTEEN

THE WEATHER SERVICE in Cairns had issued hurricane warnings for the entire week, so Mick was in danger of not seeing the reef. He hadn't come to the opposite side of the world to miss the prize. Before breakfast, he booked on the first dive boat leaving shore, a huge commercial outfit called Quicksilver.

Once aboard, he thought he screwed up. All he saw were overweight, geriatric American and European tourists. These senior citizens had no intention of sandwiching themselves between the glass bottom hull and the water.

After two hours at sea, a voice droned over the loudspeaker that anyone interested in snorkeling or diving should report to the bow. Assembled at the fore were about a dozen would be swimmers. The dive master instructed anyone interested in scuba to step to the right where Mick found himself alone.

"Well it looks like you're my only diver, the others are snorkeling," the lofty, leathery man said. "What are you interested in seeing?"

Using his vast knowledge of marine life accumulated from years of riding New York subways, Mick said, "I guess . . . I want to see big fish."

"Would you like to see sharks?"

"S—Sur—Sure, I'd like to see sharks . . . I think?"

The two jumped on one of Quicksilver's gray, 20' dinghies and ferried thirty minutes from the main ship. As he tied the launch to a buoy, the dive master said, "This is the spot."

They were geared up shortly and seated on the gunwale with their backs to the water. The dive master's left hand pulled his mask down from his forehead.

"Stick close to me underwater."

Mick's heart was beating like a bass drum.

Stay close? I'm gonna share your wetsuit.

Mick clutched his mask with his left hand and fell backward. Once the turbulence settled, a coral cathedral engulfed him. Six reef sharks circled less than ten feet away. The dive master signaled thumbs up. Mick's thumb responded all's well, but he had the unnerving certainty that his tiny trail of bubbles would only break the surface for a few seconds, and this buoy would become his anonymous tombstone.

The sleek grey predators glided around him in a deadly rhythm with Mick's wide eyes glued to the circle of perceived death, but soon a Bronx kid did the inconceivable. Boredom set in, so he turned his back and swam away to explore the rest of the reef.

He spent the next hour examining coral, mollusks, sponges, and schools of fish, every size, shape, and color. Stingrays glided and undulated like shadows down the sides of the coral, puffs of sand clouding their wings. Crabs crept slowly along the bottom following a path to a bed of giant clams.

But what really cracked Mick's egg wasn't the sea turtles, the three-foot clams, or even the sharks. The dive master picked up a sea anemone from the sandy bottom, and this strange cucumber shaped creature squirted chords of camouflage string. It had shown no life before being disturbed, but now a web of threads clouded the water.

Clusters of small blue flowers springing from the reef's walls screamed for attention. When he went to touch them, they disappeared back into the coral. He played with the foreign life form a few minutes until he sensed a shadow lurking above him. When he glanced up, his head almost collided with a huge, hovering wrasse that frightened the shit out of him. It weighed at least 1,000 pounds, two enormous frogeyes glaring over a wide mouth, which acted like some kind of prehistoric vacuum.

Back aboard the mother ship, he learned these huge, harmless wrasses were scavenger's common to the reef, often hovering near dive boats hoping for scraps thrown overboard. Yet at the end of the day, *I dove with sharks, the great predators. Holy shit. I guess a few jars of Fosters are in order.*

MICK DRANK THAT night in Cairns' with the FDNY basketball team. The women loved their height, and blacks were rare in Australia; so, like the crustaceans at the floor of the reef, Mick planned to bottom feed.

He hung out with the starting power forward, Bobby Barr. The two overspent and over charmed their way into the company of two British gals. The laughs and drinks flowed liberally enough until the inevitable coupling occurred.

The two gals wouldn't make the cover of Vogue, but each was attractive in their own way. Cecelia was formidable and had spirit. The petite, athletic one was shy, cuter than her friend, and ironically enough, named Sheila. As usual, Mick opted for enthusiasm over looks and chose the live wire.

AFTER A PITCHER of Manhattans, neither girl minded sharing close quarters. They checked into a room with two double beds, and Mick soon bedded the spunky Cecelia while Bobby ended up with the cuter Sheila.

Next morning while Bobby shaved, Mick was fiddling Cecelia under the covers and Sheila looked over, "What's going on over there?"

"Mick is giving me a bit of a pamper," she smiled.

"Why are you having all the fun? I could use a bit of a pamper myself," Sheila said.

"Jump on over," Mick bubbled.

As Bobby left to catch his plane, the look on his face was pitiful. He dragged his suitcase along the hotel room floor like a man trudging to the guillotine. After he left, the two didn't disappoint.

WHEN THEY AWOKE late the next afternoon, he called room service, ordered breakfast, and a liter of vodka with two containers of orange juice.

Might as well keep the party going.

After breakfast and only one drink, the girls said they had bought tickets for a harbor cruise on a 100' tall ship, so Mick said, "no worries."

I'll just lay back, hang, watch TV, and recharge my batteries. I could use a break, anyway.

He refilled his glass, sprawled in bed, and began to relive the past week.

Whatta schmuck. I run from a great gal in Melbourne. Now here are two accommodating Brits, and I'm delighted to ditch them as well.

Then, Grace crept slowly back into his thoughts. What was it about her? He couldn't see himself falling in love with a hooker, even a spectacular one. Not just because of her profession, but his soul was still tied to Eileen.

Grace was beautiful and amazing in bed. That certainly was part of it, but she was a born hustler, maybe an asset in her profession but not a gal you'd want to hook up with. He knew he was being played but was just egotistical enough to believe that she enjoyed their time together. The chemistry was too good.

Mullan gripped the vodka and thought of an old alcoholic trope.

Can't fly on one wing.

He snatched the ice bucket, tossed four cubes into his empty glass, and heard the familiar clink as they hit bottom. He uncapped the bottle and poured heavily.

When Mick Mullan drank, he did it methodically and with dedication, his time frame open-ended, his progress from first drink to last as steady, as unrelenting, and as disciplined as anyone's can be while systematically sawing one's brain in half. He needed booze to help soften the painful memory of Eileen's bone cancer, or that was his excuse anyway.

The first drink led to the second, the third, and eventually he'd lose track of his consumption and slip into a blackout during which his motor controls still functioned but his mind and soul wandered. A voice outside him would warn, *You're on the edge. One more and you won't remember anything.*

He heard the whisper, poured a double, and woke up three days later.

WHAT HAPPENED?

Even his hair hurt.

I remember ordering a bottle of vodka. Did I order a bottle of scotch too? I'm alone, anyway, Think, Mick. Try and remember.

Then he rolled on to that blasted prosthetic leg.

What the hell? Good God, now I have a real problem. Think, Mick, think. Did I take Percocets? Am I still in Cairns? Where's Shifty, and how the hell did this prosthetic get here?

Too many questions, no answers, he forced his feet to the floor, emptied his bladder, and gingerly hobbled to the desk where he read from a stationary pad "Dorchester Hotel, Cairns." He called room service, ordered breakfast, and then realized that he hadn't heard from Shifty in days and had better check in. He lifted the phone again, punched in the new number, and barely recognized his own hoarse voice.

"Hey Brother, how are you doing?"

"Mick, my Brother, I'm doing great. I'm hung over a bit, but great. What are you up to?" Shifty asked.

"Hey man, I'm having a ball. I dove the Reef, met a couple of crazy British broads, and I've been hanging with the basketball team. I didn't want you to worry."

"Worry? What da fuck are you talking about? You told me all this last night."

"I talked to you last night?"

Shifty rolled with laughter.

"You called me three times ya fucken screwball. You don't remember?"

"No. Did I sound whacked?"

"No more than usual. But shit yeah, you were definitely drunk. Hey Mick, I've been calling that escort service. Ya gotta see the hookers they've been sending me, gorgeous."

Now, Mick laughed.

"Hookers? What happened to the chase?"

"Extremely overrated," Shifty said between screeches. "I'm in the groove now, man."

The scraping of a plastic card entering the door's metal slot demanded attention. When it sprang open, lo and behold, carrying a large brown sack filled with egg sandwiches, and coffee, Grace. Shocked, but delighted, Mick stuck the phone in Shifty's ear.

"How in da hell did you get here?"

"You flew me in last night. You don't remember?"

"No. Did we screw?"

"You don't remember that either?"

Mick pointed his chin to the floor.

"Don't be upset, mate. You're loads of fun when you're drunk. All you do is laugh."

"Did I pay for your flight?"

"I could lie and say you didn't but of course and champagne too. You're grand when you're drinking, very generous."

"I bet I am. Tell me something." Mick hoisted the prosthetic leg as if it were an umbrella. "Where'd this come from?"

"You don't know?"

"No."

"Haven't a clue, mate. It was on your dresser last night when I came to your room. You were delighted with it. It was funny though, and what I like best about you Mick is that even when you're drunk, you aren't the slightest bit abusive. I have more fun with you than any John I've ever met."

SEVENTEEN

FOR MICK, NOTHING competed with the flavor of fine malt, smooth Irish whiskey, or for that matter, even a shot of chilled speed-rack vodka. He loved it all, the browns, the whites, and all the standard cocktails: Stingers, Manhattans, Martinis, anything and everything—even the slushy rum drinks with umbrellas.

If you placed every illegal drug on a long table: speed, morphine, heroin, cocaine, and ended that row with a half of glass of beer, for Mick, that would be the most dangerous drug on the table. Alcohol was and always would be his drug of choice.

Since Grace had arrived in Cairns Monday, the two were tearing it up pretty good. Mick was surprised at her capacity. Not many girls would even attempt, never mind actually keep up with him. She tossed back a lot of wine, but that was fine with him. Outside of food and drink, the last two days weren't costing him anything.

When Mick had told her Tuesday that he was putting her ass back on a plane, she had asked if she could stay until Thursday. He had the hotel room anyway, so why not? Those two days had altered his impression of her.

He was starting to like, even admire her. Sure, she was a prostitute, but she was free, beautiful, and amazing in the rack.

Grace used all her senses in bed, but dialogue was her strong suit. She soon got inside his head. The hoarse throaty taunts were constant, deliciously obscene, and whether true or not, tattooed his brain.

She raved about his sexual appetite while her screams massaged his ego and almost convinced him that he was the only man who had ever satisfied her.

"Mick, it's all yours." She patted her ass cheek. "Anytime you want it; anywhere you want it; and anyway, you want it."

She came with an assortment of sex toys too, which made every romp in the hay an adventure. When she climaxed, it was with a series of explosions. Mick had to keep a towel under her perfect little ass to soak up her fluids. She flooded every room they made love in.

That last morning, he rubbed a towel across his freshly shaved face and studied her. She sat high on the bed, two pillows propping up her perfect frame. Small lights played in her eyes. When she saw his vulnerable, open posture, she slid off the bed, and eased toward him. Then, she was behind him. He felt her breasts touch his back, felt her hands reach for his crotch, felt her fingers lightly trace the outline of his prick.

She pulled him to the bed and placed him in her mouth. She knew every centimeter of him and just how softly or hard to tease each point of passion. And even after he was spent, she never stopped. It was glorious.

But something was missing, something not quite right. Once his passion was spent, the deed done, he began to think of himself as Somerset Maugham's character in *Of Human Bondage*. She was a prostitute, plain and simple, and although he was totally captivated, nothing could come of this.

He knew that he was acting like an idiot, yet he knew she felt a connection. If she didn't, why was he getting a scholarship? Free wasn't a word normally in Grace's vocabulary. But why think about this? In a few days, he'd be back to reality. Suddenly craving the beach, he told her to throw on a bathing suit.

THE SANDY AIR was heated with a light wind, the clear sky crisscrossed with birds. They sat on a blanket and read and relaxed. Later that afternoon when the slight breeze had dropped, and the air had become still, Grace pushed the hair out of her face and said, "You should be flattered. I turned down a special customer who pays me $500 a session just so I could stay with you in Cairns."

Mick peeked up from his newspaper, smirked, put fire to a Marlboro, and stared out at the ocean. The evening sun was low above the water and slivered streaks of silver light crossed the breaking waves. He drew the smoke deep.

Yeah, I bet.

Grace interrupted his thought.

"So, what's New York like?"

He tossed the folded newspaper onto the sand before looking in the direction of her lovely face colored bronze from the sun's rays. Blankets dappled the sand, and a young couple behind her tossed a beach ball. Although most of the women on the beach were topless, Mick glared at Grace's yellow bikini.

"You've never been to N.Y.? That surprises me."

"I've been all through Europe and much of the Pacific, but New York is such a journey. If I go, it would have to be for a few months. Who knows? One of these days I just might show up on your doorstep." She used her chin as a pointer. "That would frighten you half to death. Wouldn't it, Mick?"

Turning his back on the couple playing catch, Mick grabbed the towel off his beach chair.

"Baby, you can put your shoes under my bed anytime. C'mon, let's get back to the hotel and get cleaned up. We'll have a bite to eat and a few bottles of wine. Tomorrow, I'll put your fine little ass on a plane."

EIGHTEEN

FRIDAY MORNING, THE sun broke hot. He dropped Grace at the airport, and then his bleary eyes read the cab driver the address of the marina. His hands shook, his head cracking like broken ceramic.

For their final days, a few Brothers had chartered a sailboat. For frugality, six men doubled up in three berths, and two more slept under the stars. They ate breakfast and lunch aboard and had dinner ashore.

The copious amount of beer, rum, and vodka practically fork lifted aboard was the largest expense. Mick already felt a dull throb from where he was fairly certain that his liver was and decided to give the drinking a break. Watching his hands tremble like a Parkinson's victim persuaded him that it was a wise move.

That first night he staked out quarters in a forward cubby-hole far from the stern and away from the inevitable all-night partying. When the sun's bright rays slanted through the bow's porthole the next morning, his eyelids lifted. He tried to grab a few more hours, but after another bout with the local spirits, the Brothers had slept late again, and the snoring, and farting echoing from the cabin made sleep impossible.

He pushed his palms against the floor, propped his body up, and stared out of the porthole. The palm trees speared in the white sand swayed and straightened in the morning breeze. The wind's gentle sounds were broken by footsteps on deck, so he leapt from his bunk, and grabbed the railing. Climbing the four metal steps, he cautiously navigated his way to the stern.

"Morning, Tommy. You're up early."

"Mick? I hardly recognized you without a beer can glued to your lips," he laughed.

"Nah, ya fuck. I haven't had a drink since we've been at sea. I was drowning in that shit ashore. I knew from the jump that Australia was going to be a fog, but I really went overboard."

"Come to think of it you didn't drink last night, did you?"

Tommy was close to six feet in height, two decades older than Mick, and wore a Marine haircut. He was lean with a slight bulge in his waist, which gave the impression that he had a small volleyball tucked under his loose gray T-shirt.

"Good for you. A couple of days sober won't do you any harm."

Mick yawned, stretched, and reached for the sky.

"But you're never without a drink in your hand, and you stay sober. How da hell do you do it?"

"When the shore patrol brought me back all banged up on New Year's Eve in a stokes-stretcher with my jaw wired shut. That did it for me. Thirty years ago was my last drink in the Navy or anywhere else."

"I never dreamt you didn't drink. You're always the last one to leave every party."

"I drink cranberry and orange juice. It looks like a cocktail."

One of the best-known and well-liked fire officers on the job, Tommy had an unflappable disposition. Because of his oversized ears, the men often referred to him with great affection as "Chief Wing-nut." Behind his head, a gusher of blush-ribboned the sky. The rainbow sluiced color across the calm, crystal waters, almost butterflying the Reef. He stretched for his Nikon and started fiddling with the lens.

"Let's take the dingy to shore and have a jog," Tommy said.

"Sounds like a plan. What's with the camera? You gonna take a shot of that rainbow?"

"No. I want to take a quick picture of your ass. Turn around and moon me."

A civilian might be surprised or puzzled but not Mick. He didn't think twice, just spun, and dropped his blue swimsuit. Tommy clicked the camera and went below to lace up his sneakers.

THE FOLLOWING MORNING, Mick was thrilled to find himself on deck alone again with Tommy. He knew the closer he stuck to the chief, the better his chances of staying sober.

"Ya wanna take the dingy into shore again, have a run, and check out the terrain?" Tommy asked.

"Sure, I'm in," Mick said. "We need ice, anyway."

Tommy twisted the protective lens off his camera.

"But before we leave, drop your bathing suit. I wanna get a photo of your family jewels."

Tommy was one of the most knowledgeable and admired men on the job. If the Chief had ordered him to follow him into an inferno with a fire extinguisher, Mick wouldn't have hesitated, but this time he balked.

"Look, I don't give a fuck, but what's with you and the pictures of everybody's credentials? You've been doing it throughout the trip, pictures of my ass, Karl's cock, Bobby's balls."

"Oh," Tommy laughed. "This isn't my camera. It's Haney's. He married a girl who just left the nunnery. He was bragging that she does everything for him, even packs his clothes. Wait till she develops these shots. She'll wonder what the hell kind of a trip he went on."

THEIR THIRD AND last day, the chief suggested a final

run, so Mick laced his running shoes and threw on shorts and an old T-shirt. Once ashore, the two jogged along the white sand before sprinting up the green overgrown trails traversing the hills. Mick was having trouble keeping up. His wind was good, the muscles in his back and thighs loose, but he still had to push himself hard to stay with the older Tommy.

He must have taken it easy on me the first two days.

Breathless, "How long have you been running, chief?"

"Since, the day I stopped drinking thirty years ago."

"You didn't go to A.A.?"

"No, I didn't have to. I went to Sports Authority," he grinned.

Mick let the wisdom seep in.

Maybe if I started running again?

Tommy's short-cropped hair never stirred as his feet beat the mountain paths in a slow lazy rhythm. Running behind him, Mick focused on Tommy's ears, marveling at their peculiar curvature, not deformed, just oversized.

"If I can stay close enough, the shadow from your ears should protect me from sunburn," he yelled.

"Don't worry about sunburn, Mickey, my boy. That's the least of your problems, and you know it."

Tommy knew that a long lecture about drugs and drink wouldn't fly with this thick, stubborn Irishman, so he tried to subtlety maneuver Mick down the right path. As another alcoholic, he knew that his disease was incapable of restraint and total abstinence his only salvation. He slowed his pace, allowing Mick to catch up.

"You're in the bar business. Alcohol and drugs are all around you. I've found out over many lost years that drinking narrows your world. If you're a juicer, you'll only hang out with other drunks. You'll end up drowning the innocent child that once lived happily within you. You're young, healthy, and you've got a great job. Count your blessings, Mick. You're a fine firefighter. I'd hate to see you throw your life away over a piss test."

"I know, Chief. You're right. After this trip, I'll get it under control." He filled his lungs with air. "But I didn't have a hope in Australia, not with this crew. I'll quit as soon as we get back to the States. I did it before, and I can do it again."

They continued to punish their calves along a thin mountain path winding through the thick woods. The more Tommy's words replayed in his mind, the more they resonated.

Mick loved the rush of slamming two c-notes on a bar and screaming, "Give us all a drink." But Tommy was right. He had to stop. Surely to God he could quit if he wanted to? But did he truly want to? At 33-years-old, could he stay sober and still have fun? He had tried abstinence, and although bearable, it definitely wasn't desirable.

His disease was an old friend, talked to him often, and persuaded him that it was the camaraderie that he craved, not the alcohol. After all, he seldom drank at home and never alone.

Oh, you have a few beers or a bottle of wine at home, but that isn't drinking. If you remember what you did the night before that isn't drinking.

His feet continued to pound the rooted, leafed, upward path, his thoughts racing in tandem with his legs. His mother had warned him, "You have to be careful. You see what the drink did to your father, and you don't know the half of it. You haven't met your cousins and your uncles in Ireland. Most of your ancestors are dead from cirrhosis. Alcohol doesn't run in our family. It gallops."

His Mom was so used to hearing that a family member had died of the Irish disease that she couldn't believe people could die any other way. Once Mick had told her that an old friend had passed.

"Fitzmaurice? Dead? Is he? But, Jesus, Mary, and Joseph, he didn't drink at all?"

THE WINDING PATH got steeper until the two broke into a clearing where sheer rock cliffs, and sharp-sided mountains ran straight down to the edge of the water. Before him was the gift of the Pacific Ocean, blue, immense, and dancing with sunlight. The view robbed him of what little breath he had left.

In the distance, a white sloop tacked between two islands. Clouds of salt water exploded off its bow. Bright green trees were rooted high among the rocks, and his eyes traced the cliff downward to study the white froth in the breakers as the waves blanketed the alabaster sands.

His calves ached, and his lungs screamed for mercy.

God, how long had it been since he had really pushed himself?

Just six short years ago, he had jogged everyday to get ready for the FDNY exam. For the past year, he was smoking and drinking again, but he had to be in better shape than this? No way he was gonna quit though. Tommy had two decades on him and was gliding along. He'd hang with the chief if it killed him.

Pain is all between the ears. I gotta let my mind drift to a happier, less painful place.

HIS MIND SOARED through a hole in the dimension transporting him back to the streets he had grown up in. It was impossible for him to think of them without smiling. His childhood memories were sweet, and he visited them often, the way a woman looks back at an old doll, or the way a man pounds his old baseball glove.

The corners they hung out on, the candy stores they drank egg creams in, the streets where they measured home runs by sewer lengths, all flashed like memory points across his brain. Bitter memories came too, most involving his dad, but who was he to judge? Big Tom hadn't had Mick's advantages, yet here he was a bigger mess than his old man. Not only was he a drunk, he was using coke.

The pain in his lungs shocked him back to reality. Wow, he was in terrible shape. Chief or no chief, he was done for the day. He bent his body, put his hands on his knees, and filled his burning chest with oxygen. All Mick wanted to do now was get back to the boat and lie down.

This run was a wake-up call. He'd get back to the States soon enough and things would be different. His vacation over, no more excuses. He'd stop the drinking, the drugs, and the smoking, and get back to the regimen that got him the FDNY job to begin with. He swore he'd run every day and stay sober like Chief Tommy.

NINETEEN

WIELDING A SODA gun, Erin hosed puddles of club soda along the empty bar. Mick climbed the cellar stairs with the day bank just as she was wiping a fresh, white towel along the pine. Before she spotted him, he darted into the men's room, ran his fingers across his hair, and tucked his shirt inside his pants. Satisfied, he sauntered behind the bar and placed the cash tray in the register with a big grin.

"How's the job working out, Erin?"

She wore a white cotton blouse and a loose black skirt exposing a dancer's calves.

"Great. How was your trip?"

"Unbelievable. I didn't think it could exceed my expectations, but it did. The sailing and diving were amazing plus nobody makes me laugh like the Brothers. That's what life is all about, the laughs."

Mick wore bottle green work boots, clean khakis, and a corduroy shirt with the two top buttons open.

"I'm glad you had a good vacation. You've got a grand color." She gave a half smile. "But surely to God, you believe that there's more to life than laughs."

"Oh sure, of course. Making sure you don't deliberately hurt anyone, improving your mind, maybe even earning a few bucks, but ultimately, nothing's more important than having a good time."

"How about leaving some kind of legacy, maybe have children, or make the world a better place? You have to have goals and purpose in life otherwise you're a man without a soul."

"Every sane man wants to make the world a better place, and I try to live by the golden rule . . . but wait a second, did you just mention my soul?" Mick laughed. "Jesus, don't tell me that you're still Catholic, an intelligent girl like you? Wow, those Dominus Vobiscum salesmen really screwed you up."

Erin's emerald eyes charged with light. The skin below her lip creased.

"Yeah, my faith's important to me, but how does that make me screwed up?" She stared hard into Mick's face, thinking a few moments, searching for the right words "How can you say something like that? You barely know me."

"You're a smart professional woman. How can you believe in that bullshit? What in the world could possibly justify eternal damnation? Science has disproved all that hocus-pocus, talking snakes, virgin births."

Erin's back teeth grinded, her words dripped.

"I'm a lucky gal to be in the presence of a man who knows all the answers to questions that have puzzled us mere mortals for 5,000 years." She tilted her head with a lopsided grin. "And to think how fortunate I am that he runs a bar right here in Queens."

"Well that bit of sarcasm put me firmly in my place. Good for you. I like a woman smart enough to call me on my bullshit. Sorry, I swear I'm not usually this arrogant. Forget this conversation happened."

He walked toward the phone and over his shoulder said, "Butch told you about the benefit this afternoon, right?"

"Yeah, he said about 150 people. I have fruit and juices set up at all three stations."

"I have to attend to a few things in the kitchen. Don't take any cash. Just mark mixed drink or beer on a sheet behind the bar. I'll figure it out later."

THE MAJORITY OF the people who showed up that afternoon were women. Some had brought their children, and the buffet that Mick served in the silver trays wasn't elaborate but sufficient: chicken and potatoes, baked ziti, sausage and peppers, three six-foot heroes, and a huge salad.

A woman wearing a white, scoop-necked sweater, and black slacks approached Erin carrying a plastic plate in one hand and extended the other.

"I'm Maria Ognibene."

Erin introduced herself.

"I just want to thank you and Mick for this afternoon. Ever since my daughter's accident, things have been rough. This benefit will help more than you can imagine. That's my daughter Donna over there in the wheelchair."

"She's a lovely girl. What happened?" Erin asked.

"Car accident, she's going to need back surgery."

"I'm so sorry, such a beautiful girl."

"Well I hardly know Mick, so when a friend suggested Nobody's, I was a bit leery. I didn't see how we could afford to pay for a hall and caterer and still make the fundraiser worthwhile. I can't believe how generous he's been. He's refused to even touch a nickel of the proceeds. He insisted it all go to my daughter. He's quite a guy your boss."

A HALF HOUR later, when Mick exited the kitchen, most of the guests were eating at tables while some clustered in small groups at the bar.

"Give me a beer, kid. All I've got left to do is keep those serving trays full."

She placed a draft Heineken in front of him.

"Everybody seems to be having a good time. They're not

drinking much though."

"This might seem counterintuitive, but for a change, I don't want them with glasses in their hand." He sipped his brew. "You look great back there, smooth as silk."

"Thanks."

"I never did read your application. How long have you been at this?"

"Only about a year, but I've been playing fiddle in and out of bars since I was sixteen. I'm comfortable enough."

"Well you handled this crew without a problem. I can't wait to see you back there when you get some real action. Do you want me to cover the bar while you grab a bite to eat?"

"No thanks. I had a big breakfast before I came to work. I'll hold until dinner."

Mick went back to his chores, and the room emptied out just as the night bartender came in early for his shift. Dewey marched behind the bar while Erin rang out the day receipts and totaled out the tab that Mick had told her to keep. When she finished and brought Mick the check, Maria and her guests had already left.

"Here's the tab from the party. You never asked me for it. I thought you'd want it earlier."

"Oh, don't worry about it. Maria and I go way back. We're practically cousins." He took the paper, folded it, and put it absentmindedly in his back pocket.

The lids above her emerald eyes turned straight as a razor's edge. She half closed one of them, nodded, and smirked.

"Yeah, Ognibene and Mullan, sounds like you could be brother and sister."

"Don't be a wiseass." He grinned, lifted his leather jacket from the back of a stool, and had an afterthought. "Hey, you haven't eaten a thing all day, and I'm starved. You wanna grab a quick bite before I head home? There's an Italian place about a mile from here. I hate eating alone. We'll be in and out in an hour, and the food is dynamite."

"I have to get home early, school tomorrow, but sure, yeah, sounds swell. Just give me a few minutes in the lady's room to freshen up and grab my coat."

TWENTY

WAITERS WEAVED THROUGH the packed room wearing white aprons and carrying hot plates of manicotti, calamari, and linguini. The odor of garlic and oil saturated the air.

"Thanks for the invite. I'm starving now," Erin said.

"No, thank you. I'm thrilled you came."

"When you said Italian, I couldn't resist. I can still remember the first summer that I ever tasted pizza out at Rockaway. It burned the roof of my mouth, and when the cheese slid off, it swung down, plastered itself against my chin, and burned that too. To this day, it was still the best I've ever tasted."

"My family used to go to Rockaway all the time." Mick beamed at the memory. "We used to stay in an old rooming house on 107th Street. Our room didn't even have its own bathroom, but it was only a short walk to Playland. The roller coaster and the ocean were all that I cared about."

He lifted two menus and handed her one. "My family didn't have much money growing up, but I never knew we were poor. Shit, we had so much fun in the streets who had time to think about money?"

"My family came from nothing too."

"That's not surprising. Who was it that said, 'The Irish are the niggers of Europe?'"

She looked over the top of her menu grinning.

"Everybody?"

He laughed aloud and said, "Remind me to keep you happy. Your eyes are like shafts of light when you grin."

The menu hid her blushing cheeks.

"So, you told me in the car that even though you earn great money, you spend it gambling and partying. Well, at least you're honest, but what the hell is wrong with you? You own a successful nightclub and have a marvelous vocation. You'd jeopardize all of that for a few laughs? What kind of lunacy is that?"

Mick loved her unfiltered honesty. He was her boss, yet she had cut to the chase and gave him both barrels in the face.

"Yeah, unfortunately, I guess that about sums it up. I'd do just about anything for a few laughs. I went to a shrink once. He said I had textbook manic depression. When I told him I never got depressed, he said I was unipolar. I don't see clouds, apparently I walk on them."

"That sounds like a blessing not a disease."

"That's what I thought, but the shrink said that my mania encourages gambling, drugs, and infidelity, all dangerous habits. He said that it's fine for me, but not for the people around me. So, I started thinking. Shit, I've got tons of friends, and as long as I'm having fun and not hurting anyone but myself, why should I change?"

"Nice attitude. Did he give you anything for it?"

"Lithium," Mick said.

"Do you still take it?"

"Fuck no. It turns out that lithium is salt. In large doses, it acts like saltpeter. The side effects make it impossible to get a hard on. If I'm crazy, I'll be damned if I'm going to be celibate too."

"I have a question for you Mister Manic. How can you be so sure that your reckless behavior never hurts anyone else?"

Mick never answered. Just then the waiter appeared to take their order. The more they talked, the more she enthralled him, belting honesty, no nuance, no treachery, just straight adorable toughness. She was so easy to talk to and such a wonderful listener. He poured from a bottle of Botticelli while she spoke.

"I love the feel of a restaurant. Growing up as a child my mother was like an overlord at the table with a wooden spoon her weapon of choice."

"Your mother? No shit? With me, it was my old man. It was like I was a plebe at West Point. 'No elbows on the table, no talking while chewing, no reaching for food.' I had to have permission to leave the table.'"

"At least you could leave the table," she said. "With my mother if I didn't like what was put in front of me, I had to sit until I changed my mind."

"Same with me. My parents were old school. They never owned a house, went to a concert, set foot in a football stadium, or even owned a credit card."

"My parents still don't have a credit card."

LATER WHEN THE food came, Mick cleared the antipasto and breadbasket to make room for the steaming hot plates. He couldn't stop staring at her. She wasn't classically beautiful, and yet Erin had something about her that made him feel both vulnerable and confident. He wanted her to know everything about him. Her eyes seemed to delve deeper into him than he usually allowed, as if she were inside him looking out. With this gal, there could be no bullshit. He took his eyes off her a moment and spun a fork in his linguini.

"I love good food, all kinds of food. I'd no more limit myself to one kind of cuisine than I would one kind of music."

She lowered her fork and eyed her plate.

"I've heard you don't limit yourself to one kind of woman either. You've got a bit of a reputation."

"Don't believe everything you hear." He lifted his glass and lied. "Besides our sexuality is such a small part of who any of us are. You and I are not about sex. I have lots of friends that I don't want to sleep with. Buffalo for one. Here's to friendship."

She clicked his glass while he thought: *Platonic relationships are platonic nonsense.*

"To friendship," she said.

"So, you teach English Literature? What are you reading now?"

"Ulysses," she said.

"Joyce? Good God, that's heavy stuff. I tried once but couldn't get through it, way outta my league."

"He's definitely tough but worth the trouble. I actually had to read it with Cliff notes to make him easier to interpret. Some think he wrote that way deliberately to confuse the scholars. Even though I teach English Lit, Irish writers are my passion."

"I've read some of them: Singe, O'Casey, Wilde, Behan, and of course I love Yeats. But history's my bag, William Manchester, David Halberstam, Will and Ariel Durant. I decided when I was a kid that it didn't matter how much I read but rather what I read that was important. Even historical fiction turns me on, Gore Vidal, Herman Wouk."

"I agree to an extent, but not everything you read has to be edifying," she said.

"Oh no, you're dead right. I read all of Ian Fleming's James Bond books by the time I was fifteen, and the Catcher in the Rye changed my life."

"Everybody loves Salinger."

"He wrote that book while part of the allied invasion force at Normandy. Can you imagine? That was his first battle, D-day. His childhood sweetheart jilted him for a man fifty years older than he was. Do you know who she was?"

"Who?"

"Eugene O'Neill's daughter, Oona."

"Holy hell, didn't she marry Charlie Chaplain?"

"Yep, the most famous man in the world at the time. Salinger never got over it."

HE FOUND IT impossible to look at her without his long-closed heart starting to creak open. The conversation flowed so easily that they seemed like two volumes of the same book. She seemed to admire honesty, so he gave her a belt of it.

"God, you're so easy to talk too. We're gonna be great friends, so let me be up front with you. I make it a point to never bullshit my friends. I know this ain't going anywhere. We're from two different worlds. You're a straight shooter, a keeper. I'm not looking for that. I was a one-woman man once, no more. I just want to scratch the occasional itch and enjoy my life."

Mick pushed linguini onto his fork and lifted it to his mouth.

"But I love good company, so with us . . . no strings . . . just good conversation and good food." Before his lips hit the fork, he said, "By the way, you're doing one hell of a job at the bar. In the short time that you've been here, the daytime weekend business has doubled."

"Thanks. That's good to hear. I appreciate it." Erin forked a piece of lasagna, but her eyes never left his. "No strings seem to be a theme in your life." She slid her eyes to her pasta and murmured, "Are you afraid of commitment?"

His deep blue eyes stared at her as though they were lidless, his face frozen, his jaw bent.

"You don't know?"

She shifted her gaze from her food directly into the fine bead of pain in his eyes, reached across the table, and squeezed his hand.

"I had heard that you lost your wife. I'm so sorry."

Mick forked linguini into the back of his mouth and chewed

silently, but his sullen eyes never left her flushed pink cheeks. He swallowed, washed the food down with wine, and said, "She wasn't just my wife. She was my partner, my mentor, my friend, and the love of my life. She gave everything eagerly, unconditionally, unrelenting love, always there. She would have given her life for me. No one will ever replace her."

"She died so young."

"And in unbearable pain. I don't ever want to watch anything like that again, ever."

"You sound afraid of life. I'd have never thought that of you."

"Afraid? No, I'm not afraid. Why would I be? On the job, I've seen unimaginable horror."

"That proves you're not afraid of dying. It doesn't mean that you're not afraid of living."

"Listen, I'm not an idiot. Only a fool runs from happiness. Nothing is set in concrete. If the right woman came along, I would even consider having a couple of kids." Mick shook his head. "But I'll never meet a woman like Eileen again. She was my moral compass, my North Star, my partner in everything, braver than me, more steadfast. Now I only date women for sex. Trust me, sex is important, but no man falls in love with a woman just because she's the best piece of ass that he's ever had. Unless he's an idiot, and I'm no idiot."

"That's the second time you said that I'm no idiot in the last few seconds," Erin said. "You might not be an idiot, but it's starting to sound like you have your suspicions." She lifted her glass smiling. "To friendship."

Mick raised his glass, clicked hers, and said, "Ouch."

She brought the wine to her lips, and her smirk skipped across the table.

TWENTY-ONE

ALL FDNY BOSSES come up through the ranks. An officer can be petty, but if he takes that route, he had better damn well know his job. Nothing pisses off the men more than a disciplinarian who's not aggressive at a fire. Having been firefighters themselves, one would assume all officers know this simple tenet.

Bosses without much confidence usually try to avoid the busier houses. But through the luck of the draw, an officer has to occasionally cover a tour or assignment in a house where he'd prefer not to work.

THE MEN OF 60-truck drifted in for the day shift.

"I heard you had an occupied last night." Mutt poured coffee for Patty and grabbed an empty cup for himself.

"Yeah, an old-law tenement, fire on the third floor, good job. Victims were hanging off the fire escapes," Patty said.

"Who was the boss?" Mutt asked.

"Covering Lieutenant, been here about a week and doesn't know what he's doing," Patty said. "We gotta make sure that when he puts his paper in for a permanent assignment, he doesn't ask for our house."

The two ambled into the dayroom for breakfast.

"What did you mean when you said that the lieutenant didn't know what he was doing?" Mutt reached for a jelly donut.

"He took his lazy ass time getting off the rig, and we were second-due truck; but this jerk stopped at the fire floor," Patty said.

More sleepy men from the bunks upstairs grabbed coffees and trudged into the dayroom.

"How could he not know that the second-due truck belongs on the floor above the fire?" Pete asked.

"We had to tell him."

"Jesus, that's scary," Pete said.

"To top it off, the guy's been breaking balls all week, looking for who's wearing white socks, editing mutual-exchange cards, chicken shit things like that, begging for trouble," Patty said.

"You working today?" Mutt asked.

"No, but this clown of a boss is," Patty said. "So, if you catch a job, watch your ass."

The Lieutenant in question came into the kitchen for coffee and then headed to the front of the firehouse to write a roll call at the house-watch booth.

The Mutt pulled Patty aside and said, "I was at a retirement party last night and got hammered. I got to take a wicked shit. Keep an eye out for the Lieutenant. I'm going to paint his bowl."

MUTT SETS OFF to punish the incompetent Lt. in his inimitable, innocuous, and ruthless fashion. After he explodes the remnants of last night's excess in the boss's toilet bowl, he won't flush it. This is a technique he has honed, mastered, and christened appropriately, "a leave."

After he wipes, he plants the soiled toilet tissue in the wastepaper basket next to the Lieutenant's desk and carefully covers the outrage with typing paper. This way the abominable stench will linger long after the toilet bowl is flushed and cleaned. The Lt. wouldn't dream of looking in the trash, and of course, the men won't say anything nor empty the basket until after his shift.

MUTT RETURNED FROM his expedition and took a seat in the dayroom. Some men jabbered about the day's schedule. Others chatted about last night's job. Because the walls separating the Lieutenant's office from the dayroom were as thin as a Japanese teahouse, the bowl next door began to sound like Old Faithful on speed—flush, flush, flush.

The frustrated officer finally appeared in the day room doorway wearing an expression that looked like someone had just told him his new proctologist would be Andre the Giant, and his anus would be stretched accordingly.

"Some fucking animal just took a disgusting shit in my bowl, and even though I flushed the bowl over twenty times, I can't get the stink out of my office."

The men acted puzzled. Eyes darted from face to face. Mutt finally hinted, "Hey Lieu, did you notice any toilet paper in the bowl?"

The Lieutenant's mouth formed a donut.

"Come to think of it, that fucking animal didn't even wipe his ass." He shook his head and plodded back to his office. As soon as he was out of earshot, the men looked at each other with wry smiles. A murmuring chorus of Mutt, Mutt, Mutt, rippled the room.

As the men paid homage to the master, Mutt tilted his chair back on two legs, crossed his arms over his chest and glowed.

TWENTY-TWO

THE FOLLOWING WEEKS, weeks, Erin discovered that she and Mick had a great deal more in common than she could have ever imagined. Both loved Irish culture, shared similar Bronx backgrounds, and even political beliefs. Against her better instincts, she was physically attracted to him and starting to find him fascinating.

On a rare night out, they entered a packed Irish pub where she was immediately hailed by a group of admirers. Mick pushed through the crowd to find an opening at the bar. Trying to secure cocktails from the frenzied bartender, he barked, "Let me have a double Johnny Walker Black on the rocks, and send that young lady at the end of the bar whatever she's drinking."

The bartender glanced to where Mick was pointing.

"You mean Erin Callahan? She drinks Bud light."

"You know her?"

"Everybody does. She's one of the best fiddlers in Yonkers."

While the bartender trotted to fill the order, Mick watched Erin work her entourage. Minutes later, he spotted an empty table and grabbed it. Half a drink in, she joined him.

"You must be damned good with that fiddle. Everybody knows you. I love that you're immersed in Irish culture. Besides loving the music, I've studied our history a bit. The Great

Hunger and Trinity are great books about the famine, and Yeats' poetry drove me to read about the insurrection."

"It's impossible to know where you're going unless you know where you came from. I have a Master's Degree in Irish History."

"That doesn't surprise me too much. I bet myself six to one that you'd dwarf my knowledge of Ireland, but a Master's, Jesus? I'm still trying to gauge the breadth of you."

"Breadth of me, is it? You better pray that you're not talking about my ass . . ."

Erin's green eyes sparkled then narrowed.

"Sure, Irish History interests me, but Irish Literature is my passion. I have a Masters in that as well."

He took a slight sip of his scotch.

"Another Masters? Jesus, how many do you have?"

"I have three," she smiled. "Don't be too impressed. It's not so much an accomplishment as indecision. I'm all over the place."

"Not so much of an accomplishment, are you kidding? You're beautiful, talented, and you have that kind of education? You're one hell of an interesting woman, Erin Callahan."

"Thanks for the compliment, Mr. Mullan, much appreciated," she hoisted her bottle in a mock toast. "You're interesting as well, but we're just so different. I don't know . . . as long as it just stays fun."

"Because of that God thing again? You gotta give that a break."

"Well, that and other things," Erin avoided his eyes and let her fingers massage the beer bottle.

"Look, Christians and Bible thumpers bother me for a reason. Most of the evil perpetuated on this planet was done by people absolutely sure that they were right. Science gave us the Age of Enlightenment, and religion gave us the Dark Ages. Every now and then, people should hang a question mark on things that they are so certain about. They'll find that every time they open their minds, sure as shit, some other fool will come along and park a thought in them." He sat back satisfied. "Whatta ya think about that?"

"I think that you need a laxative," she grinned then leaned forward. "You kill me. You think it's cool to put down God, meanwhile you admire overgrown men running around in short pants dropping a round ball through a net."

"I definitely spend too much time watching sports, but I don't worship athletes. I just gamble too much." Now Mick leaned forward. "Look, if the Almighty exists, I want him on my side, but I gather facts, use my intuition, and summon whatever little faith I have to come to a conclusion. That's logic. Your ilk believes first, and when the facts don't agree with your beliefs, you dismiss them."

"My ilk? Okay, this discussion is finished. I knew that this would be a mistake."

"Wait, I'm sorry, truly, just a poor choice of words." He got quiet and studied her in the bar's dim light a few moments. His face softened.

"Let's calm down and lighten the conversation a bit."

Mick clutched his scotch, twirled the ice in his glass, and looked intently into Erin's face.

"How do you feel about anal sex?"

"Eedgit." Erin almost choked laughing. "Look, I don't want to sound like a broken record. One more point and I'll leave it alone." She stared at him, "Do you really think that everything that happens in the universe is random? We all have to believe in something. I choose Christ. If he wasn't God, I've lost nothing. If there is a God, and you don't believe . . . well, you're the gambler, not me."

A barrel-chested, full-bearded man interrupted.

"Erin, in the name of Jesus, how long have you been here?" He was tall and dark with a broad nose and wore his premature-gray hair long and tied in the back. Erin and Mick raised their chins to the sound of his voice.

"Bobby," Erin said smiling. "Oh my God, are you guys playing tonight?"

His teeth flashed.

"You mean that you're not here because of us? I'm hurt." He turned and extended his mitt to Mick. "Sorry, I didn't mean to be rude. I'm Bobby McConnell."

"Oh. I'm so sorry," Erin stood. "Where are my manners?"

Mick rose and shook Bobby's hand.

"Nice to meet you. I'm Mick Mullan."

Each patterned weave on his thick, white-wool Irish sweater represented an Aran Island sailor's crest. Below it, he wore loose tan slacks with creases so sharp you could have shaved with them.

"We're gonna crank it up soon. If you feel like jumping in for a few tunes, Joanie has an extra fiddle."

"Joanie's here?" Erin squealed. "I haven't seen her in ages. How long has she been with the band?"

"Once you left, we had to get someone to fill your spot. It wasn't bloody easy. Come in the backroom and play a few tunes. We'd love to have you. It'll be fun."

AFTER REPLENISHING THEIR drinks, Mick and Erin walked back to where McConnell's Law was filling the air with rebel songs. The two bobbed and meandered through the packed dance floor. Erin climbed the four steps while Mick's elbows rested on the stage.

For the next half hour, her right hand raced the bow across Joanie's fiddle. When the two girls finished a fiddle duel, six songs later, the crowd clapped and screamed like Evangelicals at Sunday worship.

Mick stomped along with the crowd, his smile wide, his eyes beaming. He lifted his scotch from the floor, and as it glided down his gullet, the glass seemed to empty itself. He rapped his knuckles on the wooden stage and counted his blessings, but then a gnawing lump grew in his gut.

He began to realize that maybe all the rules of constraint, procedure, and protocol that he had previously lived by since Eileen's death might be vacuumed out of his life.

He drained the remains of his glass. The stage didn't seem nearly as wide as his grin.

Fuck it. It is what it is.

TWENTY-THREE

AFTER WORKING AN unusual, uneventful night tour at the firehouse, he entered the bar early Sunday morning and spied Erin chatting a few inches from Jamie's ear. Mick gave the two a quick, hand salute and headed straight downstairs. Erin turned her attention back to Jamie.

"You know we're dating, right? You're supposed to be his best friend? You're lucky I don't tell him about this. How can you hit on someone he's seeing?"

"Tell him if you want. He'd expect nothing less. He's shot the horse out from under my legs enough times," Jamie glowered. "Dating? Don't kid yourself. You're just the flavor of the week."

"Don't be bitter, Jamie. It doesn't suit you."

"I don't mean to be a jerk. It's just that I've known Mick a long time. A lot longer than you." He looked down pensively and used his thumb and forefinger to twirl the Heineken bottle. "By the way, what's that we're listening to, anyway?"

"Cherish the Irish," friends of mine.

"Well, no offense, but I'm the only one here. I don't mind that stuff occasionally, but could you play something a bit more contemporary?"

Erin let the affront slide, changed the music, and started cutting fruit. She filled the three trays and began filling the juices at each station. When she got back to Jamie's end of the bar, he said, "I'm sorry about that flavor of the week crack. It was childish. It's none of my business who you date. I just wanted you to know that I care for you. That's all."

He gulped the remains of his beer.

"You know what? The more I say the more I regret. I think I better get the hell out of here before I make a total fool out of myself."

He placed his empty bottle onto the return, left her a $10 tip, and twisted the handle of the back door.

MICK SURFACED SHORTLY.

"What did Jamie give me an Irish goodbye, no handshake, nothing?"

"He told me to tell you he had a few errands to run," Erin said.

"Might as well give me a beer. It's just as well he left. I need to talk to you. Paddy's Day is just around the corner. I'm gonna need a little help with the music. What was the name of the group you were listening to on my way downstairs?"

"That's Joanie Iver's band, 'Cherish the Irish.' They're friends of mine.'"

"They sounded great. Can you book them?"

Erin shook her head. "No. They're really big. You'd never be able to afford them. Irish musicians get double on Paddy's Day. Everybody wants us."

"Let me know if you can get anybody, please, and why'd you shut the tape off? Put it back on, or put on an Irish ballad or two, anyway. I'm in the mood."

Erin filled a pint glass with Heineken, placed it in front of him, and selected a Ronnie Drew CD from a large selection in a black leather case. She hit the play button and then dragged a bar rag across the space in front of him.

Mick sipped his beer, opened the New York Post, and said,

"That's better." He looked up from his paper. "Hey, what are you doing tomorrow? The weather's supposed to be pretty good. If it's not too windy, you wanna go sailing?"

"I don't know. I've never been sailing. I'm afraid I wouldn't be much of a hand."

"I can handle the boat alone. It's small. All you gotta do is bring drinks, sandwiches, and good conversation."

"I think I can handle that. Sure, why not. You've got a date."

Mick nodded and then pointed to the front of the bar.

"You've got a few customers."

Erin strolled to take their order, and Mick dove back into handicapping the day's basketball games.

But later that evening something beyond strange happened.

WHEN THE SUN set, the sky outside turned blue-black, windy, and veined with streaks of dry lightning. An unobtrusive Oriental man pulled open Nobody's large, wooden door and whipped his head to the sound of the stiff wind slamming it shut. He strode with purpose past his usual stool and marched to the back door where Mick was scribbling on a band schedule.

"You, a man I must talk," he said.

Dang was everything that Mick wasn't, disciplined, self-sacrificing, and frugal to a flaw, the kind of man who probably counted grains of rice before cooking them. Dang would show up every weekday at Mick's bar at exactly 2:30 pm.

He'd sit on the same stool by Nobody's entrance and order one glass of beer. There he'd settle, his narrow face cratered with acne scars, sipping his glass until the clock read precisely 2:50. Then he'd swallow what was left in his glass and walk the few short blocks to pick up his beautiful little daughter from school.

He was an inflexible, diminutive fellow, a hard man, tempered by trials, circumstance, and responsibility. He wore the same shabby navy sweatshirt and soiled blue workpants atop a pair of scuffed, black patent-leather shoes everyday. If a newspaper were available, he'd read it, but he'd never buy one.

Mick liked Dang. He never needed to be entertained, never bothered anyone, and never uttered more than the occasional sentence. But today was different. Today was Saturday, and Dang never came in on weekends.

When Dang placed the white box with two strips of red ribbon tied neatly into a bow on the bar, his hands were stained with grime, his nails broken and thick. A taut voice said, "God say I give you."

Mick put down his pen, picked up the box, and studied it.

"God said give this to me?" Mick's eyes shifted to his. "What's in it?"

"You open. You see."

Mick undid the ribbon, lifted the lid, and pushed aside the soft white tissue that blanketed its contents. Resting on green felt, the parted packaging revealed a beautiful beige-stone cross. In large letters emblazoned on its crossbar was a single word, "Journey."

"Nine angels in different parts of cross," Dang said. "God say I give to you to protect you."

Mick lifted the cross from the soft white tissue and read the vertical inscription.

"For I know the plans I have for you, said the Lord. They are plans for good and not for disaster, to give you a future and a hope. In those days when you pray, I will listen. If you look for me whole-heartedly, you will find me."

Below the puzzling quote was the attribution, "Jeremiah 29:11-13."

Mick placed the cross back into the box and rewrapped it. His right hand involuntarily rubbed the back of his neck. He felt a tingling sensation inside his throat, which he didn't quite understand.

"It's beautiful Dang. What a thoughtful gift, but unless you let me pay for it, I can't accept it. It looks too expensive."

Dang's coffee eyes were hollow, and wide, and blinked rapidly.

"No, me no can take money. God say I give you."

"What do you mean God say?" Mick's pulse quickened.

"I no can say," his feet shifted. "He knows. You will know."

"Can I at least buy you a beer?"

"No, no beer, today."

And with that declaration, the extraordinary fellow gave Mick a crisp nod, spun around, and marched out the front door. Mick had a strange intrusion in his stomach, a premonition of sorts. Why would a man so thrifty give him an expensive gift, and Jeremiah, why Jeremiah? He walked out the back door to the parking lot and carefully placed the box on the passenger seat of his Honda.

He dismissed the incident soon enough. It was puzzling and something that would probably fascinate Erin but not tantalizing enough to clog his crowded cranium for long.

Da hell with that Bible bullshit.

TWENTY-FOUR

IN THE FIREHOUSE the following week, the news spread like swine flu.

"A new Probie just reported for truck duty. Wait until you see this beauty. He's wearing his dress-blues, and he's got his mother with him."

"What, his formal uniform down here? Where's this guy think that he's working, headquarters?" Patty asked. "His mother? Are you kidding? He's with his fucken mother? What da fuck does he think this is grammar school?"

The men of 60-truck fought fires and didn't stand on ceremonial elegance. They worked in the ghetto and like soldiers in a combat zone couldn't be concerned with trivialities. They only wore dress uniforms at parades, medal days, and the all too frequent funerals.

They were too busy to keep their shoes shined or their rig cleaned. No one was interested in pomp. The job was to pour water on fire, and if anyone brought a woman into this neighborhood, it certainly wouldn't be their mother. In the interest of mercy, the Brothers decided to send a message. Break this kid in right. Set him straight.

"Tell the Probie the Chief wants to talk to him," Patty said. "I'll put on a chief's hat and jacket and wait for him in the Engine Office."

IMPERSONATING THE CHIEF, Patty sat behind the engine officer's desk awaiting the unsuspecting Probie. He didn't wait long. Mutt filled the doorway, jumped to attention, and lifted his fingers to his temple in a snappy salute.

"The new probationary firefighter is here to see you, sir."

The unsuspecting newcomer stiffened to attention and smartly popped four fingers above his right eye. Grinning, Patty tilted back in the swivel chair, and upturned his right hand, making cupping motions, beckoning the Probie toward him.

"At ease son. Come in. Come in. No one's going to bite you. Stand over here in front of my desk."

The rookie took the six necessary steps and stood firm.

"Now, first off, I'm pleased that you reported for duty in the proper uniform. Too many guys around here have let their appearances slip, and it's not good for morale."

The Probie's eyes gleamed, shoulders stiffening, congratulating himself on his decision to wear parade apparel.

"You can teach these veterans a thing or two, so you'll continue to wear your dress uniform until you complete your first year."

He wasn't happy to hear this but kept up a stoic facade.

"We run a tight ship around here, and we expect the men to cooperate. I don't suppose we'll be having any trouble with you?"

The Probie practically groveled assuring the chief that he would toe the line.

"Did you complete your training at the top of your class, or were you an also ran?"

He seized the opening.

"No sir. I was in the top five. I graduated right up there with the best of them."

"Good, good, how did you handle the smokehouse?" Patty asked.

"No problem, sir."

"How about the scaling ladder?"

"No problem, sir."

"This is important." Patty said. "How were you with your knots? Did you learn all your knots?"

"One of my best areas, sir," he said confidently. "I was a Sea Scout."

Patty nodded and let his fingers slowly unbutton the blue chief's jacket. When he stood from behind the desk, the white hat, blue tie, and white collar were all he had on. Below the waist, he was balls-ass naked.

He reached down, grasped his enormous weapon, and pounded it on the desk. The thud sounded like someone struck a snare drum with a ten-pound carp.

"Sea Scout, huh? Glad to hear that kid. How about tying a rolling hitch on this bad boy?"

Speechless and wearing the astounded look of a fish out of water, the Probie's eyes riveted to the incongruous sight before him. When the other men entered the office laughing, the Probie realized that he had been had. They welcomed him to the company, explained that the dress uniform wasn't necessary for the commute, and exposed Patty as a fireman.

The new firefighter was red faced, but conditioned to expect a hazing the first year took the prank in the good spirit it was intended. To insure bygones were bygones, Patty said, "Hey man, we're just getting ready for chow. Why not stay for lunch? There's plenty of food. Your mom can stay too."

"My mom?" he said puzzled. "That's not my mother. That's my wife."

TWENTY-FIVE

THE MORNING WAS a bit brisk for an ocean jaunt but bearable. Mick's boat, the *Sin Fein*, was moored fore and aft to a battered, white-planked dock out at City Island. It was 26-feet long, sleek, and could sleep two comfortably, four in a pinch, but Mick had learned years earlier that the bigger the boat, the less often it's used. He could take the blue and white sloop out alone and often did.

Erin held Oliver on her lap in the cockpit while he prepared to castoff, and in the sun's glow, her sparkling eyes and dazzling smile seemed magical. She wore a large, floppy straw hat atop a beige skirt with a buttoned-high long-sleeved, white silk shirt. A bronze drawstring bag slung from the shoulder of a tan canvass coat. Her hair was light auburn, yet the tips hugging her shoulders appeared red against the brightness of the morning.

The sloop's stern strained against its mooring, and wind gusts shook the trees causing a layer of leaves to speckle the cold gray water. A backdrop of black, rolling waves rose and fell under a mauve and pink streaked sky. When Mick ripped the starter chord, the kicker roared to life.

At the engine's roar, Oliver slipped slowly from Erin's lap and carefully navigated his four legs toward the bow. Mick cast off the lines and then cautiously steered the outboard through a nest of moored boats. Once in open water, he revved the gas and watched silently as Oliver's head appear to bounce in rhythm with the waves. Away from shore, he finally spoke.

"The bar's doing great, but I gotta slow down with the gambling and drinking. I've gotta quit the cocaine too. With that shit, I could lose my job. If I just curb a few bad habits, I'll have it all under control."

"Curb a few bad habits? Do you think they're just habits? Isn't it more likely that they're symptoms of that disorder that your doctor diagnosed, more like addictions?"

A tugboat chugged by, and his head whipped skyward. The harsh, offensive horn had caused a flock of seagulls to torment the sky. He stared a few more seconds before focusing on her question. Salt air filled Mick's nose and lungs while he broke into a wide grin.

"Disorders, addictions, nah, what are the odds that a psychiatrist knows more about mental illness than me? He only studies it. I live it."

"Listen to yourself. You might lose everything you love because of an illegal drug, yet you've got it all under control? Things are fine? If you're so together, why do you see a psychiatrist?"

"I don't anymore. I only went twice." He passed the rudder's wooden handle to her. "Here, hold this steady for me, and hold that thought too. I mean the one about my sanity."

Mick leapt up, raised the sailboat's jib, and adjusted the sheets. The ocean had turned as black as satin, only lustering whenever the sun peeked from behind a cloud. Heavy waves pushed steadily against the bow rocking the ship like a cradle. In the distance, roils of black water smashed and buried the gray rocks dotting the shore.

When the jib filled with wind, he gripped his arm firmly to the mast for balance before tottering along the cabin's roof, plopping himself next to Erin, and re-manning the tiller.

"Yeah, I'm a little whacky, but who wants to be sane in an

insane world?"

"I'm no psychiatrist, but it seems like you're attracted to drugs, gambling, and sex the way a mole is drawn to the recesses of the earth. You have zero regard for your soul."

"There's that soul thing again. How am I supposed to act? I'm not looking for a long-term relationship, but I have physical needs. I'm a man. I'm not sitting on my hands."

"That's what I mean. You see nothing wrong with casual sex?"

"What the hell? Sex is fun. Who doesn't like sex?" Mick handed her the tiller again. He didn't like where this conversation was heading.

"Just hold it steady for another minute or so. I wanna jump below and get my jacket."

He disappeared into the cabin and came back seconds later to reclaim the tiller.

"I'm just being honest. If I were in a relationship, I'd be faithful, but I'm a grown man with strong urges. There's no shortage of women in my life, but I don't mislead any of them."

He stared out at the open sea a few moments before he said, "I do what I want, and I don't have any moral qualms about it either. I tell the truth about who I am to the women I spend time with. I used to be religious. It has a certain comfort to it. But once I reached puberty, the Catholic Church's repression and all that guilt made me flee. I remember when I was a kid I used to slip in all my sexual sins at the end of my confession. Bless me father for I have sinned. I ate meat on Friday, disobeyed my parents, and oh yeah, I almost forgot," he laughed loudly. "Last month, I masturbated a couple of hundred times."

"What?" She clutched her sides and doubled over. "You better be exaggerating, or you can add an astonishing lack of self-control to the behaviors you can't curb."

Erin's unrestrained laughter rang through his soul like the

peals of church bells. When her bewitching eyes lingered on him for a minute, it made him feel rightly or wrongly that he was genuinely invited into the mysteries of her life and was surprised by how much that touched him.

"My parents were poor. I had nothing else to play with," Mick chuckled. "Speaking of self control . . ."

Mick leaned forward to kiss her, but Erin twisted her head. He returned to the rudder with darkened eyes.

"Look, I understand. You're a one-man gal and expect the same. If you and I fell in love, I'd stop seeing other women in a New York minute. But foregoing sex until that happens isn't in my nature, and even you will have to admit that so far, I've shown extraordinary restraint the few times we've gone out. You know there's chemistry between us, and we'll end up in bed eventually. Why postpone the inevitable?"

She avoided his piercing eyes and the question that came with them before measuring her next sentence.

"Look. I like you a lot. I have a ball when I'm with you, but we have different ideas of morality. I refuse to be a cliché, 'Girl gets barmaid job, sleeps with owner.' Forget that. I'm not going that route, not easily anyway, but don't have any illusions about me being some kind of a goody two-shoes. I'm hardly a choirgirl. I just won't have sex recreationally. That's not who I am, but I like to have a good time as much as anyone and would probably surprise you in the area you deem so important!"

"Surprise me?" Mick gave a half smile. "You might at that. Listen, I had no problem with fidelity when I was married. After Eileen died, I had no bloody reason to be faithful, faithful to whom, myself? I don't understand you. What kind of woman denies her desires? I know there's a connection between us. I can feel it. So, can you."

"I'll tell you what. I'll cut you a deal. If you think that I'm worth the trouble, come with me to Mass this Sunday."

"What? How will that prove anything?"

Mick pulled the mainsail's sheet, tightened, and readjusted the jib. The coastline became grayer and more indistinct and then dropped behind them altogether. He stared at the wind cutting long V's in the sea's surface and said nothing. Erin finally broke the silence.

"It'll prove something to me. I don't care about the damn sex, Mick, and you know it. I need to know that I'm not a cliché, a convenience, just a passing fancy."

He waited a long while before he spoke again and wondered if he should tell her one of the reasons he didn't believe, tell her about what had happened to his best friend Eddie. He decided against it, but on his mind now, his head replayed it.

AS A KID, he kept his problems bottled up and never discussed them with anyone except Eddie. With his best friend, nothing was taboo. They spent every free moment together, were athletic equals, had a mutual love for the Giants and Mets, and did what all best friends do, watched each other's backs.

They spent days huddled in makeshift clubhouses and romanced about these "forts" that were built with discarded lumber that they had found around the neighborhood. They'd sweep away the stones and broken glass in a vacant lot, toss down a discarded old rug, and finally throw up the wood.

"Hey, look Mick. Someone threw out a carpet. Let's build a fort," Eddie would say.

"Yeah, we'll start a club, but no one can join unless we say so," he'd answer.

Although their fort was neither secret nor hidden, except in their childish imaginations, it became a sanctuary to escape the turmoil and madness of their alcoholic homes, a place to hang out. It was extra special when it rained because they didn't have to march upstairs like their friends.

Throughout his childhood, Mick and his buddies built loads of these clubhouses, but that incident on that one dreadful day soured the experience forever. What happened to Eddie was so painful that it would sow seeds of doubt about everything that his parents and parochial school had ever taught him.

On his ninth birthday, Monica reminded him that later that morning the two would be off to Fordham Road to buy new Keds, so if he was going downstairs to keep an eye on the clock. Mick was delighted about the sneakers, but a little annoyed because he wanted to meet Eddie at their fort.

Two hours later, he had asked his mom if he could wear his new Keds out of Modell Davega's. As usual, his old sneakers were held together by magnetic tape and worn to the max.

"You'll have to. The ones you're wearing now are only fit for the garbage."

After shopping, Monica bought him hot dogs at Nedicks. The frankfurters on Fordham Road were the best, on toasted rolls, with that crisp German sauerkraut. He didn't get back to the neighborhood until late afternoon.

He asked the guys playing stickball if they had seen Eddie. No one had. Mick made a quick check inside the fort, nothing, so he went to play ball with his buddies and show off his new Keds. After a few games of stickball, still no sign of Eddie. Like most parents on the block, Eddie's mother and father worked. Mick didn't expect them to be home but hiked the four flights of stairs and rang his bell anyway, no answer.

Mick assumed that he'd see him later. He was wrong, dead wrong.

THE NIGHT EDDIE disappeared police scoured the neighborhood. Two squad cars at first, but later hoards of detectives knocked on doors and made inquiries. He had just vanished. Even though no ransom notes ever materialized, the cops called it a kidnapping. Most disappearances in those days were, few used the term sexual predator. All that Mick knew was that Eddie was missing.

If I hadn't needed sneakers, would I have been there? Would I have been taken too? Could I have prevented it?

Monica had told him that all he could do now was trust The Lord, and pray hard because God did everything for a reason. So, to save his buddy, Mick turned to his Creator and prayed harder than anyone had ever prayed. Every waking moment, he prayed.

He never saw Eddie again. Neither did anyone else.

The seeds of doubt planted, Mick realized that prayers weren't magic, so he'd never pray as hard or as often again. The "benevolent" Supreme Being had taken a fine boy, who had done Him no harm, and the irony of that wasn't lost on Mullan.

He grew up, and married Eileen, and the day that she died was the last day Mick ever spent on his knees. He'd finally had enough of all that Big Man in the sky bullshit, but maybe now wasn't the time to tell that tale to Erin. For now, he'd just make it short and sweet.

"LISTEN, I WAS devout as a kid. I prayed hard, and your God never listened. This God of yours is not a merciful one, and his universe is a world of war, drought, agony and famine, not a pleasant place."

"I can't explain why there's such suffering in the world . . . or why children get cancer, or starve," she said. "But you can't second guess God. We just have to trust our creator and his infinite wisdom."

"Yeah, I've heard that bullshit from the pulpit before, usually just before church minions pass around the wicker-collection baskets. The funny thing is that those self-righteous hypocrites never ask the faithful to make their checks out to Jesus."

Erin averted her eyes and said nothing more, just staring out at the waves splashing against the bow.

When they stopped talking religion, the next few hours flew.

They ate from a bucket of chicken, chatted, and enjoyed the sleekness of the boat as it cut through the choppy waters. She was a great storyteller, so interesting and charming that Mick had no alternative than to fall in love with her. But toward the end of the day, his big mouth got him in trouble again. Erin lobbed a sentence at him about principles, which he swung at and whiffed badly.

"I admire your ethics. I really do, but shit, it's the 21st century. Wouldn't it just be easier to let yourself be a woman?"

Erin opened her mouth to respond but bit her tongue. The weather had started to change. A heavy bank of gray clouds stretching from horizon to horizon was moving out of the West, and as the first shadows passed across what was left of the sun, a heady breeze began rocking the boat. She turned her collar up and commented on how cold it was getting.

"How long will it take us to get back to shore?" she asked.

TWENTY-SIX

THE FOLLOWING MORNING, Mick was shoving a bagel in his mouth when a familiar drone blasted over the firehouse intercom, "Mick Mullan, outside phone."

Mick lifted the receiver.

"Hey boss, some chick called for you," Butch said. "She said that you met her in Australia. She's staying at the Regency Hotel in Manhattan and wants you to call her."

"A gal for me? What's her name?"

"She didn't say, but she said that you'd definitely remember her."

Mick yanked the phone from his ear and stared at the mouthpiece in disbelief.

"You didn't get her name? What room number is she in?"

"I didn't get that either."

"What the fuck kind of an eedgit are you?" Mick asked his bartender. "A woman calls and tells you to have me call her, but you didn't get any other information? So, you expect me to call the hotel and say, 'I need to talk to a girl, but I don't know her name or room number? Can you just connect me with all the girls in the hotel?'"

Mick felt trapped in a Cheech and Chong routine.

"Sorry boss, but don't worry. I gave her your number at the firehouse. She'll probably call you there."

Mick's jaw clenched, and a vein in his neck throbbed, but he didn't want to act like an asshole, so he said, "Yeah, probably."

When he hung up, his mind raced.

How many girls did I give Nobody's number to in those three weeks?

Except for Grace, Diane and the two Brits, the other girls whom he had romped with were blurs. He wouldn't have been able to pick them out of a line-up.

As callous as that sounds, many Australian nights he had drank to unconsciousness and when drinking heavy, he seldom remembered much. Sick and hung-over the following morning, the only knowledge he'd extract from the previous night came from an empty wallet, or two or three crumpled singles, on whatever nightstand, next to whatever bed, in whatever hotel room he awoke in.

AN HOUR LATER the "bitch box" again, "Firefighter Mullan outside phone."

"Hey boss, it's me again. That chick called back. She wants you to meet her at the Regency tomorrow morning at nine a.m. and take her to the Empire State Building." Mick started to bark but Butch interrupted, "I swear boss, she wouldn't give me her name, but she said that once you saw her you'd recognize her."

"Again, you didn't get her name? What da fuck, man?"

"I swear. I asked her six times. She wouldn't say. She said it's a surprise; just tell Mick to be there. He won't be sorry."

Once Butch hung up, he started piecing Australia together.

It wouldn't be Grace. She's about money. It wouldn't be Diane. We said our goodbyes, and she's too grounded to chase me halfway across the world. Maybe it's one of the girls I met up in Cannes when I was diving the reef and hanging around with that screwball, Bobby. Fuck it. Tomorrow morning will be here soon enough. If she's a drag, I'll take her on a quick tour and shove off.

THE FOLLOWING MORNING, Mick wheeled through a lobby of strangers. He was early and cooling his heels until laughter pouring from the lounge distracted him. He followed the noise past the thick leather seats, cherry wood walls, and brass fixtures to where five guys were huddling at the center of the bar.

Chest high amidst the business suits, and barely visible in the circle, Mick glimpsed a shock of bleached-blond hair. As the huddle shifted and elongated, he spotted a bright red mini-skirt. He didn't just spot it. He couldn't take his eyes off it, nor could any man in the room. The miniskirt barely concealed her upper thighs.

Under her neck sat a pair of perfect nipples wrestling to burst out of a black bodysuit. Cream lace stockings accentuated her flawless legs and lured his eyes down to her pink, six-inch heels.

Holy shit, Grace, what the fuck?

No wonder the bar had so many customers so early. He couldn't believe his eyes. A lucky smile etched his face when she squealed, "Mick."

When the red meat the jackals had been feasting on swam through the sea of suits to get to the schmuck wearing jeans, the five men glared at Mick like he had just pissed in their martinis. Grace glued her body to him and captured his mouth with a lingering kiss. The moment their lips broke, she grabbed a black leather jacket, and spun him toward the exit.

"Now, you must take me to the Empire State Building."

"Baby for you, I'll climb the fucking thing."

He glanced over his shoulder to break some balls.

"Thanks for watching over my niece boys. Damn nice of ya's."

Grace wore the costume of high-priced company, so as soon as they hit the street, the hoots and whistles began. Mick had never experienced this before but lapped it up. Every few catcalls, he'd just turn his palms outward with a smirk on his face and shrug his shoulders.

Their entire route had suddenly turned into a testosterone charged construction zone, but Grace wasn't fazed. She courted the attention, indeed thrived on it. When the elevator doors to the observatory closed, she jutted her ass against his groin and jiggled.

She was driving him nuts and knew it. He wanted her more than a cold beer after a softball game, now right here in the elevator, and he knew his hunger would only get worse. While he still had a shot-glass of willpower remaining, he decided to fill Grace in on an old New York custom.

"Baby, we have a saying in N.Y. called, 'on the arm.' You're on holiday. You ain't working, and I ain't paying. 'On the arm' means free."

"Of course, no worries, Mick. I get it," she chuckled. "Don't worry, Yank. I definitely get it."

After an hour at the landmark, they cabbed it back to the Regency, opened the door to her room, and nearly broke a window. It looked like a phone booth. It barely had space for the bed, which Mick nevertheless immediately put to good use.

He asked afterwards what was she was paying for this closet, and when she told him, he spat, "Are you kidding, $400 a night? This room's so fucken small you could bump into yourself in here."

One of his friends from the old neighborhood currently ran one of the most prestigious hotels in Manhattan and was hardly a prude.

"Let me make a call."

He punched his cell.

"Hey Jake, Mick here. Listen, I need a favor. I got this working girl from Australia with me at the Regency. She's a knockout, a real doll, and a hell of a worker. Her room looks like a coffin. She's in town for a year. Can you put her up a few weeks until she gets settled? She'll do us both a few favors."

"If she looks as good as you say, I'll put her up for a few months," Jake snorted

"Thanks man." He hung up and smirked. "Pack a bag, sweetheart. We're checking out of here. We've got much better digs, and here's the best part. He tapped three fingers from his right hand across his left forearm and beamed, "On the arm."

WHEN THEY WALTZED into the hotel, the concierge greeted them like royalty. He was instructed to make sure they were comfortable in every way. The bellhop led them to same suite where the Beatles stayed on their N.Y. visit.

The door opened to four bedrooms, three bathrooms, an enormous kitchen, and a living room with a wrap around terrace overlooking Park Ave. Even Mick couldn't believe the layout but tried to act nonchalant.

"Here you go baby. This is more like it."

She paraded through the rooms like a proud, pedigreed pigeon, and Grace was the kind of girl who could strut sitting down. She belonged in digs like this and knew it. Mick couldn't resist repeating the coup de grace.

"And like I said, Gracie baby, 'on the arm.'"

"Oh my God, Mick. It's beautiful. You're so influential. I can't believe it."

"One thing honey, you're gonna have to take care of Jake."

"Don't worry. I'll send your Jake to heaven."

With a pout on her mouth like an adolescent girl, her eyes fastened on his face, she lifted her sweater, unhooked her bra, unbuttoned her jeans, and stepped out of them.

"But first, let me take care of you. Can I please suck your cock again, Mickey? Please?"

He grabbed her hand and led her to the enormous acreage that the rich call a bed. As his head lay on three stacked pillows, Mick looked down at Grace's blonde crown.

"If other men knew what I know about you baby, they'd be fighting wars over you."

"Mick, you make a working girl feel like Helen of Troy."

"Why wouldn't I treat you good, baby? What you do for me is a minor miracle. Anything else you need while you're in New York?"

"Can you get me some cocaine?"

Mick had four or five phone numbers that would solve that problem. He dialed one and soon after made a call to another buddy who was the day manager at one of the best steakhouses in Manhattan. A restaurant table secured, he concentrated on the moment at hand. Grace's head bobbed in perfect rhythm and didn't disappoint.

THEY CABBED IT to Smith and Wolenskys where his buddy had hooked him up with a table by the fireplace and a complimentary bottle of Dom Perignon. Grace's dress left little to the imagination. Cheap and classy at the same time, not an easy look to pull off, but her body would have looked good in burlap.

Mick knew Grace was bright but in time discovered that she was also well healed. Every time she left the hotel suite, she bought back bags of expensive clothing from many of the best-known stores in New York.

But after a week of ravenous sex, something was missing. Worn out, and tired of catering to her, she didn't seem quite so special now that he wasn't on holiday. He had a life he loved and two jobs. With her charm fading fast, he asked if she would be interested in picking up a few bucks while she was in town. She could turn a few tricks and do his friends a few favors. She was all for it.

He called two of his bartenders, and they were at the hotel almost before he cradled the phone. Why not? He was offering a beautiful blonde and rails of blow. They gave her $100 each and did the deed. After they left, Mick attempted another session, but the coke had kicked in. His ability to perform depleted, he asked was there anything else she'd like?

"I've never fucked a black man."

One black guy in Mick's firehouse was an incredible athlete, 25-years-old with muscles in his hair, a real ladies man. So, Mick called the firehouse, and by a happy coincidence, Chris was working. Mick told him that when he got off duty tomorrow morning, come to the hotel, and then ran Grace's tale by him.

Chris thought that Mick was putting him on.

"I'm not kidding man," Mick said. "I've got a beautiful blonde in this hotel room who wants to screw you. If I'm lying, you can kick my ass all the way up Fifth Ave."

After he hung up, Grace said, "You're so cool. I never met a man who didn't care who slept with me."

He looked at her as if she were nuts.

"You're not sleeping with him. You're a pro in the oldest profession in the world. Who the hell am I to pass judgment on you? This is your livelihood. If you were a plumber, would I care if you fixed someone else's pipes?"

"At last," she said. "A man who understands me."

Mick knew then that Winston Churchill was right. Women were puzzles, wrapped in enigmas, and surrounded by conundrums. He had just called a stunning blonde a whore, and she couldn't wait to prove him right.

TWENTY-SEVEN

MICK AND MUTT were carving a blueberry pie in the firehouse.

"You know how with women you get those hills and valleys? I'm on some roll, man."

Mick forked a huge piece between his teeth, wolfed it down, and paused a few seconds before finishing his thought.

"This hooker from Australia showed up in New York. She's amazing, no bullshit, and just pure unadulterated sex. Every man's dream."

"Not every man's," Mutt laughed. "But definitely yours."

"No, man. I'm not kidding. The shit this broad says is unreal. She asked me if I would mind if we threw another girl in the bed every so often just to keep things fresh." Mick's right thumb pointed to his chest. "Asked me? Imagine?"

His left hand wagged an empty fork to emphasize his next sentence.

"I asked her about her first sexual experience, and when she told me it was with a woman, I said, 'cool. Tell me about it.'"

Despite piling pie onto his plate, Mutt was listening.

"She said that she and her girlfriend were watching porn, and then they started playing with themselves. From there one thing led to another, and by the end of the week, they had bought sex toys and were going to town on each other."

"Holy shit, man. This chick really does sound wild." Mutt sipped his coffee.

"Wait a second. You ain't even heard the kicker. When I asked her how old she was when this happened, she didn't flinch. She said twelve."

Mutt spilled coffee on his shirt.

"Fucken twelve-years-old?"

"I know. I couldn't believe it either, and she said it like she was talking about a pedicure, totally uninhibited about sex."

"She sounds like a trip, but I guess a hooker can't be inhibited, bad for business."

"You have no idea. This chick absolutely ruins me. She brain-fucks me

The things she says to me are absolutely filthy, so erotic."

Mick pushed his plate aside.

"Get this. We were playing blackjack at a casino in Australia, and she tried to pick up the girl in the seat next to me. When the gal said that she had an argument with her girlfriend, Grace asked her about her plans for the rest of the night."

Mick reacted like a tickled child.

"She's so fucken cool that it's hard for me to remember that she's a prostitute, especially because thanks to Jake I ain't been paying for shit since she hit N.Y. She makes me believe that she likes it and that I'm making it good to her. I can't figure out why she's doing me for free. She usually has a dollar sign where her heart should be."

Mutt pulled his coffee toward him and laughed.

"It was inevitable. We always knew that you'd fall in love with a prostitute."

"Yeah, right, like I'm gonna fall in love with a working girl. I don't give a damn who she sleeps with, but shit man, where do I go from here? What woman is gonna be able to follow this act?"

"What about this Irish goddess that I've heard so much

about? When does she start?"

"She's been working a couple of months, but she's a different kind of chick, a straight shooter. She's a knockout too, but that's not it. I've seen women that I'd look at quicker."

Mick took a healthy swig of his coffee and wiped his mouth with a napkin.

"But not since Eileen have I met a woman that I'd look at longer. There's just something about her."

Mutt tilted his chair and let the corner of his mouth form a smile.

"You haven't slept with her yet, and you hired her before you left? That's some kind of record for you. Ain't it?"

"Yeah, but I was in Australia, so ya gotta make allowances," Mick said. "I'll close that deal yet. It's just a matter of time. She'll cave. Women like to have fun just as much as men do. I'm guessing that Erin's no exception, plus she's smart. Why would anyone with an inquisitive mind embrace celibacy or monogamy?"

"She's not the type of gal that you're used to Mick."

"I don't get the double standard. If a man wants to have consensual sex without commitment no problem. If a woman wants the same, she's a slut. Bullshit. We're all one species with the same appetites, sexual, and otherwise."

Mutt's eyes froze. His voice rose, "She's not the type of gal you're used to Mick."

Mick let the sentence resonate a bit, stared at Mutt with an empty look, and abruptly changed the subject.

"What do ya hear about Paul?"

"Great news, man. He's coming back to work. He had his big toe amputated and transplanted to where his thumb was. Can you believe that shit? Some balls, huh?"

"Wow, whatta piece of work. He could've gotten out of the job with a three quarters pension but decided to come back to work? Whatta stand up guy. Yet, he's so quiet, so introverted compared to the other lunatics in this house."

A devilish gleam lit Mutt's eyes.

"I gotta figure out a way to really break his balls."

TWENTY-EIGHT

TWO DAYS LATER, Mick drove down the Grand Concourse, exited at the hub on 149th street, passed Lincoln Hospital, and steered past the vacant, burned-out blocks of the South Bronx.

He parked in one of the few designated spots in front of the firehouse, signed in at the house-watch booth, and strolled back to a crowded dayroom during the change of shifts. The Brothers gulped morning coffee and eyeballed the dayroom door, awaiting fresh meat to carve.

As soon as Mick walked in, Pete started, "Hey, Mick, when's the wedding?" All the men looked up grinning.

"So, the ultimate hedonist is finally turning monogamist," Patty said.

"Wow, hedonist, monogamist, that's a hell of a lot of syllables just to break my balls. You'd usually just call me an asshole. Fuck you, Patty, and fuck the rest of you pricks. It's no big deal, and I'm hardly at the altar. I won't bore you with the details of my recent escapades, but just check with Chris. Ask him about the blonde at the hotel." Mick laughed. "I just got this chick, Erin, on my mind at the moment, and what's weird is that she's the opposite of every woman who has ever attracted me. Even her annoying traits intrigue me. She's on Irish time, always late, and the strangest thing of all is that she hasn't let me seal the deal."

"No sex?" Patty said. "Get the fuck outta here."

"No, but I ain't pushing it; besides I'm on a roll right now, anyhow."

Mick splattered cream cheese and a slice of tomato on a bagel.

"I'll crack that vault soon enough."

He waved the bagel like a baton.

"I don't know what da fuck it is about her? She's smart as hell though, man, and funny." Mick barely took time to swallow. "There's just something about the way she talks, the way she holds her head, the way she walks. Every joke I crack seems funnier when she's laughing."

Mick stopped ranting. Face flushed, he clutched his Adam's apple.

"Listen to me. I sound like a ten-year-old. I'll be having trouble breathing next."

"Whoa, you're way too excited about this chick. You sound like you're in deep," Mutt said. "What happened to the stay unattached at all costs philosophy?"

"Yeah, I say a lot of stupid shit, so there's no chance of getting hung up."

"Keep me posted on this," Pete said. "I'm dying to see how long this "Irish goddess" puts up with your extra curricular activities. Old married guys like me live vicariously through you."

His face reddening, Mick escaped to the kitchen. While pouring coffee, he thought about the extraordinary friendship that firefighters have. It seemed eternal and not subject to the laws of mutability. It was improbable that all of them would finish their careers, but if they ever did experience visions of mortality, they only had to look into one another's faces to assure themselves that none of them would ever die.

He sensed Pete's broad nose pushing air over his shoulder and turned.

"Shifty was telling me some lieutenant made a comment about that shit you've been shoveling up your nose. Get some help. Guys are talking. It just fuels your drinking, and that's the last thing that you need."

The skin around Mick's mouth tightened.

"I know Pete, and you're right. I was just telling Erin that the other day. I'll get my act together. It's just that in the bar business, it's all around you."

WHEN THE TWO re-entered the dayroom, the door burst open. Back from sick leave after a successful thumb transplant, a smiling Paul slammed a dozen donuts on the table.

"Make sure the miserable sonofabitch who sent me that script of *Edward Scissorhands* with 'Thumb through this asshole' written across the first page doesn't eat any of my donuts."

All the men jumped up, surrounded him, shook Paul's hand and patted his back.

"Jesus welcome back, man," Patty said.

"Oh, my God, ya made it." Mick hugged him. "So, glad to see ya, Brother."

Paul showed everyone the newly grafted toe replacing his thumb and then sat and began buttering a bagel.

"The place wasn't the same without you," Kingsley said.

"I couldn't wait to get back to work and see you guys." His elbows supported his two hands, which stretched across the table. "The whole ordeal sucked."

"We're all thrilled to have you back, man." Mutt sipped a can of coke and paused to give emphasis to his next sentence. "But let's get one thing straight . . . What are you a fucken animal? We're trying to eat here. Get your fucken foot off the table, or put a sock over it. You're gonna give us all a case of athlete's hand."

Paul swung a mock smack that crossed the thin air in front of Mutt's face.

"Fucken Mutt, I never thought I'd be glad to hear your bullshit. I know it was you that sent that script to the hospital, you sonofabitch."

Bent over with laughter, Mutt barely spurted, "I thought up a nickname for you, too." He wiped tears from his eyes. "From now on, you're Thoe. Get it, thumb and toe?"

Mutt's chest heaved with laughter . . . "Aaaahhhhhh," he grabbed his sides. "I hope it sticks."

Three air born blasts interrupted Mutt's self-induced hysteria. The house watchman's voice filled the room with the familiar refrain, "Everybody goes. Everybody goes. Truck, engine, chief, get out. Get out."

Men scrambled from the table. Some slid poles. All jostled to don their turnout gear and board the trucks. The apparatus doors lifted. The sirens roared, and the two rigs sped to the box.

The Engine rolled up to a vacant. Tinned windows and broken fire escapes hugged the burnt-out structure, and flames roared through the roof. The chauffeur hooked the apparatus up to a hydrant. While the engine stretched their lines, Pete and Mick boarded the Truck's bucket.

Scurrying to secure the Tower Ladder's steel supports, the Truck chauffeur failed to notice that one of the metal legs had inadvertently landed atop a manhole cover. While the bucket was climbing, the flames burnt through an electric power line. After the wire severed, it settled against a metal fire escape.

The metal bucket, metal manhole cover, and metal fire escape had completed an electrical circuit and were now charged.

"Last time this building had squatters," Pete spoke into his handi-talki. "Mick is going to make a quick search on the floor above. Hold water until I give you the word."

As Pete maneuvered the bucket close to the fire escape, Mick reached out and clutched the metal railing. When the wire's voltage hit him, the blood drained from his face. His mouth quivered, body stiffening, shaking like it had a violent life of its own. His blue eyes webbed with red lines, his face contorted like he was having a seizure, yet his voice didn't make a single sound.

His head reared back instead, and his mouth spread in a silent, twisted yell. That first red-black rush of pain seemed to seal his eyes and steal the air from his lungs. He froze while his mind slipped gradually downward from darkness and pain into a warm, comforting pool of blessed unconsciousness.

Behind Pete were three different sized hooks. He snatched the one with the wooden handle, turned and slammed Mick's forearms upward. When he broke the connection, a tongue of smoke curled from Mick's fingernails. His insides turned to pudding, his legs liquid. The bucket's steel floor met his chin, knocking his helmet off. Pete saw yet another alarming tuft of smoke rise from Mick's sweaty-blond hair and screamed through his handi-talki, "Code Red, firefighter down. Call E.M.S."

TWENTY-NINE

THAT SAME AFTERNOON, Erin and Linda ate lunch on Arthur Ave, an Italian neighborhood near the Bronx Zoo. The most consistent Trattoria on a street well known for homemade Italian dishes, Dominick's had been in business more than seven decades. Diners received no printed menus, no written checks, and no ambiance, only superb cuisine.

Before slipping the spoon between her lips, Erin blew on her pasta fagiola.

"Why is it all the guys that I'm attracted to are a mess?"

"Join the club," Linda said. "Who's the culprit?"

Linda was a shade under medium height. A thin physique, mousy brown hair, and bright eyes made her look considerably younger than she was, which was 36. Although a keen mind and quick wit made her a fine catch, Linda was "nice looking" rather than pretty but a wonderful teacher.

"My boss at the bar has enormous potential, energy, sense of humor, smarts, but he's borderline psychotic," Erin said.

Linda's green eyes sparkled a bit.

"Psychotic? Just the kind of guy I'm attracted to. He sounds like the perfect fit for me. Does he slow dance?"

"No, really. It's sick." Erin's nose crinkled. "Even though I know he's poison, I can't stop thinking about him. This guy's a storm but not the kind we run from. He's the kind we chase. He has a well-deserved reputation, and I'm determined not to join the rank and file; but in this day and age, who doesn't have sex? I'm gonna have to sleep with him soon or lose him, yet if I do that, I'm really gonna be in deep."

Linda's eyes formed an unnerving and unattractive narrowness.

"You think that if you sleep with him that he'll be a pain in the ass to get rid off?"

"No. Just the opposite, I think that if I sleep with him, I'll be a pain in the ass to get rid off. I think I'm falling in love with him."

Linda's squint betrayed a literal-mindedness, or matter-of-factness, or whatever it might be called, but as soon as her tight lips cracked, Erin knew that she was in for a lecture.

"Listen to yourself . . . You know that he's no good for you, but he's all you think about. You sound like a heroin addict." Linda poured a smidgeon of oil and vinegar on her salad. "You've got too much going on for yourself, Erin. The last thing you need is melodrama. Take my advice. Dump him." Her voice rose, "Now, before it's too late."

Erin bit into her pasta, chewed slowly, and sipped her coffee. She reflected on Linda's words a moment before she spoke.

"But when he talks about his ex-wife, he seems so vulnerable, so helpless."

"Baby, they're all vulnerable. That's how they get us." Linda forked a piece of Romaine and used it like a pointer. "Take my advice. Get rid of him."

THIRTY

EVENING VISITING HOURS had just begun. Grace checked the room number she had written on a small business card against the arrows on the wall and then turned down a brightly lit hallway littered with wheelchairs and gurneys. It led to a semi-private hospital room where Mick was propped up on two pillows, smiling and alert with the Georgetown, St John's basketball game muted on the television.

"Oh Mick, I came as soon as I heard," Grace said.

Mick's eyes shot to the sound of her voice, and his face broke into a wide grin.

"Baaabbbyyyyy," he sang. "How sweet of you to come."

"What did you expect? You must know how I feel about you by now."

"How you feel about me?" He sat forward on the bed. "I love you too, baby, but you're in town for a year. Are you losing your mind? You know how we roll."

"I know we're not gonna play house, Mick. That's not what I meant, but you know damn well that when we get together, it's not about money anymore."

"Yeah, of course, I know there's more there than sex, Grace. But shit, we're just two adults having a good time. Come on. I thought you were cool. You know we aren't exclusive. You're still screwing Jake."

"You know that's only for room and board," she spat. "Although, he is damn good to me."

A loud voice from the doorway turned their heads.

"How ya feeling, Mick?"

"Pete, Jesus, so good to see you, man. My back and my chin still hurt a bit, but that's nothing." His lips turned stiff, his eyes intense. "I owe you my life, Brother. Thank God, I was lucky enough to have you in the bucket with me. I doubt that anyone else would have reacted that quickly."

"I just did what you'd do for me, man. As for luck, you're the gambler. I don't believe in coincidences. I saw Mike Weldon almost die like that three years ago, so I knew how to react. Another few seconds . . . well, I guess the Good Lord decided that your time just wasn't up."

"I'm glad you were in the bucket with me, Pete, but for the love of Jesus, don't start preaching." Mick reached for a plastic cup of water and sipped from it. "Ya know, I have had people come up to me all my life and tell me that I was blessed. And shit, although I'm a half-assed atheist, I'm starting to believe them."

"You must be 'Perfect Pete.' I'm Grace. Mick talks about you all the time."

"So, you're Grace? Mick doesn't talk about you enough." He shook her outstretched slender hand before turning back to Mick. "When are they letting you out of here?"

Before Mick could answer, a panicked Erin blew through the open door and rushed to his bedside.

"You're safe. Thank God, when I heard—"

"I'm safe enough baby, thanks to Pete here."

Erin put both hands over her heart and gave Pete a nod of her head.

"So, you're Erin. You're all he talks about."

When Grace heard that, her eyebrow raised, and she leveled Mick with a look that could have peeled the skin off his face.

Pete let his eyes slip from Erin's and turned to lecture Mick.

"You're a pisser." He aped Mick's accent. "Thank God, you were there, Pete, but for the love of Jesus don't preach." Pete smiled at Erin and canted his head. "He uses God in two sentences, but he's an atheist?"

Mick ignored Pete's dig and attempted to smooth over the tension between Erin and Grace.

"Baby, this is my friend Grace. We met in Australia."

Erin extended a wooden hand. Her face tensed.

"How nice, pleased to meet you . . . How long will you be in N.Y.?"

"At least a year, I work for the U.N."

Erin noticed her high heels, low cut top, and heavy makeup, bit her lip, drew her mouth into a pleasant smile, and said without sarcasm.

"That's impressive. I think you're in the right place. I'm certain the majority of diplomats will pay very close attention to whatever you have to say, the men anyway."

She turned back to Mick.

"What did the doctor say? When will you be released?"

"I'll probably be out of here tomorrow. I guess they just want to run some more tests. I feel fine."

"Well, atheist or not, you promised that you'd come to Mass with me, and I'm holding you to it. I sure as hell have something to thank God for, and you do too, even if you're too obstinate to realize it."

Grace stared at Mick in disbelief. She mouthed her next sentence silently, "Mass, are you fucken kidding me?"

THIRTY-ONE

IT HAD BEEN years since he had seen the inside of a church. St. Philip's was packed, and Mick felt intensely awkward amid the faithful. He had married Eileen here, and even that moving memory was soured by church hypocrisy. He remembered his feeling of disgust when told that he'd have to pay for a pre-cana conference.

Five hundred bucks to have a celibate tell me what to do on my wedding night?

Once settled in a pew with Erin, his cynicism softened as the altar boy swung the three chains holding a golden bowl-shaped vessel of incense. About two hand lengths from the ground, the child intermittently opened its top flap, swinging it gently, slowly, letting the charcoal refuel with oxygen. The unique smell brought back pleasant childhood memories.

Later, with a full contingent of choirboys behind her, and accompanied by Erin's violin and an organist, a marvelous diva sang Ave Maria. The splendor of the scene grabbed Mick's emotions and triggered the memory of he and his mother on their knees. His eyes moistened before his inner cynic warned him to snap out of it.

You're too smart to buy into this shit.

But then another echo surfaced. When he was little more than a teenager, four different adults had told him that God had laid hands on him. One was an Irish cousin, another a priest, and the oddest of all, two total strangers. Instead of frightening him, it gave young Mullan a strange comfort, as if he were invulnerable until he fulfilled whatever plans that his Creator had in mind for him.

As the choir raced to the crescendo, another thought surfaced. Falling in love with Erin would be a betrayal to Eileen's memory. That unalterable reality remained. No one could take his ex wife's place, so why go through the inevitable pain and disappointment that another relationship would bring?

When the Mass was over, Mick found himself sleepwalking from the wooden pew and shuffling to the front of the church where he found her surrounded by a few friends. He came up behind her, kissed her hair, clutched her waist, and pulled her to him. He could feel her heart beating beneath his arm.

And whether it was his brief brush with death, the week of sobriety, or the wisdom that comes with age, Mick was suddenly overwhelmed with the feeling that he could be true to this remarkable woman. He could put Eileen behind him and build a future with her.

What was he running from? She was brilliant, beautiful, and had all the qualities a man could want in a mate. It dawned on him how lucky he was to have her in his life. How many chances at real love does a man get?

Erin was blessed with the same glorious Celtic lust for life that he had. She had a gypsy's soul and was so down to earth that she would have been more comfortable in a mariachi band than an orchestra.

Erin spun, and when Mick looked down into her lovely face—a mere vestibule for a scholar's mind—her eyes were clear, as though a breeze had blown a dark object away from her vision. She smiled, and a single tear slid down her cheek.

Mick knew then that he could keep up this mask of indifference and pretend that he was a freewheeling soul. But down deep, he knew it was a lie. He could stay a jumble of sorry fictions, and live his life in regrettable pretense, or he could just admit that despite all that he had done to prevent it, he was in love.

Erin wasn't just another woman. They hadn't even had sex yet, except when the two embraced in his imagination, yet in his thoughts, one face shimmered above the rest, more beautiful than all the rest, and that face was Erin's.

He bent down and kissed her tenderly and wondered how the world could become a better place, how he could feel so good about himself, and how he could forget all his hesitations in the short moment that it took for two people to press their lips against one another. In that very instant, Mick realized that although love was a fool's game, in the end, it was the only game worth playing.

THIRTY-TWO

ERIN PICKED HIM up at his apartment the following afternoon knowing that they'd end up in bed together. Something about that moment that they shared together after mass had clinched it. Mick had told her about Grace's profession and their history. She had waited too long already, and so had he. She had surrendered all thoughts of postponing the inevitable.

After all, it was just sex, and she knew that if anything were ever going to come out of this, Grace had to be out of the picture. She had verbally fenced with Mick long enough and had her own sexual urges. She knew the time was now but was anxious as well. How in the hell could she hope to compete in bed with an Australian prostitute?

She needed neither romance nor prodding and had figured out the perfect way to blow his mind. She planned to expose a side of her that he had never seen before, a side of her only one man had ever seen before.

THEY ATE AT Rory Dolan's in Yonkers and sat opposite each other in a back-corner booth. Erin's shoulders were smooth, tan, and muscular, the tips of her auburn hair burned almost red, her breasts and hips tight against a blue cotton dress. After two Sheppard Pies and four Bloody Marys, they sat in silence and seemed to read each other's thoughts. The tryst's inevitable acceptance slowly oozed from their souls to their loins.

Then, true to her instinct and intellect, Erin astonished Mick by doing the single most erotic and revealing act he had ever seen displayed in public. She lifted her hips a few inches, reached below the table, and clandestinely pulled her purple g-string down both legs, out over her shoes, and crumpled it into a ball.

Mick drained his drink and broke the silence.

"We have the whole evening ahead of us, baby. What do you wanna do?"

Erin leered brazenly a moment, reached across the table, and stuffed the contents of her right hand into Mick's astonished mouth. The coyness dissipated, the veil lifted, Mick suddenly saw the depth of her. Her sense of humor, playfulness, and intellect exploded in front of him with that single wanton act.

Mick never needed nudging for sex, but this time around, it wouldn't be just physical. He knew he was falling in love. Not just falling but rushing into it with both eyes wide open. He removed the strip of silk, formed a broad smile, and responded predictably.

"Waiter, check."

HE TUMBLED THE lock, tossed his keys into a glass dish by the door, and reached down to knead the fur on Oliver's neck. Racing to the refrigerator, he loaded two pint glasses with water and carried them to his bedroom nightstand.

Her left palm grabbed the back of his neck. She kissed him hard and hungrily, loins pressing hotly against his, tongues probing feverishly. He bussed her hair, nibbled her ears, and kissed her neck carefully, glacierly, before raising the hem of her dress over her smooth legs and taut hips.

He kissed the tops of her breasts and then ran his hands

along her bare back and down her shaking muscular thighs. She gaped at him strangely, her mouth slightly parted, her face suddenly vulnerable.

Every time their loins touched, their bodies became points of fire. When he mounted her, Mick knew that he was entering a territory where the rules that had previously governed his life were about to irretrievably disappear.

Her skin was warm and cool at the same time. Her hair had the odor of hothouse orchids, and when her lean, strong legs wrapped around his, Mick arched his back and drove himself into her, slowly at first.

Any anxieties or apprehensions she might have had disappeared in his rhythmic motion and her passionate breathing. She pressed hard against him, tucking her feet inside his calves. Their gentle cadence quickened, and quickened, until the tempo was more like two wild animals in the heat of procreation.

She felt him tense, slow up, and try to hold back from that bursting moment of fulfillment, but Erin wouldn't slow her motion. Her groin felt like a hot flame was burning through her. When the moment came, and Mick went weak inside, she felt the sweat break out on her forehead but forced her hands to grip his back and pull hard as though some part of his climax might elude her in that final, heart-twisting moment.

When the explosion took place, Mick knew that something special had happened. This wasn't just another conquest. Life had magically restored in him something that he had lost way too soon somewhere along the way. She had strengthened his willingness to reopen his life to the possibility of love, a chance to get back what the universe had stolen.

Afterwards, she saw his look of contentment and knew something had changed.

"After Mass that day, did you feel the way that I felt?" she asked.

He couldn't get past her eyes, inches from his. He saw her soul through those two hypnotic jade portals shining a spirit so vast that he feared his heart couldn't contain it. Her essence just gushed out through those two magnificent green globes. No, this wasn't just another conquest, but Mick, being Mick downplayed it.

"I don't follow. What did you feel?"

"Like there was no past, no future, just that moment.

So many thoughts and emotions ran rampant inside him. Men fall in love with women for different reasons. Sometimes they are so beautiful that you have no more control over your desires than you do in choosing your nocturnal dreams. Then others earn their way into your soul by being kind, protective, and loving, the way you imagined your mother.

Then there were women like this, women who walk unexpectedly into your life when you have no intention of falling in love. These were the special ones. Not the women you want to live with but the ones you can't live without. But an old habit, his hesitancy to commit, made him blurt.

"I'd like to be more romantic or more 'the earth moved,' but I didn't see this coming."

She jabbed his naked thigh with her knee.

"You're as romantic as a slug, but at least you're consistent. You don't pay much attention to the details of life. Do ya, Mick? You just live it."

She took one of the tall glasses of ice water off the nightstand, sipped it, and handed it to him.

"I suspected it the minute we went out to eat that night, Mick, right then, right at that moment. I had that incredible certainty that the universe had created the both of us for a reason. God created a twin soul for each and every one of us, and I knew that soul was you, Mick. I really did. I knew."

A wry smile crossed his lips.

"It took you bloody long enough to do something about it."

"Don't make a joke. Not now, Mick, please. What do you think that we should do about it?"

"What do you want to do about it?"

"I want to hear you say that you're done fooling around."

"I said I'd take a shot. What more can I say?" Mick's face brightened, but his sentence had no humor in it.

"I want you to take more than a shot. I love you more than you can imagine, but you don't have a clue how special you are." Her eyes looked deep into his. "All this hooker business, the drinking, drugs, and gambling, you've lost respect for yourself. If we're to be together, we have to make each other better. It has to be symbiotic."

What little smile he had collapsed when Erin lifted her lovely head and her steel eyes stared up at him. "No shots. It's all or nothing. I'll say this in a language that you can understand. If you want this to happen, you'll have to go all in. That libido of yours has led you on a merry little chase, but that's all over. No more Grace's. No more one-night stands."

He knew better than to run from this kind of happiness. Whether Mick liked it or not, he was indeed, all in. His face suddenly turned rigid and glazed, his expression flat.

"Baby, I was just breaking your chops. I'd have to be an absolute fool to screw this up, and no one has ever called me a fool."

Erin's emerald eyes glowed.

"There's that I'm no fool again."

He gave a half smile and reached for a Marlboro light off the nightstand on his side of the bed. Before he touched the lighter to his smoke, he said, "I'm still hungry for you. I don't know if I can even give myself time to smoke this."

"Smoke later tonight or better yet early tomorrow."

Erin rubbed the inside of her thigh up and down his leg and moved the flat of her hand down his chest and stomach. She bent down and pulled him into her mouth. Mick let his fingers flip the unlit cigarette back onto the nightstand.

When she took him from her mouth, she continued to stroke him, her eyes climbing his chest, halting inches from his. His eyes were half-closed with passion.

"Open them wide, Mick. I want to see your blue eyes dance when it happens."

Once it happened, she had climbed so deep inside his soul that he felt like the two of them were joined. When he took her again later that evening, she came again, and again, something that she had never done before, as though an entire race was being conceived inside her.

She felt spent and chilly after and pushed her bottom against his pelvis. He cocooned her in his arms, and she wriggled and molded into his belly like the two were made of wax. She faded into sleep with sighs of deep contentment and swore she could hear the sounds of Irish fiddlers playing tearful ballads.

THIRTY-THREE

HE SAT AT the end of his crowded bar the following evening nursing a bottle of Heineken and a double scotch. Nobody's back door opened, and Grace glided in beside him.

"Grace, how ya doing, sweetheart?" His face brightened. "Butch, get Grace a taste."

She removed her Ralph Lauren fur-collared walking coat and hung it on the high-backed barstool behind her. A tight white shirt was tied below her generous breasts exposing a muscular midriff, the leather skirt below it too glossy, too blue, and way too tight, in other words, perfect.

"Where have you been hiding? Are you trying to avoid me?"

"I ain't avoiding anybody, honey, especially you. I've just been crazy busy."

"Well, it's been a while since you've stopped by the hotel. A girl has to take a cab to Queens to get a cock in her mouth?"

"Gracie, my love, you really know how to turn a phrase." He grinned, lifted his glass, and threw back half his scotch. When he placed the glass back on the bar, his mouth straightened. "Normally, nothing would make me happier, but I've been seeing Erin."

"So, what? You know me, no strings."

"I know honey. But this time, I'm playing it close to the vest."

"What? Why?"

Mick's eyes went flat. The way eyes go when someone has no intention of allowing another inside their thoughts. Grace let her gaze slip a moment to order a whiskey sour. When Butch left to build the drink, she stared hard into his face.

"Smarten up, Mick. You're heading for a fall. This chick is a holy roller, not your type. You and me are whores at heart. We both know what you like and how you like it. Stop kidding yourself. We even like the same type of girls."

"How in the hell would you know that?"

"If you jumped in the mix, I'd give your Erin a tumble. If you tell her that I'm keen on her will she play?"

He shuffled a step back from the bar and swiveled his head back and forth, using his index fingers to form the sign of the cross as if to ward off a vampire.

"Jesus Christ, you've no idea what kind of girl she is." The corners of his mouth curved downward. "Don't screw this up for me, baby. I would never do anything to hurt you, ever."

"C'mon, mate, lighten up. I know that she's special to you."

"Yeah, she is honey. I don't know where this is going, but I gotta see it through."

Grace shrugged, lifted a dollar from Mick's change, uncoiled from her stool, and ambled to the jukebox by the bar's entrance. After selecting a few tunes, she came back and fired a shot across Mick's bow.

"Does Erin suck cock as good as me?"

"That's not fair, Grace," Mick laughed. "I'll just take the Fifth on that one."

"So, you're sure that you don't want to go down the basement to see if I still have what it takes?"

"Gracie baby, you could empty the cargo hold of an oil tanker with a soda fountain straw. I know you still got it, but I just wouldn't feel right about it.'

"Okay, Mick. If you change your mind, you always know

where to find me."

Grace picked up her drink, and before wending her way toward the dance floor executed a delicate about face. She flashed Mick a coy glance.

"Watch your step. This offer might not be good much longer. Jake's awful good to me."

"Gracie, baby, if you and I lived together, I'd need an extra room just for your shoes." When she disappeared through the crowd, he drained his scotch, hailed his bartender, and bobbed his index finger up and down at the empty vessel.

"Another double boss?" Butch asked.

"Bring me a double every ten minutes, until I pass out, and then every five minutes after that. I think I must be losing my mind. I just turned down a blowjob from the best piece of ass that I've ever had in my life."

THIRTY-FOUR

WEEKS FLEW BY and life was good. The two still had fundamental religious differences, but their tangible bond far outweighed any metaphysical disagreements. Neither could do anything about their circumstance now. It was way too late for that. He and Erin had grown so close that Mick felt they should be brushing each other's teeth.

Whether they wanted it or not, they were hopelessly linked; yet every now and then that one big conflict would resurface, especially if they weren't in bed. That Saturday afternoon, Nobody's was slow.

"I'm an empiricist, honey. I've got nothing against your faith. Believe what you want," Mick said. "But my mother tried, twelve years of Catholic school tried, and now you're trying. You want me to lie to you and say I'm a believer? You'll have to take me as I am, baby, or not at all. Science has disproved all that earth is 5,000 years old nonsense."

Piled atop her head, Erin's hair made her appear ageless and magically enhanced her features. She wore white slacks with a faded cobalt peasant blouse. An indigo bandanna tied her strawberry colored hair.

"Your arrogance surprises me. You're usually open-minded. If brilliant saints like Augustine and Thomas Aquinas believed in God, men who were brighter than either one of us could ever hope to be, what makes you so certain?"

When she talked, small lights played in her eyes, warm, lustrous, and charged with energy. Her expressions were so sincere, and she seemed so genuinely concerned for Mick's welfare that he would have done anything for her.

"Don't patronize me, baby. Of course, I'm not certain. No one's certain about anything." His jaw stiffened. "I've just had my fill of these pious, two-faced, medieval ass rapists to last a lifetime."

He used the back of his right hand to slide his empty glass towards the bar's edge. She strolled to the taps, refilled his Heineken, and placed it in front of him. He sipped the foamy head.

"When I tried to buy a condom in Ireland ten years ago, the chemist looked at me like I was trying to buy heroin. Imagine? I think that the sexual ignorance that Mother Church has kept Ireland in throughout the centuries is responsible for the inordinate amount of pedophile Irish priests. Come on, the silk slippers, the gold dripping from their necks. You know Irish history. No organization has done more to keep Ireland in the Dark Ages than the Catholic Church."

He reached into his shirt pocket and fingered a cigarette out of the box.

"I swear. I believe that. Think about it. A 13-year-old boy finds that he's not attracted to girls, so he figures that he must love God, believes he has a vocation. So, he enters the seminary and finds out too late that it's not God that he was attracted to after all."

"That's some theory. You're full of unproved presumptions. You should write a treatise." She said sarcastically. "No organization is without corruption. Why paint the many with the brush of a few?"

"I have had too many examples of the futility of prayer to even discuss, but I won't go into them now." Then a devilish gleam crossed his eyes. "Look, I can believe Jesus was born of a virgin, or that Noah took two of every species aboard an arc to save life on the planet, but how in the hell did Jesus manage to find twelve guys in the Middle East named: Peter, Matthew, Mark, Luke and John and the rest of that unemployed outfit?"

Erin didn't smile.

"I can handle your doubt. What I can't fathom is the constant jokes and your blasted arrogant certainty. As if you're the only man who has ever given the matter serious thought and your conclusion the only acceptable one."

He shrugged, grabbed his cell phone, and searched for a number.

"Hold the assault for a second. I need to make a doctor's appointment for my Mom. She called me yesterday. Her blood pressure is high, and she's been light-headed lately. After this call, I'm gonna take a ride over to her house." He let his voice flood sarcasm. "Or I could always go primal, forget the doctor, and just kneel down and pray to bundles of sticks and mud?"

She stared at him hard, pushed her tongue to the back of her cheek, and let her gaze roll over his face, but after a quick sarcastic leer, her eyes softened and morphed into sincere concern.

"Sorry about your Mom, baby, even sorrier than I am about your cheap cynicism. Call me at home later, and let me know what's going on."

AT THE CALLAHAN home later that evening, Erin's mother stacked dishes in the plastic drainer atop her sink and looked at her disgustedly.

"So now, you're going away with him?"

A short woman of compact wiriness, with alert, bright green eyes, and taut ruddy cheeks, Nora wore a stiffly starched white apron over a black housedress.

"I have a week break from summer school, and I'm a big

girl, Mom."

"Too big and too smart to be running around with a bloody bar owner."

"He's a firefighter too, Ma."

"I've asked around about him. He's a sinful, soulless, selfish git, and a drunken womanizer. Even if he wanted to marry you, I'd try to break it up. He's not for you, Erin. You can do better. But sure, what's the sense of talking to ya. I'm wasting my breath."

"People change mom. You hardly know him. What have you got against him?"

"I know enough about his kind to suit me. Do you think I never had me own Mick Mullan? Mine was a Godless, hilarious, carousing, selfish scoundrel. In short, he was bloody marvelous. But I knew that he was killing me soul. In time, I met your father, a good solid man. When you were born, I forgot all about that blasted rogue. When your time comes to make a choice, I pray you're smart enough to make the right one."

"I'm still not sure how I'm gonna handle this, Mom, but I'm a grown, educated woman. Whatever decision I make, it'll be me that makes it. You've already lived your life. How about you let me live mine?"

THIRTY-FIVE

IN LOWER MANHATTAN the following morning, Jamie's boss, Sam, stopped by his cubicle. Sam was a sleek, stylish, smooth-haired, well-mannered man of 50. He wore a Gray Armani suit and black Gucci loafers, the kind with the little gold tassels across the top.

"Jamie, I want you to push some of those derivatives. The quicker we get rid of that junk the better."

Jamie wet his lips. His hands clenched.

"Some of my old clients trust me like a son. I can't bury them, but I guess I can spread a little around."

"The more of that shit you dump the bigger your bonus."

Jamie had wanted success, and this was the path he had chosen. But damn it, he despised this part of the job. He spent the rest of a painful afternoon on the phone.

"I don't see how you can pass this one up Mr. Greenfield." Jamie had never met Greenfield, but his aching conscience visualized some weathered, misfortunate wrapped in a shoddy bathrobe, hanging on his every word with stained yellow teeth. "All of our brokers are in on the ground floor on this one."

When the clock finally freed him, his cheeks dented and pooled with relief. He needed a drink and fast.

Once he shifted his BMW into first and heard the powerful engine roar to life, his mood changed.

Fuck Greenfield. He's trying to get something for nothing, and he's probably hanging at the pool sipping cocktails and smoking a cigar with his other hand on a fine-looking woman's ass.

He parked the Beamer in back and entered Nobody's through the unmarked black metal door and stood beside Mick. Erin tossed a bev nap in front of him.

"Give me a Heineken, hon, and back Mick up." Jamie took off his brown-tweed sports coat, hung it on the back of the stool, and collapsed on the seat next to Mick.

"I swear to Christ, sometimes I hate my fucken job, but what the hell, that's why it's called work. Other than ballplayers and entertainers, who da fuck loves their job?"

"I love my job. I don't earn the dough you do, but I get to make a small difference. It might be only a drop of bleach in a world full of stains, but it makes me feel good." Mick lifted his scotch to click Jamie's green bottle. "A couple of months ago, our forcible-entry team rescued a child. You can't put a price on the expression on that mother's face. It'll stay with me forever. Have you ever seen a woman who has found her missing kid in Wal-Mart? Well, multiply that by a million."

"With my job, I don't get that opportunity." When he flexed his thick arms and neck, his tapered, white dress shirt suddenly appeared too small. "So, I'll just have to make due with six figures and my yearly bonus."

"That kind of sensitivity would bring a tear to a glass eye," Mick said.

Jamie's caustic comeback would have to do for now, but Mick's words stuck like shards of porcelain in his stomach, then he doubled down.

"Profit doesn't have much room for sentiment. I have a friend, a litigation attorney. One day after a car accident, he cheered when a child in intensive care died. It meant a larger lawsuit."

"That's disgusting. What the fuck happened to you, man?"

Mick looked at him coldly. "I'm going to take a piss. The air's better in the John."

"Don't give me that holier than thou bullshit. I know better," he shouted at Mick's back. Mick glanced over his shoulder but kept walking.

Jamie's self esteem needed whiskey and fast. He called for Erin to bring him a shot of Jack Daniels. When Erin appeared with the bottle, he shook his head in disgust.

"So, you're going away with him, huh?"

"Not you too? You don't mind if I run my own affairs, do you? Just because I serve you drinks doesn't qualify you to psychoanalyze me or give me advice."

"Look, I'm not telling you how to run your life, but I know Mick way better than you do. He has a zest for life. We all love him for it. He's just not a one-woman guy. After Eileen passed, something inside him died. I think that he attacks life because of that inner pain. It's just a matter of time. He needs women the way a junkie needs a fix. You know you could do better."

She wore a long gray skirt, over calf-high black boots. Her blouse was bright emerald like her eyes—eyes she now used to scrutinize Jamie.

"And I suppose that better would mean you?"

"It might be. If you gave me a tumble, you might be surprised. At least, I'd be faithful."

Erin ignored his remark and built a bourbon and soda for another customer. After returning, she said, "I know you mean well, Jamie, but you sound like my mother. He's good to me, and I love him, and there's nothing you or even I can do about it. You're a nice guy, but the chemistry's just not there."

"I've known him longer than you. When he's drunk, he's not the same guy. One night, he'll gallop through that looking glass. Mark my words."

Mick came out of the men's room and moseyed toward them.

"Not now. Here he comes," Jamie said.

"I see you bought a drink, ya cheap prick. About time that you filled my register with some of that Wall Street cash."

"You criticize my ill-gotten gains, but you don't bitch when I spend them. Come on. I owe you a steak. We'll go to Ruth Chris."

"What little old lady did you bankrupt to pay for this feast?"

Jamie smiled, but the irregular downward slope of his eyes gave his expression a negative cast.

"Do me a favor. Don't break my balls with that shit, okay?"

"Relax. I was just fucken around. I don't think you're a swindler. You're one of my best friends. Shit, I'd trust you with my life. I trusted you with Oliver's." He emptied his drink, placed the glass back on a damp bev nap and grinned. "I wouldn't trust you with my wife, if I had one, but . . ."

Mick lifted his brown leather jacket from behind the stool.

"Baby, I'll be back to pick you up before you get off work. Daddy Warbucks here is springing for an early dinner."

THE TWO HAD been friends forever and said what they meant. Jamie's dad was a drunk too, so when they were kids, the two were always there for one another.

Mick had spent the first week after Eileen's burial in complete emotional exhaustion curled in the fetal position on his couch. The tears came in pulsating waves. Although he kept telling himself that she was better off, a part of him blamed anyone and everyone. He deeply resented whatever negative energy could create such disorder in an orderly universe.

Why her? She was a beautiful, vibrant woman, with a heart as big as the Coliseum. After the funeral, the first week of depression led to a month of drinking and slipping in and out of consciousness. His friends knew the state that he was in, but few called, and none visited. It was as if they feared his grief would be contagious.

Somewhere in that foggy world between sleep and consciousness, Mick heard the lock turn on his apartment door. Seconds later, his bloodshot, soggy eyes set upon a large man with a bottle of scotch in each hand and a carton of Marlboros tucked under his right arm. He wore a Yankee cap, a blue sweatshirt, and jeans.

"Eileen was one hell of a woman. Let's give her the sendoff she deserves," Jamie said. "Let's do this, Mick."

For the next twenty-four hours, they laughed, reminisced, and mostly cried. Mick never forgot that. Anybody can be a friend when it's easy. The places where no one wants to be are where the true ones show up. Jamie was there. He was always there.

Down the block from the famed steakhouse, Jamie parked in a corner garage. At Ruth Chris's crowded, crescent-shaped, cherry wood bar, they plopped onto the only two stools available.

"What are you gentlemen having?"

The bartender wore tidy black trousers and a red striped tie over a neat white shirt rolled up at the cuffs. A white apron hugged his hips.

"Give us two Heinekens and a menu," Jamie said.

The lithe, mustached man slung two coasters in front of them and turned to fill their order.

"I'm not preaching, but I fight fires in the ghetto. The poor are just mirrors of the slums. You can't see it from Wall Street. All children are reflections of their parents. Children mirror what they see, good or evil, and shit man, face it, schools cost less than prisons."

"You bleeding-heart liberals don't realize that money thrown into the system gets lost in the system. Government can't do anything right. Free enterprise is the only way to go."

"That's not true, man. Sometimes the problems are too big for private enterprise. John F. Kennedy got nothing done in his

1,000 days. He couldn't get anything through Congress, nothing but twenty percent tax cuts for his rich cronies, but he'll go down as a great President because he pushed the space program. The unintended consequence of our race to the moon is why we now lead the world in microelectronics. You know how many jobs that created? Silicon Valley happened because of Kennedy's foresight. If it weren't for the space program, we'd be eating each other."

"Fuck that phony womanizer. You liberals believe man is basically good. That's bullshit, man. It's a dog eat dog world out there."

"Complex issues aren't that simple. You're talking in absolutes. We all have good and bad in us, a constant battle between Jekyll and Hyde." Mick's blue eyes got merry and full of light. "Although my Hyde seems to have substantial more influence than most."

"Tell me something I don't know."

"The problem in the ghettos is poverty and the lack of education. These kids just imitate what they see. If you take an immoral person and put him around a moral one, Cain takes down Abel every time. You can make book on it. It's easier to be corrupted than cleansed."

"Alright, spare me the bleeding-heart crap for a while." He picked up the menu, made a selection, and almost as an afterthought finally said what was really on his mind. "You and Erin are getting to be quite an item. Why don't you give her a break? Leave her alone, Mick. You know you're gonna fuck this up."

"Where da fuck did that come from?" He set his beer on the bar and leaned forward. One eyebrow arched. "What are you, getting cute?"

"You're a fool, and she's amazing. Simple math."

"Maybe I'm not as stupid as you think. Since I've met Erin, I haven't had or wanted another woman. Shit, I haven't even fooled around with Grace." Mick scratched the top of his skull, cocked his head, and planted his eyes in Jamie's face. "You're reaching a bit high for your grapes aren't you?"

Jamie slumped forward for balance, one black Florsheim on the brass rail below him, and put his sneering lips inches from Mick's ear.

"That's where the sweet ones are."

"They are indeed." His eyes seemed to go inside Jamie's.

Jamie dodged his glare and glanced through the framed window out at the Manhattan Street, "You've always scorned morality. She has it sewn on her like her skin. She has a stable of admirers on and off the stage. No one, including me, can figure out what the hell she's doing with a rake like you, so let me be up front with you. After you fuck this up, and you will, I'll be on her like white on rice."

Mick froze. "So, the court of envy delivers its verdict. Bullshit, I won't fuck this up."

The bartender returned with two menus and placed a green bottle in front of Jamie.

"Here are the menus, and here is your Heineken sir."

The bartender turned to Mick.

"I'm sorry, sir. I forgot your order. What were you drinking again?"

"I ordered a Heineken too." Mick raised his eyebrow.

"Heineken got it," the barman said.

Mick stared at the cold sweat dripping down Jamie's green bottle, licked his upper lip, and shouted at the bartender's back.

"And do me a favor. Bring me a glass."

He turned to Jamie and said sarcastically, "Jeese, what a professional, can't remember two Heinekens? He wouldn't last five minutes at Nobody's."

He wiped his palm across his mouth and yelled again, "Bring me the cleanest glass in the joint." Then he lowered his voice to Jamie and smiled. "Bring me your tip jar."

THIRTY-SIX

THE SUMMER AFTERNOON sun was white-hot and the air that night so hazy with humidity that even a T-shirt would stick to your body like wet tissue. As Mick's customers fled to nearby Long Beach or the Hamptons, his business suffered. After another slow Friday night, Nobody's was closed.

At the end of the bar, Erin and Mick drank alone. Although tired and half loaded in the early morning, she looked fresh and clean in a yellow sundress with her hair pulled back. Mick pulled a carefully creased $10 bill from his pocket. He rubbed a quarter along the bill's edge to crush the crystals into a fine compact powder.

"I thought you were gonna pack that in? What do you see in that stuff anyway?"

Mick scooped the coke out of the bill and then used a credit card to chop and separate it on the bar's surface. He bent over, inserted a cut soda straw up his nose, and sniffed. His nostrils twitched and turned wet.

"It just helps me stay awake. Try it."

"I'm afraid," Erin said.

"You're afraid of everything. Try it once. It won't kill you. It's no big deal. You're not gonna hallucinate. It just gives you an energy boost."

"I suppose once wouldn't hurt."

Erin took the cut straw and bent cautiously to snort a line.

"Thank God my poor old Irish mother can't see me now."

She did one line, threw her head back, and shook it. She bent down and did another and was pleasantly surprised. Any fatigue she felt faded, and other than a slight numbing of her teeth, no side effects were noticeable.

A SHORT TIME later at Mick's apartment, she came to him and they lay in each other's arms above the sheets. The window was open, and the wind billowed the curtain, drawing the breeze across their naked bodies.

"Let me try a little bit more of that coke," she said.

"I told you," he laughed. "It's no big deal. It just gives you an energy boost."

She did a few more lines, and afterwards, he kissed her thighs and her stomach, and put her nipples in his mouth. Whether it was the cocaine or not, when he entered her, she felt like she was burning up with a high fever. Their pelvic muscles sought each other's and joined in a ritual as ancient as creation.

Her blood-red nails scrabbled against his taut back muscles while his long fingers entwined in her mass of auburn hair. The heat and passion burned brightly from one completion to the next and the next until finally Mick lay exhausted. Beside him her breaths deepened. His eyes closed as he savored the last lingering sensations of her giving and surrender. He trembled on the edge of consciousness in the aftermath.

Love was so much better than sex, so much more than sex, and he wondered how he could have ever fooled himself into forgetting that. With sex it was about him, with love about her, and then he had another eye-opener. He realized that for him to even think like that, to want her happiness more than he wanted his own, Mick Mullan must be hooked and hooked but good.

THIRTY-SEVEN

"GET OUT. GET out. Everybody goes, Truck, Engine, Chief, everybody goes. Multiple calls. People trapped. Everybody goes."

While Mick was having his epiphany in Queens, evacuated tenants wrapped in blankets dotted a Bronx sidewalk and watched heavy spirals of smoke darken the clear morning dawn. Red flashes of flame dimly glowed through a blackened storefront window on Brook Avenue.

Inside the bodega, tongues of flame snapped and popped. Thick, evil smoke bulged and throbbed against the heavy plate-glass window, pushing dense, caustic gases into the storefront's voids. Trapped, terrified victims screamed from open windows on the floors above. Above the din, Pete yelled at Mutt, "That sonofabitch is really charged. We gotta get those poor bastards down and fast."

While Patty and Joe Sullivan jumped into the bucket, Mutt and Pete leapt from the truck to position portable ladders against the fire escapes. The engine stretched a 2½-inch line toward the deli's entrance for a frontal assault. No fire was visible yet, but the devil's pal was churning merrily inside, blackening the plate glass, building up pressure, and starving for oxygen.

In five minutes, the interior of a building can heat to 1,000 degrees, and this fire had been smoldering at least a quarter of an hour, well above ignition temperature. If the men advanced a line through the entrance without letting the gases escape chimney-like from a crosscut in the roof, massive amounts of oxygen introduced through the front door or window would cause a back draft and make the whole building blow. This structure needed vertical ventilation and fast.

Mutt placed a 35' ladder against the third-floor fire escape. He turned and cupped his eyes against the blackened storefront before screaming, "Holy shit" and sprinted for the other side of the street. He hadn't reached it yet when the space behind him filled with a violent, brilliant fireball. The storefront hurled glass like shrapnel from a howitzer round.

The explosion's force lifted Mutt off the pavement and catapulted him to the distant sidewalk. He landed on his shoulder to the pain of a giant's fist. On bruised knees, he painfully crept behind the engine for cover. A massive paw gripped his shoulder.

"Mutt, you okay?"

He saw Jack's lips move but couldn't hear a word.

HIS BROTHERS MEANWHILE were left to face the crackling fury shooting from the empty space in front of them. Engine-17 was dragging limp hose toward the blown-out store window, the deafening flames bellowing like some kind of giant demon.

"Water, dammit. We need water before we lose the upper floors," Lieutenant Mitchell yelled.

Twiggy, the nozzle man, finally felt the hose harden. The confined power that the charged line contained jerked him forward, almost knocking him to the floor. When he opened the nozzle, the stream pushed him sideways staggering him again.

The heavy bolt of water ripped into the churning guts of the inferno, caromed off the ceiling, and dissected the vortex of fire that was spreading to the apartments above. A solid wall of bright flame crackled in front of him, hurling thick black smoke as if it were trying to choke anyone it couldn't reach.

The physics of water pressurized through an engine's mighty centrifugal pump, and then forced through a 2 ½-inch nozzle produces a force that could kill a man, tear down walls, or in this case, knock down an astonishing amount of fire. The nozzle's heavy stream crashed, splashed, and cut through the smoke, turning it a foggy white as the pressurized water knocked a path through the inferno.

Mitchell screamed above the roaring flames, "Put your masks on. We're going in."

The hose carved a thin path through the entrance, and Mitchell's tiny band of smoke eaters fought their way inside. The earlier explosion had blown out the windows of the floor above, and the flashover had lit the grocery aisles and walls. Banking down from the ceiling, heavy smoke filled the store with a choking, lethal fog.

Paper products and cereals flared up intermittently and fell off their shelves eating at the floorboards. Charred debris from the ceiling rocked and rattled Twiggy's helmet. Patches of red were bleeding down the store's walls, yet still he advanced, hosing down bright bursts as he went.

The heavy stream slung canned goods and obliterated displays. With visibility near zero, Mitchell and his men lurched toward the dim glow and into the heart of the fire. The smoke closed in around them, isolating them, but they kept dragging the bloated hose through the blistering ruin that was once a deli.

The inside of the store appeared to be carved out of soft coal, the canned goods superheated, exploding glass from jars and bottles embedded like teeth in the walls. Twiggy whipped the wide-open nozzle clockwise along the ceiling in front of him. Window glass shattered, cans flew, shelves toppled. As they fought for inches deeper into the darkness, streams of water puddled their rubber boots, the sound of fire hissing at them before turning into dense clouds of steam.

The floor suddenly hiccupped under Twiggy's feet, forcing him to grip Mitchell's turnout coat to avoid falling. When the floor shuddered again, they heard a deep rumble that seemed to start in the bowels of the fog and work its way out until the entire structure shook.

"The roof's coming down. Let's get the hell out of here, now," Mitchell shouted through his mask.

The red devil had lured them into a trap. The flames they could see and fight weren't the problem. The fire had spread through the pipe shafts, and ventilation ducts, up between the partitions, through the ceiling, and had eaten away at the bones of the building.

Assing and elbowing their way to freedom, stumbling and staggering along the hose for guidance, survival now their only thought, a second quake knocked them off their feet. The roar sounded like a plane landing hard on a runway. Debris fell like sheets of rain in a typhoon.

The team ducked instinctively to protect their faces, but there was no place to hide, the blocked storefront their only chance out. Mitchell led the way along the limp hose line, which was pinched off by the collapsed roof. Without water, the fire crackled behind them with renewed energy, licking the heels of their boots, and just when things couldn't get worse for Mitchell's crew, their Scott Pack alarms started to screech, alerting them that they were running out of air.

Through the soupy tomb, Mitchell spotted a small ray of light. He fell to his knees and frantically crept toward it. He and his men pawed, scraped, and widened the small opening until it was as large as a manhole cover. With masks useless now, Mitchell stood and told his men to drop their Scott Packs, acting like a hallway monitor hustling them toward the small gap that was their only way out.

After his men were out safely, Mitchell dropped to his

knees.

Then the second collapse came, burying him under a shower of stone and plaster. The debris chicken-winged his left arm, pinning it and his back against a hot metal joist. A pile of cinder blocks had crushed his vertebrae, preventing him from pulling air into his lungs. Before he lost consciousness, his mouth turned bone dry as the fluids leaking from his crushed legs formed a slow disgusting pool in his boots.

THE HIERARCHAL STRUCTURE of the FDNY borrows terms from the military. Terms like operations, tactics, and strategies might be found in any army field manual. Companies attack, troops advance. The major difference in fighting fires and a human foe is that the military chooses where to make a stand. With firefighting, the enemy chooses the time, location, and conditions, and it always ambushes, always attacks with surprise.

Mitchell lived unconscious for days with internal burns so severe that morphine didn't help. Mostly to comfort the heartbroken wife at his bedside, Mick and the Brothers made alternating visits to the hospital. Towards the end, lying lifeless, writhing in pain, even Mitchell's wife prayed for it to end.

WHEN THE BLACK Hearse carrying Mitchell's gallant body crept to Yonkers for the wake, thousands of firefighters, policeman, and civil servants lined both sides of the route. All the way from the medical examiner's office in lower Manhattan, along the West Side Highway, up to and including the Major Deegan Expressway, fire, police, and E.M.S. trucks with men both on and off duty saluted solemnly and stiffly to pay final respects to the fallen hero.

His body was waked two days.

Outside the funeral parlor, mourners stood for hours under pelting rain. Beneath their dress blue hats, rigid firefighters had streams of water streaming down their cheeks. The Brothers queued separately from civilians, lining up four abreast to present a quick salute and make way for the next wave.

Mick and the men of 60-Truck did all they could to comfort Dolores. FDNY support teams saturated the stricken widow's home. The mayor, fire commissioner, and the chief of department all offered somber condolences. Bagpipers flooded the cemetery.

The fire department chaplain, Father Mychal Judge, delivered a powerful eulogy while Mick and Erin stood silently in the rear of the church. Tears swam down the sides of his cheeks when he saw the commissioner quietly call aside the lieutenant's son, little Danny, and hand him a small white box wrapped in a yellow ribbon. The six-year old opened the box, but his trembling frame found his father's badge little comfort.

THE BURIAL BEHIND them, Mick and Erin, Patty, Mutt and their wives had finished lunch and were waiting for their cars from the valet. Another firefighter and his wife had joined them.

"It was great seeing you again, Sammy, even under these circumstances," Mutt said. "Glad you're feeling better. We'll be having our company picnic next week. If you're up to it, you and your family should come. You've got my number. Give me a call. Stay in touch, ya hump."

"I've been a bit under the weather, but I'll try and make it for sure. I still can't believe that's Mitchell's gone. Hanging with the Brothers becomes more and more important. Here comes my Toyota. Take care, and stay safe, love you guys."

Sammy tipped the carhop, and he and his wife drove off.

"That could have been you we were burying today," Mick whispered into Mutt's ear.

"Yeah, one more minute and I was toast." Then Mutt lost the solemnity. His elbow nudged Mick's side, and he winked.

"Thank God Sammy left," he said loudly. "I hate that prick."

Patty chimed in.

"Me too. You ever see such a cheap cocksucker? I was thrilled to hear he was sick."

Mick didn't miss a beat. "Sick? He should've died before he was born. I hope I never see that bastard again."

The burial a memory, the Brothers used the only anesthetic they knew. The three men roared with laughter. The women just shook their heads.

"Firefighters . . . they crack themselves up," Erin said.

MICK AND ERIN parked around the corner from his com-lex and trudged the three flights of stairs. When he sprang the lock, and lobbed his apartment keys alongside a picture of Eileen, Oliver's two front paws punched Erin's lap, his brown and white tail wagging while she rubbed his head.

He ripped off his uniform tie and shirt, slipped off his black shoes and socks, and nabbed a porterhouse bone from the refrigerator. He tossed it in the microwave for 20 seconds and waved it at Oliver. The Jack Russell sprinted to him, took the bone in his teeth, and ran toward the balcony. Mick opened the door, and Oliver ran outside to gnaw his booty. Stretching on his stomach, dripping saliva, his paws held the bone like an ear of corn. Back arched, fangs exposed, he began turning the treat into a fossil.

Mick closed the balcony door and turned to Erin. His hungry eyes inches from hers, mouth open, he grabbed her by the waist and reached under her black dress and began to caress her.

When they kissed, her mouth felt cold and dry at first. Then he felt her tongue turn wet, slide past his teeth, and probe deep inside his mouth. It stirred a heat in his genitals that he hadn't experienced since Eileen, not with Grace, not with anyone. He unbuckled his belt and let his pants slide to the carpet.

He slid the white panties from under her slip. With a wide sweep of his right hand, he brushed away the clutter on the dining room table. When he lifted and entered her, he swore he could hear a plane revving its engines, rattling with light, and roaring with sound, before finally rumbling down the runway and lifting itself into a clear, dark night, lit with stars, and a bright full moon.

Her fists grabbed his hips. The corner of her mouth bit white. She begged him to keep fucking her, as she bucked in desperate passion.

For the second time in his life, Mick felt that fate had dealt him a royal flush. He couldn't believe his luck nor could he explain her attraction to him. Here he was making love to a woman he had never wanted to meet, never searched for, and never thought existed, a woman who finally made him realize that life hadn't ended with his wife's death.

THE TYRANT OF lust satisfied, they shared a cigarette.

"Thanks for coming with me tonight, baby. It was a long night, and you hardly know my firefighter friends."

"I want to meet all your friends. I want to know everything about you."

"Some of my friends are real screwballs."

"Your friends are screwballs, and you find that strange?" Erin asked. "You have any mirrors in your apartment?"

"Hey, easy. You might hurt my feelings."

"Right, a fireman with thin skin, I thought this relationship was based on truth?"

"Don't kid yourself. I have a very fragile ego. That's one of the reasons I love you so much. With you, I feel like a giant."

She had heard him say, "I love you" before, but things had changed. The past and the future meant nothing anymore. It was only about Mick and the now.

"Say that again," Erin said.

"Say what again?"

"That you love me so much," she said.

"What? You know I love you, baby, head over heels."

She raised the stakes.

"Where do you see it going, Mick?"

"What do you mean?"

"What do you think I mean? I mean us. Do you see us getting married?"

Her belting honesty intimidated him. Here was a woman incapable of lies, games, or nuance, just straight-shooting adorable toughness.

"Married? Slow down a little. Let's not put our wagons ahead of our horses. Who knows? Let's just see how it goes."

"You mean you're not sure?"

"What's the rush baby? Let's just enjoy what we have. Down the road we can think about marriage. I'll even get down on one knee."

"I was half-assed breaking your chops," she laughed. "I'm not looking to get married, but you know damn well that I'll never live with you. My problem now is that I'm not quite sure that I can live without you."

Mick averted her eyes and snatched a book to change the subject.

"Speaking of weddings, you remember that we have one next month, right?"

Erin snagged a book from the oak end table on her side of the bed, and spun the lamp's switch, the soft light reflecting disappointment in her eyes.

"Another wedding? Yeah, I remember. You know what? Screw you, Mick Mullan." She mockingly stuck her nose in the air. "I wouldn't marry you now if you got down on three knees."

THIRTY-EIGHT

MICK CRADLED THE phone and lifted the small blue notebook containing his band schedule off the bar just as an elderly couple walked through his door. The woman led the way. Her hair was a coppery red, her eyes a deep green made more vivid by contrast with the scramble of freckles and sunburn that formed her complexion. But the most noticeable thing about her was her bearing. She strutted with an erect, purposeful, arrogant haughtiness that bordered on slapstick.

"Can I help you?"

"Are you Mick Mullan?"

"Guilty as charged."

"We're Erin Callahan's parents. You've been seeing our daughter. We were heading out to Queens after Mass anyway, and we thought that it was time we met."

The smile dripped from Mick's face.

"Mr. and Mrs. Callahan, wow, nice to meet you. Let me get you something to drink."

"We'll have two coffees, if you have it," Nora said.

"Of course, of course, come over here. Have a seat."

Mick glanced at the clock and noticed it was just after noon. He returned from the kitchen with a full coffee pot. When Nora Callahan's harangue ended, the pot was empty, yet what Nora said next implied that she hadn't said enough.

"I don't believe in beating around the bush. She's our only daughter, and I don't think you're the right man for her. I know you're sleeping together. Now you want to take her to Las Vegas. We're a religious family, and you're hardly a practicing Catholic. Just so we understand each other, I'll be doing everything in my power to bring her to her senses."

"I know this wasn't an easy conversation for you, Mrs. Callahan. I appreciate how much you love your daughter. I love her too, but things are a bit different here in America than they were in the old country."

"Whether Ireland or America, the church is the church, and sin is sin. I wanted to get a look at you for myself and see what I thought. I've said what I came to say. Now, I'll be on my way. Come on Brendan. We're done here. We'll both pray for you."

Brendan Callahan was a short-necked, pie faced man, with thick curly brown hair, who hadn't spoken much throughout his wife's tirade but seemed content to merely nod his agreement every third or fourth sentence. Both stood, but only Brendan shook hands with the dumbfounded Mick. Nora merely grunted before storming off.

THIRTY-NINE

THE ROLLING CHERRIES, stars, and bells of the slot machines spun to the sounds of coins clanging onto loud metal plates. Mick hurried Erin past the banging bells, whistles, and sirens, dodged the gawkers, gamblers, and waitresses, and steered her directly to the crap tables.

"If you know what you're doing, this is the best bet in the casino. There's free odds on all the come bets, and the don't pass only allows the house a 1.44 percent advantage. Of course, some bets are larcenous, big six, big eight, and the field, all terrible odds."

They had decided that rather than dealing with Nora's hostility, an overnight trip to Atlantic City might be more prudent than Vegas. Mick clutched a cocktail while navigating between the blackjack tables.

"Used to be when the mob controlled the casinos, ya got a fair shot. In those days, you could count cards and have a reasonable chance to come out ahead. They got your money but slowly. They greased the pan, so the cookies wouldn't stick, ya know? But these MIT boys are too smart. They want it all at once. For example, they changed one little rule in blackjack that tilted the odds insurmountably in the house's favor. Dealer must hit soft 17. When I have time, I'll explain why you can't beat that rule. That's why I don't play blackjack here or Vegas."

"Imagine if you used this knowledge for something useful."

"Don't kid yourself. I made a lot of money playing cards. Of course, I blew it on sports, blow, and women," he smiled.

"We're from two different worlds."

"You're a smart girl. I'll teach you how to count cards, and play poker. You'll be great at it. But avoid sports betting like the plague. My bookie, Fruity, has been killing me for years. I love that bald-headed little Jew, but no one can beat a 10 percent edge."

She sipped a screwdriver and spun in a circle soaking it all in.

"I've never even been inside a casino before. It's electric."

LATER THAT NIGHT, Erin stared into a make-up mirror on the dresser. She lifted a tiny spoon attached to an amber vial of cocaine from her pocket. After the snort, she pinched her cheeks for color. The liquor and cocaine had started to etch their lines on her face one ounce and one gram at a time. Disgusted, she turned the mirror face down and headed to bed where a smiling Mick awaited holding yet another screwdriver.

"I'll say one thing about your mom. She ain't bashful."

"No, she's not."

"I tell you, baby, she read me the riot act."

"I'm sorry honey. I never know what she'll do next."

"If my own mom couldn't sell me on that Bible thumping bullshit, your mother certainly can't. Pray for me? Why can't people just leave me the hell alone? Take me as I am, or don't take me at all."

Erin sipped her screwdriver and artfully switched subjects.

"I was thinking. You know, I could help you schedule bands. I have connections with the Irish music network."

"You would do that? That would be great."

"You want to sell alcohol? Nothing makes customers drink like Irish rebel music. That's the way to fly, besides I can always jump up there and jam with them. You wouldn't have to pay me a nickel. Another thing, when we advertise future bands, you should post your flyers in the rest rooms. Everyone who drinks, male or female, eventually ends up there."

"You're really something else, ya know?"

"Just make sure you remember that."

"Oh, I know what I have, honey. Believe me. I know. Let's get a few hours sleep. I'm exhausted. We have to check out at four a.m. and drive back. I have a shift tomorrow, and I ain't pulling an all-nighter."

As they lay in each other's arms, Mick said, "Move in with me. I want to spend every minute with you. I want to know your voice the way I know my own. When you're not near me, I feel like I'm suffocating. I can't breathe. I'm not kidding. I'm useless without you."

"No one's ever talked to me like that before. I never knew that I could feel like this. But, I'll never move in with you. It'll never happen. You met my parents. I could never embarrass them by being anyone's mistress."

FORTY

HE MADE IT to work on time the following day still beat from the long drive. Mick did a few hours committee work and had just stretched out on the couch when the alarm came in around midday. The dispatcher had received multiple calls, so Mick and the Brothers pulled up to the box pumped and ready for action.

They turned the corner, and sure enough fire roared from the top floor windows of a row frame building. It had started in the kitchen, probably by a dishtowel left beside an open flame. The fire had climbed the wall, flattened on the ceiling, then spread through the hallway and was sucked up by a draft near the entrance to the attic.

In the older parts of N.Y., frame buildings were often erected in rows and have a common attic or cockloft. If fire spreads to this open space between the top floor ceiling and the roof, the additional fuel and oxygen allows flames to spread unimpeded and could quickly involve every building on the block.

Mick and Pete climbed in 60-Truck's bucket and waited for the Lieutenant to give the all clear to open the Truck's powerful Stang nozzle to knock down the flames. The second due truck's outside team raced to the roof with a partner saw to cut a trench in hopes of creating a firebreak, anything to stop horizontal spreading.

Seventeen-Engine stretched their line through the entrance, up the interior stairs, and into the hallway of the fully involved third floor. Incoming units stretched their lines to the building's adjoining exposures. Hoses spider-webbed the entire Bronx Street. Flames engulfed the top floor and roof, pushing black, dense smoke from the roof's eaves painting the afternoon sky.

FIVE HOURS LATER, the fire out, the soot-covered Brothers backed the rigs into quarters.

"Great job, men. I put us in for an hour clean-up time," the Lieutenant said.

Mick turned to Pete, Thoe, and Kingsley.

"Hey, it's 5:15 now. With the hour clean up, we're finished. Wanna grab a beer?"

"I can't. My wife has plans, but I gotta get this stink off me," Pete said.

"I would man, but they charge too much in those honky bars that you go to. For what it costs me to get wired, I'd be broke for the week." Kingsley was one of the company's five black members. A slight paunch hung over his belt. "I'm gonna just head home to mama. She ain't to happy with me right now anyway."

Thoe also bowed out. "No thanks man. I'm heading to the gym to play a little hoop."

"Come out to Nobody's, ya fuck. Saturday night there are plenty of chicks. I'll fix ya up. Next company dance you won't be stag."

"Fuck you, Mick. I'll do my own fixing up."

"I've never seen you with a date, man," he laughed. "You ain't too good at it apparently.

AFTER A SHAVE and a shower, he sat in his car and dialed his cell. While awaiting the connection, he reached for the glass vial inside his dungarees and inserted a cut off straw.

"Fruity? Mick, whatta ya got in the N.B.A.?" He scribbled the lines Fruity droned on the edge of the New York Post. "Give me the Knicks, Portland, and the Bulls a nickel a piece."

Satisfied, he snorted a short blast up each nostril, recapped the amber vial and drove toward the Whitestone Bridge and out to Northern Boulevard.

THE NIGHT BEHIND him, the customers long gone, the entrance double locked, Mick sat at a table in the basement with Buffalo and Grace. He crushed a white pill and melded it with lines of coke. He snorted two thin lines and handed the bill to Grace.

"The coke brings you up, and the Percocet brings you down. It's like going sideways," he quipped. "This blow's so damn good. I need something to take the edge off. I can't do this shit when I'm not drinking heavy." He turned to Buffalo. "I bet three NBA games tonight, and they all went in the toilet. Unless I bail out by Monday, I'm going to need cash. Thank God we were busy tonight."

"You lost all three?"

"That's why they make the ball round. I'll get it back tomorrow."

"You should quit that shit," Buffalo said.

"I should quit a lot of things."

WELL PAST DAWN, Mick turned the key to his apartment and was surprised to find a pissed off Erin in his bed.

"Baby, you didn't tell me you were coming over."

"I woke up and couldn't sleep. I thought I'd surprise you. I'm glad I'm here. Jesus, Mick, it's seven a.m. What are you doing? You're killing yourself."

"Don't break my balls honey. I got a package of blow and just got caught up in conversation with Grace and Buff. You can have what's left out of the eight ball."

"You come home in this condition and tell me that you got caught up talking with a prostitute that you used to screw?"

"I told you I'd always be honest," he shrugged. "Why would I mention Grace if I had something to hide? I didn't do anything that I'm ashamed of."

Erin flew out of the bed and raced to the chair where Mick had thrown his jeans. She ripped the package out of Mick's pants and held it up.

"And then you have the gall to try and buy me off with this? I'll show you what I think of this shit."

She headed for the bathroom, opened the plastic baggie and shook it down the bowl.

"Honey, calm down. You're over-reacting. Grace's nothing to me. She's a hooker for Chrissakes, I was the one who fixed her up with Jake."

"It's not just Grace, Mick. I can't put up with this madness much longer. I love you, but Jesus, you're drowning your soul and dragging me down with you."

"Honey, with you it's better than it's ever been. With her and the others, it was always about sex. You know when we look in each other's eyes that there's no bullshit there. I love everything about you. It's real, baby. I know it, and you know it. I gotta few bad habits. I can change."

"You'll have to change, Mick, not for me but for yourself. You have to get help. You don't have a few bad habits. You're out of control."

She threw on her jeans, grabbed her keys, and left. After she turned the SUV's ignition, she realized that it was Sunday and decided to seek some spiritual re-enforcement, so she drove to St. Philip Neri.

AFTER MASS, SHE knelt in the first pew, her head buried in her hands, glancing up occasionally to study the giant crucifix above the altar. The worshipers long gone, she prayed for answers and guidance. She had a big decision to make and daren't make it without being sure.

A supple hand on her right shoulder broke her thoughts.

"I hope this doesn't sound too strange or that you think I'm some kind of nut." She was heavy set, over 50, her bright yellow hair waved and molded into place with too much chemical spray. Erin's puzzled eyes fixed on her.

"I was on the other side of the aisle, and the Lord told me to come over and deliver a message. I hesitated because I thought you'd think that I was crazy. But he said that you'd understand."

Erin's mouth formed a small circle. Her brow wrinkled, but her eyes were sincere.

"No. I don't think you're crazy. I'm a very spiritual person. It's a bit strange, but I have an open mind, and considering where we are . . ."

The woman's eyes were shiny behind heavy lashes, and her mouth opened to let perfectly white teeth gleam through. "My message is short, only three words, but I always listen to my inner voice."

"What's the message?"

"He will change," she said.

"What?"

"He will change."

Erin tortured her lower lip with her teeth.

"Does it mean anything to you?"

"Yes, yes, it does," she murmured.

"Good. I'm glad you don't think I'm crazy. I can see by the lines around your eyes that you're a troubled girl. You're at some kind of crossroads. Prayer will help. I'm many years older than you, and I always pray on my troubles. I hope now that I've done my duty everything works out."

And with that she turned and marched back to her pew.

Erin wasn't sure how long she knelt there after that. She didn't even remember getting up from her knees, leaving the church, or starting her car.

LATER THAT AFTERNOON, Erin pushed a metal cart down the grocery aisle while Nora studied a label.

"You don't think that's scary? A woman I don't know sits next to me in church and tells me something she has no business knowing."

"You won't tell me what she said to you, so how can you expect me to give you an answer? I don't see anything so remarkable about a stranger telling you that God wants to reach you and has a message for you. Why would that be scary? We all need God in our lives. Sure, you've always known that." Nora said. "Some things are just too big for us. Sooner or later a time comes in everyone's life when they realize that only God can help."

FORTY-ONE

THE STRANGER'S MESSAGE and a night's sleep had cooled Erin a bit. The acreage surrounding New Rochelle's Iona College that Monday morning was bright green and plush. Mick walked across the great lawn, opened her classroom door, and slipped into an empty desk in the back.

"To oversimplify, Hamlet is essentially a play about a man who couldn't make up his mind whether to live or die. We'll have a quiz tomorrow on what we covered today."

The bell rang, and the summer school students rushed the door.

"I want those papers, Thursday. Don't forget. Every day that you're late will cost you five points," Erin bellowed as she packed her books.

Mick slogged down the aisle.

"I'm really sorry, baby. I used all the wrong words the other night, but I swear nothing happened with Grace or anyone else. If it did, I would tell you. You're my best friend. I'm not ashamed of what happened. I just got a little drunk. That's all."

"I know nothing happened, Mick. It's not about that. It's about you. You've got to get your life back on track."

I'm a work in progress." He smiled and let his eyes slip to the papers on her desk. He stared at then absentmindedly. "No bullshit, honey. I'm really sorry. I tried to call you last night, but your phone kept going to voicemail."

"That was no accident, Mick. I needed time to think." Before he could lift one of the papers, she put her hand over his. "I love you, but I won't enable you. You can't joke or charm your way around this. You gotta grow up."

She was right. His vices were getting worse and had to stop, but one pesky question kept resurfacing. Could he?

"I won't try and joke about it, honey. As usual, you're dead on."

His picked a paper from her desk and scanned it.

"By the way, I loved watching you in front of your class. You're in complete control. I think half of your class is in love with you."

"Only half? I must be slipping," she smiled.

"Well you have one listener's adoration for sure."

"You know you should think about going back to school, Mick. That's exactly what you need to knock off this madness, all of that wasted time camping in front of a television gambling on sports. You could be anything that you want. You're as bright as hell and would make a fine teacher. Getting a degree would keep you too busy to fool with that other crap."

"The bar and the job keep me busy enough. Besides, I thought we agreed that you won't try and change me."

"I know, but I hate seeing you waste your life. You have something special, and you're throwing it away. Everyone listens to you. Everyone loves you, Mick."

"Everyone listens to me? God help their heads."

"Don't try to laugh it off, not this time. Life's not a joke. It drives me crazy that you have such low self-esteem. It's not just about having fun, Mick. It goes deeper than that. You know it does. You're a good man, yet you constantly debase yourself with all this talk about drugs, hookers, and alcoholic benders."

Mick's eyes softened.

"I believed that once." He felt a warm glow, put his arm

around the back of her head, and pulled it gently to his chest. "If all it takes is the love of a good woman, I got it made. Don't worry, honey. I swear. I'll put all this shit behind me."

FORTY-TWO

THE SUMMER WAS fading, and the job they caught that Wednesday night should have been routine; but when Mick and probationary firefighter, Julio Jimenez, forced the apartment door, it dislodged a bicycle propped against it. The bike fell and bounced across the hallway into the kitchen, rupturing a gas line, a dangerous harbinger.

While flames surged from the apartment below, the two made a primary search on the floor above. Unaware of the rupture, they fingered the smoky hallway to search the back bedrooms. Toxic smoke fogged the kitchen and combined with the leaking gas, which hungered heat, all the components necessary for a fatal cocktail.

"This bedroom is clear," Mick yelled. "You find anything, Julio?"

"No, all clear." When Julio rejoined Mick in the living room, he said, "So now we transmit negative on the primary search right?"

"Yeah, you transmit. I want you to get used to using your radio. It's important that . . ."

Mick never finished his sentence.

When the gas reached ignition temperature, it was if a bolt of lightning had struck inside the building and burst into a blue and white blaze. A flash of light exploded from the kitchen, racing a red and yellow ball of flame up the long hallway.

Mick spotted the death storm and instinctively threw his body into Julio's, crashing them through the living room window. When the glass burst, the two tumbled onto the fire escape, their bodies framing the blinding flash that lit the room.

They rolled from the glassless window and watched fire lick the empty space behind them. The blowtorch had missed them, but the intense heat had smoked their turnout coats, and singed their hair. The two stunk like scorched cats.

As he watched the dirty strings of smoke rising from his turnout coat, Mick had trouble keeping his heart in his chest. He could feel Julio eyeballing him, so he peeked over at his ash and charcoal covered face.

The skin on Julio's lower mouth was dry and tight, sweat gushing from under his helmet, crawling across his forehead. Fear flooded his saucer-sized eyes. Julio stared trancelike and muttered, "Holy shit. That was quick thinking. Hhhhooow did you know that the window had a fffire eesscape?"

Mick gulped for oxygen. It was all he could do to spit out the sentence.

"Don't kid yourself. I'm not that good. I didn't know."

Julio's singed eyebrows climbed his forehead. The blood drained from his face. He clutched at his neck, gave his scapula a kiss, blessed himself, and stuttered, "But if you were wrong, we would have sssplattered all over the pppavement."

"And, if I did nothing . . ."

Mick watched him kiss the scapula and thought the ritual pure superstition, but after their miraculous escape, a crack of doubt crept into his psyche.

If there were forces of good and evil, would they have had time to worry about the likes of him and Julio? God didn't put that fire escape there, kid. No fucken way. That was pure luck.

But lately, he had his doubts. What if Erin were right about his arrogance? She seemed to know more than him about everything else. What if because of his mother's prayers, God really was watching over him after all?

FORTY-THREE

IT WAS THE last party weekend in Long Beach before summer faded to fall. Mick, Buffalo, and Twiggy rounded Pennsylvania Avenue and strolled down Beach Street past the many bars and restaurants.

"Mutt said he'd meet us at The Beach House for some oysters. It's a few blocks down."

The three dodged frenzied revelers overflowing onto the blocked off streets. Sweet sounds of Irish music and rock and roll streamed out of the bars they passed. After a few blocks, they hit Lido Avenue and found Mutt in a beef with three gruff bikers.

"I am minding my own business. That's not how the game is played." Mutt screamed. "She's fucked up man. She can hardly stand. Let me put her in a cab."

"What's it to you? You don't even know her," the biggest one said. "How about we just kick your fucking ass?"

Mick, Buffalo, and Twiggy jumped in front of Mutt.

"How about you dirt bags rethink that?" Buff said.

The guy who looked like he signed his name with a baseball bat sized Buff up while his pals evaluated the sudden change in odds.

"You okay, Mutt?" Mick asked.

"Yeah, everything's cool. These gentlemen and I were just

having a discussion about this young lady's welfare. They seemed to think she'd be better off under the boardwalk. I disagreed."

Mutt yanked the girl from the gorilla's grasp.

"Let's walk her down to the Beach House, get her some coffee, and put her in a cab." He stared at the three. "You gentlemen cool with that?"

Not waiting for an answer, they helped the staggering girl down the street.

AFTER POURING A keg of coffee into the over-served brunette, they helped her into a cab, and later nursed beers at the bar.

"You believe this shit, Mutt? I'm out in Long Beach all the time. I say goodbye in Shine's and nobody cares." Mick nodded his head toward Buffalo. "He says goodbye, and everyone acts like their mothers died."

"No wonder. He spends money like he's running for mayor," Mutt said. "Every five minutes he tells me to give him another $40 for the pool."

"Tell me something I don't know. You see him once in awhile. I drink with this fat bastard all the time. When we go on a bender, he drinks Johnny Black neat with Heineken chasers," Mick said. "I drink white wine watered down with club soda. Imagine, fucken spritzers, just to hang on? Three or four days later, I still end up tossing him the keys to my car. I'm lucky that I don't get cirrhosis."

"Cirrhosis? That's the least of your worries." Buff laughed. "Your head slams the bar so often that you're lucky that you don't get a concussion."

"You toss him your keys? You let that crazy bastard drive drunk?" Mutt asked.

"I gotta drive," Buffalo laughed. "I'm too drunk to walk."

"Ya see what a sick fuck he is, Mutt? It ain't me that's nuts. It's this prick."

He pulled from the bottle.

"After this beer, I gotta hit the road. Now that summer's finally over, the bar starts to get busy. Time to get back to civilization."

The four split for their cars.

"It's a good thing that you guys came along when you did." Mutt said. "I thought for sure that beef was going down. But fuck it. I've had my ass beat before. No way I'm walking by and letting a chick get raped because she's drunk. I'm no bargain. I get plenty drunk, but there are rules. We've all got to live with ourselves."

"And live with your wives as well," Mick said. "That reminds me . . . Hey Buff, I hope your wife doesn't blame me for this two-day fiasco."

"Well, who the hell do you think I'm going to blame? You don't think I'm going to tell Mary that this was my idea?" His face lit up. "And who are you kidding? You might not be married, but you've gotta check in too."

"When you're right, you're right." Mick reached for his cell, but before he could dial, it vibrated. He read Erin's name and said hello.

"Mick, I've got bad news. I'm calling from Bronx Lebanon Hospital. How soon can you get here?"

"What? Why? What happened?"

"It's your Mom. She collapsed in the supermarket. They said she had a heart attack. Hurry."

THE NEXT TWO days, Mick wrote his memory a bum check. He'd pay later for whatever the cost of burying the depression would be. He just couldn't deal with it. The pain came in waves. He'd cry for ten minutes and then be fine for a few hours and then more uncontrollable sobs.

Inside the funeral parlor, along with throngs of others, his staff and friends celebrated Monica's life and mourned her passing. Mick shook hands and accepted condolences from the long line that came to offer comfort.

"She was a great old broad, my mom, and tough," Mick said.

"I'd take 72 in a second," Mutt said. "Women come and go, but we only have one mother. I dread the day mine dies. When she goes, I'll lose what little moral compass I have left."

"It was just so sudden," Mick said. "And where was I when she needed me? Out on Long Island, tying on a load."

"It's sad, Mick. Everybody's sorry as hell for your loss, but you couldn't have done anything unless you were standing right next to her when it happened; and shit, Mutt's right," Dewey said. "She had a good run. God bless her."

"I guess I'd take that age myself." Mick slanted his head toward Buffalo and released his remorse the only way he knew how. "And this big prick should be dead already."

"If I die, they better have one enormous oven to cremate my fat ass," Buff snorted.

The four men laughed, and Mick headed off to greet other mourners. More than a few were strangers from Monica's youth, half-remembered faces now grotesquely marked by time. Flowers and cards surrounded the casket. Buffalo and Dewey stood in the back of the room against the wall.

Another bar owner, Kevin Collins, sauntered in to pay his respects. He spoke a few moments with Mick, said hello to Dewey and Buff, and headed for the open coffin to say a prayer.

"There's Collins. I could use a few days behind the stick," Buffalo said. "Maybe I can pick up a few days at his joint."

"Now's your chance. He's alone. It's quiet enough, a bit inappropriate, but what the fuck, it's Kevin," Dewey said. "He won't give a shit."

Buffalo seized the opportunity to wend his way to the front and knelt alongside Kevin at the casket.

"It's a bitch ain't it?"

"Yeah, Mick's mom was a grand old dame. Lying here, she doesn't look anything like the woman I remembered."

Monica's corpse had a blanched white face and a pasty unnatural smile, as if her mortician specialized in pleasant expressions.

"Yeah it sucks," Buffalo said. "Hey man, I was wondering. I'm a little short on cash. How about giving me a few days tending bar?"

"My joint?" Kevin asked. "You want to work for me, in my joint?"

"Yeah, I could use a few days."

Kevin stood, made the sign of the cross, kissed the four fingers he used to bless himself, and then touched the corpse's lips. He pointed his index finger at Monica.

"She works before you do."

As Kevin walked away, Buff cheeks filled with air and a huge grin crossed his mug.

He got me good, the sonofabitch.

ERIN MEANWHILE HAD seized the opportunity to introduce herself to Kingsley's wife, Barbara.

"I'm Mick's girlfriend, Erin."

"Oh, I've heard so much about you. I'm sorry we had to meet under these circumstances. Kingsley thinks the world of Mick. I know you haven't been dating him long, so you barely know my husband."

Barbara looked toward Dewey and Buffalo, who were both trying to restrain themselves from raucous laughter.

"Those two certainly seem like a trip," Barbara smiled.

"All of Mick's friends are like that. They're all crazy."

"Kingsley used to be too. I wouldn't put up with it. Thank the Creator he's changed. What's it like going out with Mick?"

"So far, it has been an emotional roller coaster, lots of wonderful moments but so many concerns. We're so different. I don't know. I just don't know . . ."

"If it's meant to be, it'll come to pass no matter what you do. If it isn't Allah's will, it won't. I'm afraid it's that simple."

Erin thought, *Allah?*

She followed Barbara's eyes. Mick was biting his lip, bending over like a man with cramps, gripping his sides, holding his hand up, almost begging Buffalo to stop.

THE FOLLOWING DAY at the funeral Mass, half of St. Philip Neri's pews were packed with mourners. An alter boy rang Sanctus Bells in cadence with Father Moriority lifting the gold chalice skyward.

"I am the resurrection and the life, saith the Lord; he that believeth in me, though he were dead, yet shall he live; and whosoever liveth and believeth in me shall never die."

It wasn't the words. It was Moriority's tone that pissed Mick off. He had expected something different, something warm, something soothing, not this flat, faraway whine with its dreadful note of cold finality. The ceremony was supposed to comfort him, ease his pain, but the priest delivered the words in a monotonous murmur as if he were addressing an assembly of comatose hospice patients. It only made Mick feel worse.

But habit being stronger than malice, he bowed his head and began shuddering from the oppression of the religious rituals the clergy had used to smother his childhood. Then in front of the packed church, Erin began to fiddle and her poignant rendition of "Danny Boy" transformed the service from grim to glorious. As he listened gratefully and adoringly, Mick felt cocooned in peace.

The ballad was the purest of tributes to the mother he had worshipped, and once more, agonizing, emotional, heat flashes started to flicker within him. His lips began to twitch. He bit his inner mouth, and although he fought to suppress them, tears streamed. He realized then that if any good would come from this, it would be that he knew now that Erin was his rock, his comfort, and his strength.

After Erin's solo, the priest dropped his voice, adopted a softer more sympathetic tone, and Mick caught the final familiar words, "The Lord is my Sheppard. I shall not want."

Before the church could empty, Mick and Erin approached Father Moriority.

"I'm going up to the lectern to deliver my mother's eulogy, father."

"I'm sorry, Mick. The church has eliminated that part of our service. It's not allowed."

"But it would provide closing for her family and friends."

"I'm sorry. The church has banned that part of the ceremony."

"Father, you're our parish priest. Can't you bend the rules a little? I wouldn't feel so powerless."

"The rules are made in Rome, Mick and not to be bent by the likes of me."

Mick bared his teeth.

"How about I just go up there and start delivering it. How many altar boys you gonna need to tear me off that rostrum?"

Erin jumped between them.

"Mick, you'll do no such thing." She turned to face the priest. "He's sorry father. Sometimes he hasn't the sense he was born with."

Mick acquiesced but his throat burned with more pent-up contempt for the cloth.

THE WORST CAME after the burial. He was left alone with Erin in the limo, nobody to console, nobody to be brave in front of, and nobody to face but himself. Water poured uncontrollably from his eyes. Erin, suddenly frightened, yet also inspired, stared hard at him.

"Listen to me, Mick. Block everything out of your mind, but

what I'm about to say. Listen to me, now."

Startled by her urgency, Mick held her hand and gazed at her through tears.

"If ever a woman deserved heaven, it was your mom. She's there now."

Too realistic and too literal minded to be stirred much by the idea of heaven Mick nevertheless craved relief from the aching void inside him. The implications of Erin's words offered solace and helped soften a pain too great for him to bear, yet her words were counter intuitive to everything that he previously believed. He listened but couldn't bridge his skepticism.

"I want you to let your mother go, Mick. There's nothing you can do." Her voice changed a beat when she grabbed his wrist. "Promise me. Promise me, right now, this minute, that someday you'll let her go."

"I'll try." But his words were empty, choking back tears. "But my mother is dead."

Erin tightened her grip.

"You can't bring her back. No one can. Promise me."

His voice turned bitter. "She lived her whole life for others, a totally selfless woman. Where did it get her?"

He took his hand from hers, his words intense.

"I tell you one thing. I'm not going to make that mistake. Live hard. Play hard. That's been my motto, and I ain't stopping now. Dylan Thomas had it right. I'll be damned if I'll go softly into that good night."

FORTY-FOUR

WHEN THE BOX came in that afternoon, baseball season was winding down, and the Brothers were watching a Cubs game. Mutt and Mick used the truck's Stang-Nozzle to pour water through two windows of a top floor walk up. They had been operating a few hours when Mick checked his watch.

"Shit, I left my cell phone back at the firehouse. It's almost game time. I'm down $3,000 this week. I've got to get to a phone."

"You crazy? We have to put this fire out," Mutt said.

"It's under control now. No one is in danger. It'll just take a second. Keep the Stang pointed up at what's left of the fire. It's mostly smoke anyway. I'm taking the bucket to the floor below."

"Are you fucken crazy? What are you gonna tell the chief?"

"I'll tell him I had to take a piss, and I couldn't hold it any longer."

Mick took the bucket lower and started banging on a window. A frightened woman opened it.

"Am I in danger? Should I evacuate?"

"No, lady. You're fine. I just need to use your phone."

"Of course, climb in."

She opened the window wide, and Mick crept from the bucket.

"Over there on the table, do you need more fire trucks?"

Mick placed both hands up to calm her.

"No, no, you're fine."

He rushed passed her and dialed the phone.

"Hey, Fruity? Mick. Whatta ya got on the Mets? Okay, give me N.Y. minus the $140 for a dime." He hung up, thanked the perplexed women, and jumped back in the bucket as if nothing had happened.

LATER THAT NIGHT, Mick was plastered to his usual stool.

"Hey, Butch. This would be a nice place to open a bar. Jesus, I can't even get a drink in my own joint."

"Hey, boss. It's none of my business, but ain't you been hitting it a little hard the last couple of weeks?"

"Do I pay you or you pay me? Damn right, it's none of your business."

Mick staggered to the bathroom and felt the floor tilt. He finished his business, paused to shove a few bumps of coke up his nose, and marched to the middle of the bar where a well-dressed bald man, about 60, sat nursing a beer.

"Hey, Fruity. The Mets lost, huh? Shit. Who are the Dodgers playing?"

"Houston," he said.

"What's the spread?"

"L.A. minus $180."

"Give me the dog for three dimes," Mick said.

"Since when do you bet $3,000?"

"Jesus Christ, another fucken moralist, you a bookie or not?"

Fruity shrugged and removed a small pad from the pocket of his sports shirt.

"I'm a bookie. I'll take your bet, but I'm also quite a bit older than you, my friend. Here's some free advice. Stop gambling. Get a little something for yourself. You could have it all, but you're throwing it away."

"Thanks for the lecture. Do I have a bet or not?"

Fruity scribbled on a small assignment pad and shook his head.

"Here's your repeat. You've got Houston plus $160—600 Times . . .Wait, let me ask you a question."

"Yeah?"

"Name one player on the Astros."

"I can't." Mick cackled.

"That's what I thought."

Imitating a football referee, Fruity enthusiastically threw his hands into the air.

"Touchdown."

Mick ordered another double scotch.

Butch grabbed the empty old-fashioned glass, packed it with ice, and poured the Johnny Walker. Mick stopped him, plunged three fingers of his right hand into the glass, and clawed the ice out.

"What's with all the ice? Ya want me to catch cold?" Mick's face seemed filled with a merry, self-ironic glow, like a man who has become an amused spectator at the dissolution of his own life. He cackled, cawed, and despite gasping for breath, threw back the double.

THAT SAME NIGHT in the Bronx, Erin's mother was on her knees. Above her bed hung a picture of Saint Jude. Rosary beads slipped through her calloused thumb and forefinger. She was praying to the patron saint of lost causes that her only daughter would finally come to her senses.

FORTY-FIVE

IT RAINED THAT Monday, a week that would start badly and only get worse. Mick carried Oliver into the Vet's office and ran his sleeve across his eyes, making the drops a memory, before settling Oliver gently onto the black industrial rug.

"He won't eat doc. He's half blind, and he's starting to crap in the house."

"How old is Oliver?"

"I've had him since he was a puppy, around thirteen years."

"I'm afraid the humane thing to do is put him down."

Mick felt his stomach curl.

"Ah, no doc, don't tell me that. He's my best friend."

"If he is, have the courage to do what's right. Don't make him suffer."

Mick nestled Oliver peacefully in his arms while the vet got the I.V. going.

"You're just going to sleep old buddy," he said through tears and had actually believed that until poor Ollie let out a deep guttural yelp, a pitiful sound that Mick had never heard him make before. He steadied Oliver's lean, old body, petted him, and whispered assurance, "easy, buddy." When the drug flooded Oliver's bloodstream, the pup went limp in his arms.

His heart was broken, first his mother, and now Oliver. Despite the nasty weather, he left the Vet's office and sped to

Nobody's. He needed scotch and fast.

Torrential rain hammered the pools of water surrounding Northern Boulevard's swollen sewers. He parked his car in back, tiptoed through a large puddle, opened the back door, and sat on his usual stool. When he swallowed the Johnny Black, it rushed through his body with the intensity of an orgasm, a violent hammer, first pounding and then anesthetizing his consciousness.

LATER THAT EVENING, he fed the jukebox a buck to play Louie Armstrong's It's a Wonderful World, which only made him more maudlin. A circuitous mental tape of a wide-eyed puppy cuddling in his lap and licking his face tortured his psyche. A half dozen shot glass stains chained the top of the bar.

Mick's eyes were red, moist, and sloppy.

"Butch, take the air out of this glass, will ya. Killing your best friend is thirsty work."

His bartender snatched the Johnny Black from the top shelf.

"Whiskey won't drown your troubles, boss. Real troubles can swim."

Mick tipped the small glass to his lips.

"Always worried about me, huh pal? Don't. I've got this."

He swallowed the ounce. The whiskey warmed his heart. A few more would deaden the pain.

Mick's head whipped when the door creaked behind him. His face brightened when Grace walked in wearing tight jeans and a navy windbreaker.

"Baby, am I glad to see you. Just what the doctor ordered. Come over here. Boy, do I need cheering up."

He placed his arm around her tiny waist and pulled her to his hip. Grace saw the thin red veins threading the whites of his eyes and the discoloration of his skin.

"No wonder you're so happy to see me. You're pissed

drunk." She placed her wet umbrella against the wall. "Where's the love of your life?"

His expression was flat.

"Oh, she's in Washington this weekend for a conference, so I'm getting loaded, looking for a few laughs."

Grace had one eye on Mick and the other on her image in the mirror behind him.

"Well, you're out of luck tonight, lover," She said casually. "It's that time of the month."

"Honey, you got me all wrong. I don't give a shit about sex. I just need some cheering up from an old friend. If you hadn't walked in that door just now, I would've sent a limo for you. I had to put Oliver down, today."

"Awwwwww, Mick." Grace pulled up a stool, ordered a whiskey sour straight up, checked the mirror once again, ruffled her damp hair, and as an afterthought said, "I really am sorry, mate. I know how much you loved that dog."

Her indifference obvious, Mick changed the subject.

"It is what it is, Gracie. We're all heading to the same place eventually, so how are things going with you and Jake?"

"Things are getting serious enough that I'm sure he'd freak out if he knew that I was sitting here with you."

"Oh, he's getting possessive, is he?"

"They all do, darling. All of them except you."

"We understand each other, baby. We're both whores," Mick slurred. "Hey, cheer me up a bit. You've told me stories about when you were in sex clubs with two men. Have you ever been with three men?"

Grace thought a minute, sipped her drink, and looked at Mick with an eyebrow raised but said nothing.

"C'mon. On the level, have you?"

Grace smirked and took another short sip of her cocktail.

"Maybe."

"Maybe?" Mick laughed. "What the fuck, Grace. I thought

that would be a yes or no answer."

"Well, one time I was bent over in a sex club taking care of some girl, and some guys entered me from behind." Grace shrugged. "Different guys, two possibly three, but I never turned around to look. I was too busy."

"Jesus, Grace," Mick laughed. "You're the most uninhibited woman I ever met. I fucken love your attitude, no shit."

He reached over, pulled Grace to his hip again, and this time planted a kiss on her mouth.

"Butch, give my gal and me another drink, only laugh I've had all day."

He took his shot of scotch, tipped it into his beer, and watched it balloon into a brown cloud off the bottom of the glass. His empty stare never wavered or hand never paused. He just hoisted his glass and swigged the boilermaker to the bottom.

THE SUNDAY MORNING air was cool and still smelled of last night's rain. From Erin's windshield, the storm clouds were so thick and swollen that she couldn't even tell where the sun was in the sky. She had returned from Washington a day early and decided to skip Mass and surprise him with breakfast. She stopped at a local deli, picked up two tall white-Styrofoam cups of coffee with three ham and egg and fried tomato sandwiches, Mick's favorite.

When she had spoken to him last night, he had told her about Oliver and sounded like he was on a bender. She knew the grease from the ham and eggs would be the perfect hangover cure. After placing the brown bag on the passenger seat, she made the engine roar to life, and turned the white SUV onto the Bronx River Parkway towards Mick's apartment complex.

She walked up the three flights and used her key. When she opened the door, Erin saw a light blue windbreaker and a handbag on the living room chair. The remnants of some pink concoction rested on the miniature bar, a metal strainer still parked atop the glass shaker. She marched to his bedroom, held her breath, and peeked in. He was alone and fast asleep.

Rushing to the back bedroom, she saw Grace, and a bitter tang filled her mouth.

She had trouble catching her breath but beat back the impulse to flee. She regained her composure, staggered to the kitchen, put the sandwiches on a plate, and walked to his bedroom with the face of a zombie.

"Get up, Mick. I've brought you a cure."

Still stewed, he awoke groggy.

"Oh, hi baby. When did you get here? I thought you were in Washington?"

"I bet you did," she said sarcastically. "I finished my business early. Get up. I brought you breakfast."

As he reached for the container of coffee, he tried to put last night's pieces together.

"Wait," she said. "What happened to your hand?"

Surrounding the Styrofoam, Mick's fingers were covered in dried blood.

"I don't know. I must have cut myself."

"Baby, there's blood all over the pillow cases." Her voice rose, "Let me look at your hand."

Mick pulled it back.

"No, it's nothing. I'm fine."

"Honey, there's no cut or anything. Where the hell did all the blood come from?"

"Baby, stop it. Will you? It's no big deal. I'm fine."

Erin pulled back the covers. The sheets were caked.

"What the fuck happened Mick?"

As last night's events became clearer, Mick panicked.

"I don't know, baby. Let me think."

Erin stood stoically and stumbled to the back bedroom. She stood over Grace and quietly pulled the bed cover back. Bloodstains soiled both Grace's white panties and the sheets.

Erin calmly replaced them and started for the front door. As she opened it, a frenzied Mick charged out of his bedroom.

"Wait, baby, wait. I can explain."

Her stomach churned bile, and she shot him a contemptible sneer through her tears.

"I was a fool. I should have known better. Goodbye, Mick. Don't ever call me or try to see me again."

She turned and ran down the stairs. A naked Mick stood at the top of the stairwell and yelled to her back.

"Baby, wait. Come back. Let me explain. I'm sorry. I was drunk. I didn't even remember anything happened until I saw the blood. If I had realized that I had fucked up, I would have told you. I'm so sorry." His sentence fell on a hallway as empty as his words.

FORTY-SIX

TWO WEEKS LATER, Jamie's tightly cropped hair was damp and freshly brushed, and he had shaved so close that his cheeks glowed with color. The Italian restaurant he chose was packed.

"I needed to get out, thanks," Erin said. "I'm still devastated. I can't believe it."

"I tried to warn you. He's not himself when he's drunk. It's like he has a death wish. He's self-destructive almost like he wants to screw things up."

"I just don't want you to get the wrong idea. You're a nice guy. I don't want to jerk you around. I'll never love anyone the way I loved him. We're friends, and that's all, okay?"

"Sure. I get it. You're vulnerable right now. You don't want to get into another relationship, no pressure. Let's just hang out and see where it goes."

Jamie talked a great game, but he couldn't take his eyes off of her. Her lips were delicate, peach-toned, and expressive. The dimness of the lighting and the way the candle on the table flickered in the reflection of her eyes turned them a greenish gold as cloudless as a spring day, then those colorful eyes began to flood.

"How could I have loved someone so short-sighted, so stupid? The two of them were playing me for a fool the whole time." She wiped under her eyes with her napkin. "He talked about honesty? I'll never get over it."

"You both have to move on. Besides, Mick has other problems. He's letting cocaine ruin his life."

"He almost had me going down that same dead end. I can't believe I was so myopic. I'm going to Mass tomorrow and do some serious soul searching."

"Listen, I don't want to be a pest, or a jerk, but do you mind if I share the pew with you?"

"Suit yourself. I'd never stop anyone from going to Mass, if you don't mind sharing it with my parents."

THE FAITHFUL FLOCKED four at a time to a padded kneeler by the altar. The priest took two thin wafers from a golden chalice and placed them in Erin and Jamie's mouth.

"I'm glad those two are spending some time together," Nora said quietly in Brendan's ear.

"She'd be better off alone for a while," Brendan whispered.

"Nonsense, she's a smart, strong girl and knows what's right." Nora said too loudly. "The other one was a fool. This one's not. From what I hear, he's carrying on now worse than ever."

FOUR MILES SOUTH of the church, the fool in question answered the firehouse phone.

"Hey, I hate to call you at work, but I wanted to invite you to my wedding," Grace said.

"Your what?" Mick asked.

"Jake and I are getting married."

"Well, congrats to both of you. I guess?"

"He's good to me, Mick, and you and I aren't going anywhere. Are we?"

"A writer I admire, Nelson Alger, had three rules he never ignored. 'Never play cards with a guy named Doc. Never eat in a place called Mom's, and never, ever, fall in love with a woman who has more troubles than you do.'"

"Don't laugh it off, Mick. You've got your own flaws and plenty of them. You and I are a perfect fit, but you won't admit it. We get each other. You're me in trousers. Come on, this is your last chance to tell me what I already know."

Mick held the receiver a little farther from his ear and stared into it as if he couldn't believe what he was hearing. The cord dangled and stretched as he paced.

"Honey, you've got looks, and smarts, and I'm not with Erin anymore; but you're still selling your ass. Either you're crazy for money, or you've got a lot more problems that I don't know about; and problems that for damn sure, Jake doesn't know about." Mick rested his elbow against the wall. "And let's be honest. I don't care, and it's none of my business; but you're still screwing Bobby on the side too."

"How did you know that?" Grace laughed.

"C'mon baby, he's a fireman. Nothing's sacred in the firehouse. We talk. Don't worry. I ain't saying shit to Jake. It's your body. Do what you want with it. I hope the two of you are sincerely happy."

"I know. I'm a mess," she laughed. "I swear I don't know why I do what I do, but I do get to shop at Bergdorf's like it's a supermarket."

"Well, you were always practical, sex for cash. But I never figured you'd get hitched for money. You didn't seem like the kind of chick who screws down and marries up, too fond of the laughs."

"Me either, but his family has money too, Mick," she laughed again. "I guess it depended on how much money."

From the housewatch, three familiar blasts filled the firehouse.

"Gotta go. We got a run but good luck. I'll be there with bells on. Make sure you wear white. It'll put a smile on both our faces."

He racked the phone back on the metal.

AFTER THE FALSE alarm, the afternoon dragged and led to a rare slow night. Mick was hoping for a few runs to distract him from the knot in his stomach and take his mind off his spirals. Too bad the Mutt wasn't working. He could use the laughs. The apparatus doors were up, and Twiggy came out into the clear night sipping coffee.

"Have you met the new probie yet?" Twiggy asked.

He was long, and sinewy, deceptively strong, hence the nickname.

"Not yet. Nice guy?"

"Nice guy? This guy Reilly's a prince. I told him casually in conversation that I was paying points to a shylock on $10,000. He asked me what points were, hadn't a clue. Can you believe a guy that straight? So, I filled him in. You pay three points for every $1,000 borrowed. That's $30 for every $1,000. Because I borrowed $10,000, I have to pay $300 a week "juice" with nothing coming off the top."

"Wow, this guy never heard of vigorish," Mick's mouth hung. "A real boy scout, huh?"

"Yeah, but Reilly's all right. He asked me why I'm paying $300 a week in juice while he had $10,000 in the bank doing nothing? He said he'd loan me the money, and I could pay him back the same way, three bills a week but no interest."

Twiggy was one of the best friends Mick had in the world, another childhood buddy, and a guy he'd go to war for.

"He wasn't bullshitting either. Very next morning, he took me to the bank and handed me $10,000. The kid's saving me $1,200 a month."

"Wow that's fucking great, Twig. He barely knows you."

But Mick's inner demon whispered,

I bet I can fuck this up.

THE FOLLOWING SET of tours, he met the beardless, boyish Reilly. He had the parted brown hair and the good-natured smile of an Indiana farm boy. Any minute Mick expected him to shout,

"My Dad's got a barn. Let's put on a show."

After the meal that night, Mick smoked a Marlboro in front of quarters, the McDonalds across the street long closed, the block, normally noisy, now deserted. The night was hazy, dark, and moonless with a warm August breeze. Reilly joined him.

"Welcome to the firehouse, Tom. We get plenty of fire to keep you busy, and the guys are great. Make sure you show up at the softball games. You'll bond with the brothers quicker that way."

"Thanks a lot, Mick. I'm assigned here at least a year. The Brooklyn commute is not that bad, so I'll see how it goes."

Banal conversation continued.

"Are you single or married?"

"Engaged." Reilly had the skeletal frame of a lad racked together from the slats of an apple crate, his stomach and ass flat, his face eternally young, his mouth as small as a child's, his eyes bright with eagerness.

Then Mick lowered the boom.

"Yeah, you'll like everybody here," he looked up at the stars and almost as an afterthought said, "but be careful of one guy."

Riley eyes narrowed, neck stiffening.

"Who?"

"There's this guy, Twiggy. He's a compulsive gambler, and he owes everyone in the firehouse money. Whatever you do don't lend him any cash. It would be like throwing it in a fire."

Reilly's eyes widened and riveted on Mick's. Every word Mick spoke after that drove another stake into Reilly's bankbook. Although Twiggy wouldn't pick a penny off the floor without looking around for its owner, and Reilly's money had never been safer, all he could think about was his blunder. He was so rattled that his foggy brain could barely make out Mick's silhouette.

TWO DAYS LATER in the firehouse kitchen, Mick was buttering an English muffin when Twiggy stormed in.

"What did you say to Reilly you Irish cocksucker?"

"Reilly?" Mick looked up puzzled. "Oh, you mean the new kid?" Mick's right cheek filled with air. "Why? Whatta ya mean?"

"Don't give me that new kid, bullshit, you Donkey, bastard. I know it was you."

Twiggy was one of the sharpest guys Mick knew. He had figured that it would take him all of five minutes to finger him as the culprit. That was what made the whole scheme so delicious to begin with.

Mick dropped the butter knife on the stainless-steel counter, grabbed his knees, and started cawing. He shuddered a full minute before finally catching his breath and said, "Tell me what he said." He started shaking again and said through tears, "Ya gotta tell me what he said."

Twiggy began laughing too.

"He said his fiancé pushed up the wedding date, so he needed the money to buy a ring."

"His fiancé, a ring?" Mick lost it again. Twiggy started to shake too. Both gasped until Twiggy finally caught his breathe.

"Where can we get a drink after work?"

Later at the bar, Mick told him that he'd loan him the money on the same terms. Gags like this momentarily took his mind off Erin, but Jamie had been anything but idle.

FORTY-SEVEN

JAMIE SAT IN gray boxer shorts on the side of his bed, his thoughts hopping like a bag of frogs.

"I've been crazy about you since the day I first saw you. I know this is impulsive and comes quickly after your breakup, but marry me," he begged. "I'm killing it on Wall Street. I'll always do right by you."

"You're killing it on Wall Street? That's what you say after we make love for the first time? That's how you propose? You think that I'd marry you for money? You think that little of me?"

Despite the affront, her mind flashed back to her mother's warning.

I had my own Mick Mullan. I hope when your time comes that you make the right decision.

"I didn't mean it like that. You know I didn't. I just wanted you to know that everything I have is yours. That's all. I love you."

"I need more time, Jamie. It's too soon, and you've got too much going for you to settle for a girl on the rebound. We both have to be sure."

"Of course. I get it." He leaned over to kiss her again.

"Not now. I'm starving," she said. "Let's head out and get something to eat."

IT WAS AFTER midnight when Erin pulled her SUV into the Callahan driveway. She put the gearshift in park and opened the door to find her mom sitting in front of the television.

"Jamie asked me to marry him."

"Why wouldn't he? He's not a fool. Wonderful. He's a good, solid, church-going Catholic man. I couldn't be happier. You said yes, of course."

"No, ma. I said I'd think about it."

"You said you'd think about it? Surely to God, what's there to think about? Don't tell me that you're still thinking about that other eedgit?"

"He was never a fool, Mom. Maybe I was. I thought I could change him . . . But this is not about Mick. It's about Jamie. It's not the same, and I have something else to think about . . . something that I can't talk about right now."

"Another thing to think about . . . and what could be so important that you couldn't share it with your own mother?"

FORTY-EIGHT

WHILE THE OTHER firefighters sat calmly and watched the Yankee playoff game, Mick was pacing the floor screaming abuse at the umpires. His ranting was interrupted by three short blasts of the air horn.

"Get out. Get out. Get out. Everybody goes. Truck, Engine, Chief, everybody goes."

They sped eight blocks and rounded a corner. Thick smoke pushed from the eaves of a brownstone. A reddish orange bloom from two windows roaring flames lit up the sky. Victims screamed and hacked from two other windows while foul clouds pushed ink-black smoke above their heads. The officer peppered his gloved fist on the Plexiglas separating him from the men.

Mick leapt from the rig, sprinted to one of the truck's compartments, and grabbed the partner saw. The roofman, Joe Sullivan, flew up the stairs of the adjoining building with Mick close at his heels.

Following the harsh sound of Pete's axe clanging against Mutt's Halligan crowbar, the enginemen slogged up the interior stairs to the fire apartment. When the locks finally imploded, the engine officer called for water, and advanced the charged line. Pete and Mutt crawled in shoulder to shoulder behind the hose. Mutt fumbled left. Pete groped right. Both inched into the darkness to conduct a primary search.

Mick and Joe had reached the adjoining roof meanwhile; and spotted tar bubbling at the rear of the fire building. They both hurdled the parapet, and while Joe pried open the bulkhead door, Mick started a crosscut above the fire to relieve the toxic, pent-up gases and help the search team below.

The interior support beams suddenly buckled. The roof bent soft, and the tarpaper vanished like burnt paper. Mick's eyes closed, opened again, and then glazed over. His lips parted languidly. A muted sound escaped from his throat. He skidded, flailed, and slipped into the inferno as easily as sliding onto the edge of an orgasm.

THE FOLLOWING MORNING, his hands and head were bandaged, but he was conscious and alert on a raised bed watching television. The nurse propping up Mick's pillow was tacit, tough, and wide. She could've been a piano mover had she not pursued her vocation in medicine.

"That's great, thanks," Mick said to her deaf ears when the door burst open.

"Oh, my God. Are you alright?" Erin asked. "I came as soon as I heard."

Mick felt a flush of color like windburn bloom in his throat. His face turned sour.

"You shouldn't have bothered."

He snatched the remote and turned up the volume.

"Does your boyfriend know you're here? You two didn't waste a day. I'm starting to think you were back-dooring me the whole time."

"That was a shitty thing to say. I thought you were better than that. I came to see if you were all right. I didn't come here for an argument. Remember, you were the one who cheated. Don't make me out to be the one who ruined what we had. I wasn't the liar. You were."

"Look, you've got the man who'll make your mother happy.

That's what it's always been about, right? Your mother, your faith, how things look to everybody else? So why the fuck come to see me; what can you possibly tell me that I don't already know?"

Erin felt his rancor and bitterness but stiffened. Swallowing her pride, she blurted, ". . . I'm pregnant, Mick."

His ears heard the sentence but refused to send a response to his brain. Mick's mind raced to find words before letting his pride bark, "Lovely. I'll round up the usual suspects."

Her insides ripped.

"You damn well know it's yours."

He saw the shards of pain in her eyes.

"And how would I know that?"

"I know it's yours. The only time I didn't take my pill was the morning after Rory Dolan's. Jamie understands and doesn't care. He wants to marry me anyway. That's something you'd never do. Even if you were sure it was yours, would you, Mick?"

His eyes squinted with suddenly secreted venom. He could feel the words binding his throat so spit them out.

"Marry you? I can't stand the sight of you. Do me a favor. Marry that double-crossing prick. You two deserve each other. Now I need to get some sleep, so if you don't mind."

His voice was full of nails and foreign to his own ears. He flipped over, his heart filled with guilt and self-loathing, his body hot with self-pity, but despite his rage, his thoughts raced to her playing fiddle at his mother's funeral. The memory rooted in his soul, digging deep, refusing to fade.

He kept his back turned deliberately. Fearing that if she saw his face, she'd see the enormous hole in his heart. His throat throbbed. Tears swam in his eyes. He knew his words were insincere, bitter, and filled with pride, but fuck her. It was his valedictory, and his privilege to deliver it any way he chose. He didn't get to see her vision cloud, or watch her stumble, as she dashed for the door. He couldn't see her heart break or acknowledge his own.

RUSHING FROM THE elevator, she almost collided with Pete on the ground floor.

"Erin, what a surprise. I'm so glad that you came to see him. How does he look?"

He noticed the pools in her eyes, her shaking hands, but still rambled. "He was insanely lucky. A kitchen table broke his fall just when Mutt and I started our search. He almost fell into our laps. He's got more lives than a cat."

Stunned, Erin didn't speak.

"What's wrong with you? Mick's alright isn't he?"

Then, she found her voice.

"Oh, me? Nothing, I'm just wonderful. Everything's perfect, lovely." She stiffened. "And Mick? Oh yeah, he's in fine form, perfect, just fucken like him. A fucken asshole, I hate him." Hysteria hit, and she started to sob with the relentless and unstoppable cries of despair that come from deep down in the soul.

"Before you go, answer one question. Are you happy?"

She gulped and sputtered.

"Happy? Yes. Yes, Pete. I'm happy, or I will be soon enough. As soon as I put that aggravating bastard in my rearview mirror."

"Give it time. You'll be fine. You're an amazing gal." Powerless to help, he bussed her maternally on the cheek. "Well, I better get my ass upstairs."

Pete punched three. When the elevator door closed, he began rehearsing how he'd handle this. Minutes later, he stood stiff as a post framing Mick's door.

"I saw Erin on her way out."

Mick's heart had yearned to reconnect with her, but no way his pride would let him.

"Fuck her. I don't know why she came here to begin with."

Mick looked healthy enough, but his eyes had changed, not as alive. Pete could see that he'd been crying, but they were dry now. Dry, red around the rims, and so very, very dead.

Pete dropped into the wooden chair next to the bed.

"I'm glad you feel like that."

"What do you mean? You're glad?"

"It'll make it easier for you to let her go. She's way better off with Jamie."

"That's a hell of a remark. You're supposed to be my pal. Why?"

"Because he can't hurt her. You know she doesn't love Jamie."

"Fuck that broad. I lived without Eileen, and I can live without her."

"Eileen's death took a bigger bite out of you than even you know. I watched it eat you alive. And even though you think that you're made of steel, losing a woman like Erin is gonna tear another gigantic hole in you. Stop lying to yourself, Mick."

FORTY-NINE

OUT OF THE hospital and sober five long days, Mick stopped in Queens and sipped a large club soda with lime. Three empty stools away, a customer drank Bud, and the bottle beaded with moisture. As the foam slid down the glass neck into the man's mouth, Mick felt his tongue slithering across his dry lips, the smell taunting his nose and mouth.

He could envision the amber color inside the aluminum barrels, the bead it made inside the bottle's neck before being poured, the splendid little splash it made when it slid down the side of a tilted glass. He had to get out of there, and fast, so he pushed $10 across the bar, jumped in his Honda, clicked the headlights, dropped his transmission into gear, and drove south.

HE ARRIVED AT the firehouse early and found a noticeably slimmer Vernon Kingsley sitting alone in the dayroom.

"But Vern, man, you were a heavy hitter. How the hell did you stop? You didn't go to A.A. or nothing? You just stopped?"

"Sure, I went for a while. I would have gone anywhere to stop. I was running out of dates."

"Running out of dates? What the hell does that mean?"

"I had already mortgaged too many tomorrows. I knew eventually the bill would come due. We're all heading for the same place, Mick. I didn't think it made much sense to ride the express. It was stop or die, so I quit."

"I tried A.A. for a month or two. Granted, there's a lot of wisdom in those rooms, but it just wasn't for me," Mick said.

"A lot had to do with my faith. I became a Muslim. They don't allow alcohol," Vern said.

"You're a Muslim? No shit? How come you never said anything?"

"It's not something I broadcast, not too many Muslims on the job. Besides, guys would confuse the issue. They'd think I was a Black Muslim. I'm not. I'm black and a Muslim."

"You lost all that weight after you got sober?"

"Drinking takes up a lot of time. When I got sober, I needed another outlet, so I started running."

"You too? That's what Chief Tommy does. I wish I had your willpower. I was sober a week, but I broke out a few days before I fell through that roof. I can't seem to flush the habit."

"Do you still go to A.A. meetings?" Vern asked.

"Not anymore. It's not my bag, all that higher power bullshit."

"You do know that your higher power doesn't have to be God?"

Mick parked his ass in a chair and lit a Marlboro.

"I know. I know. I met an old buddy at the gym who told me that too. He's sober fifteen years and said he'd take me to a meeting out on Long Island. Apparently, they have a better class of drunk in Great Neck." Mick inhaled the smoke and chuckled at his own joke. "I hadn't seen him in ages. He wasn't even a member, just using a guest pass, lucky coincidence."

"If you get back into the program, you'll learn that cocaine, alcohol, and weed are just symptoms of your disease. Your real problem is guilt about the past and anxiety about the future," Vernon Kingsley swiped a slow palm across his chin and leaned forward on both elbows. "So, you met an old friend at a gym that he doesn't belong to, and he wants to take you to a meeting? I thought you were a smart guy. You still believe in coincidences?"

FIFTY

THE SUMMER A memory, September roared in like a hungry polar bear. When the sun disappeared that evening, the darkness turned the wind cutting raw. Erin raised the collar of the long, gray-wool coat covering her barely visible pregnancy and climbed the two-dozen slate steps leading to the church's vestibule.

She dipped four fingers into one of two, white marble receptacles guarding St. Philip Neri's entrance, which held the holy water. She crossed her right hand north to south, and then west to east in the familiar ritual before pulling open the large wooden handle on the inner door.

The wealthy Parish was ornate, and the two walls bordering the pine pews were lined with expensive hand-carved mahogany Stations of the Cross. A frescoed ceiling canopied the shiny gold tabernacle, and lavish enclaves enveloped sandstone statues of saints and martyrs.

Like most churches, St. Philip's was built in cruciform design. Erin walked down the nave, genuflected in front of the tabernacle, and spun to her right to kneel in front of a life size statue of the Virgin Mary. She lit a votive candle and prayed.

"Lord, guide me to make the right choices. Let my decisions be your decisions. Let your will be my will. Help me to see your light."

Streetlamps flooded the sidewalks of the Grand Concourse. Headlights speeding by the boulevard cast their thin-beamed shadows on the church's facade. Erin prayed in front of the Virgin's image long after the traffic had thinned.

Miles south near Mick's firehouse, traffic was nonexistent, the streets unlit, the dirt yards weedless, and hard packed. Mick pulled into a tight parking spot, killed the ignition, and noticed two torn bed sheets on a filthy clothesline flapping in cadence with the strong wind.

Three buildings away, an automobile repair shop was plated with hubcaps from the concrete foundation to its metal eaves, and right next to the shop was an inconspicuous two-story house, its white paint worn and blistered. Two large ashtrays, the kind that you see outside public facilities, defended the entrance.

Mick walked up the six skewed steps and opened the unlocked door. It led to a large dining room that doubled as an Evangelical Mission. In front of rows of gray folding chairs, a dozen men held hands in a circle and bowed their heads.

"God grant me the serenity to accept the things I cannot change, courage to change the things I can, and the wisdom to know the difference."

Minutes after the prayer, "My name's Mick, and I am an alcoholic."

The "Plug in the Jug" beginner's meeting responded in chorus.

"Hi, Mick."

While he spoke, men drank from cans of soda. Some ate chocolate bars.

"Just in case some of you don't think I belong here. Let me clear that up right away. I once woke up after a three-day load in Australia with a prosthetic leg in my bed and no memory of how it got there."

That first sentence led to the second, and the third, and when his soliloquy was finally finished ten minutes later, his limitations, faults, and failures had flown from him as freely as water pours from a burst damn. Mick had finally admitted that he was powerless over his addiction. He reached out to a higher power and took his first giant step toward sobriety.

FIFTY-ONE

SOMETIMES THE DECISIONS that you ponder long and hard don't matter nearly as much as the ones that you hardly think about at all, those moments when you make decisions that seem inconsequential yet mean everything. Tuesday morning was like that.

Vernon Kingsley needed the weekend off, so Mick had worked his Saturday shift; and Vern was paying Mick back today. This common FDNY practice is called a mutual. With the day off, he and Buffalo were going to play golf upstate. Mick awoke before the sun to get on the road before morning commuter traffic became unbearable.

The two raced up the New York State Thruway just after the sun had started its slow climb into a clear blue sky. A beautiful September morning, perfect for a round of golf.

"Nothing's more annoying than a reformed drunk preaching sobriety. I'm just saying I feel better, and I'm thinking clearer," Mick said.

"Everything is relative, clearer than what?" Buffalo asked. "Clearer then me carrying your unconscious ass from saloon to saloon and propping you up on a bar stool?"

"Fuck you. I know it has only been a little over a week, but this time I'm determined. When you stop drinking, you start thinking."

"Thinking? Well, that's a start anyhow," Buffalo's eyes crinkled at the corners. "Do me a favor. Pull over at an exit by a grocery store. I wanna buy four bacon and egg sandwiches and a case of light beer for the golf cart. When Mick pulled into the 7-Eleven fifteen minutes later, Buffalo opened the car door and grinned back through the open window. "You do the thinking. I'll do the drinking."

"Fuck you, ya fuck. I'm trying to be serious here."

He watched the big man enter the store and did some of that thinking. His drug of choice lately had been guilt, the hard stuff, pure, and uncut. That baby Erin was carrying had to be his, and when she had reached out, he had acted like a jerk.

Then he began to wonder why any of us are what we are whether good or bad. He didn't choose to be an alcoholic, to have the oral weakness of a child for a bottle; nevertheless, that self-destructive passion, that genetic or sociological wound had festered since puberty and had grown into an abscess that both dictated and threatened his life.

Just thinking about alcohol made his body crave sugar, so he reached into his glove department and unwrapped a Nestles Crunch. He swallowed the last of the candy just as Buff left the store, chewing on a sandwich, and slugging a Miller Light. As soon as the Big Man fastened his seat belt, Mick threw the car into gear, pulled out into traffic, and picked up the conversation where it had left off.

"No, really, compulsions narrow perspective. Gambling and drinking make ya selfish. I look back at the damage I've caused, and it makes me want to make things right, especially with Erin. I wouldn't dream of getting in touch with her. She's better off marrying Jamie, but still . . . every time I think about her, or picture her face, my fucken heart breaks. There were times she could finish my sentences."

MICK AND BUFFALO had just paid their green fees when the pro shop's television blasted the news alert.

"We interrupt this program for a breaking story," the anchor said. "We have reports that a plane has crashed into the World Trade Center. Stay tuned. NBC News will take you live to the scene."

"Can you imagine a pilot so oblivious this early in the morning? How can you not see something as big as the Twin Towers on a clear day like this?" Mick began to pick golf balls from a jug-sized glass jar. "I think I remember reading about a plane that hit the Empire State Building back in the '40s."

"We switch to Manhattan for live coverage." The screen showed thick black smoke churning from the Trade Center, the jumbo jet an avulsion exposing the wounded skyscraper's skeleton.

"Holy shit. That's not a private plane. It's a commercial jet. What the hell? Oh man, I wish I were working. Every fire company in the city will be in on this one."

"Wish you were working?" Buffalo said between double takes. "You firemen are fucken crazy. What if that building collapses?"

"That building won't collapse. I've been to hundreds of high-rise fires. It's standard procedure. No big deal. We hook up a couple of floors below. We put them out. It's what we do."

Despite his bluster, Mick had never seen anything like this, and as far as he knew, no one else had either. He swallowed hard and looked at his palms. They were bright with a thin line of sweat.

"Granted, this will be the biggest high-rise fire in the history of the world, and the key will be trying to evacuate the floors above." He wiped his hands on his thighs. "It's already too late for those poor bastards where the plane hit."

"Do you want to watch this or tee off?" Buffalo asked.

"Are you kidding? Wait a few minutes. Let me see this play

out."

The two stood for close to thirty minutes mesmerized by the disaster . . . then the second jet hit the South Tower. Mick watched the point of impact, the amount of fire pouring from the hole, and the columns of dense black smoke.

"Holy fuck. Do you believe this shit? Something's going on Buff. Screw the golf, man. We're under attack. I've got to get down there."

ON THE ROAD to the disaster, his speedometer was reading 90 when he suddenly heard a loud pop. His knuckles whitened on the steering wheel while the car fought to respond. The tires shrieked loudly, but the spin had it now. It careened into the other lane where he barely managed to avoid a collision. He lifted his right foot from the gas, pumped his brakes slowly, and thump, thump, thumped to a halt.

He looked disgustedly at the back wheel, punched his flashers, slapped on the donut, and limped the Honda to the first exit where he found a cheap roadside tire shop. Mick explained the urgency and told the pudgy, wide-nosed Mexican that he was heading to the site of the disaster.

"I feex you right up, senor," Jorge said.

True to his word, Jorge put the car on a lift, removed the donut, and pulled the damaged tire from Mick's trunk. He submerged it in a round metal tub of water and rotated it, but then something odd happened.

Jorge approached Mick and Buff. "I weesh to show you somethееng."

Jorge handed Mick a small piece of scrap metal bent perfectly into the shape of a cross. As Mick took it from the man's grimy hands and held it closer to his eyes, his mouth fell open. His eyebrows creased when he turned to Buff.

"You believe this, man?"

Sure, as shit, there it was, a miniature crucifix had punctured his tire, plain as day. Was this yet another coincidence, or was it the universe's design to ensure that he wouldn't reach the site of the disaster for an additional thirty minutes? How many times had he tempted fate already, or could this be an omen that he shouldn't go at all?

Screw that. Staying away would be bullshit, a cowardly cop out.

He paid for the tire, tipped Jorge liberally, and shoved the car in gear. He was still thanking the Mexican from his open window as he rolled out of the service station. Once again on the thruway, he floored the accelerator.

"My turnout gear is in my trunk, so after I drop you off, I can shoot right down there. I can't believe this is happening. I wish I had a broadband radio. Keep screwing with the dials, Buff. Get as much info as you can."

"The hell with that." Buffalo took his cell phone out of his pocket, his face ruddy from years of alcohol, his belly hanging over his belt like a sack of flour.

"What's the number of your firehouse? I'll dial. You talk. They'll have more information than the fucken radio."

"Great idea."

Before Buffalo could dial, Mick's own cell phone vibrated.

"Hold that call, Buff. This could be news."

Mick pulled it from his pocket and glanced at the screen. The caller ID read unknown. "Who the fuck is this?" He barked into the cell, "Hello? Hello?"

"Hello, Mick Mullin? This is Nora Callahan, Erin's mother. Are you working? Are you down at the Trade Center?"

"I'm driving back from upstate. I'll be down there as quick as I can. Why? What's wrong?"

"It's Erin. She told me that she was meeting Jamie this morning at the Trade Center. They were going to the Diamond District to pick out a ring. I dialed her number over and over, but I can't get through."

Something in his mind, like the click of a camera, flashed back to the hospital and his false pride.

This is my fault.

He tried to ignore the knot in his gut, the dryness in his mouth, the rancid odor rising from his armpits.

"What time was she supposed to meet him?"

"Early this morning. I'm frightened to death. The police are only letting rescue workers travel into lower Manhattan. I was hoping you might have more information." Her voice trailed to tears. "Please, God protect her."

A creeping river of pain flowed from Nora's frightened words to Mick's consciousness. He ignored the chirping of Buff's cell phone and gripped the steering wheel hard hoping to steel himself.

"I'm still an hour from the Bronx. I'm going to drop my friend off and rush down there."

"Thank you. Thank you, so much. Bless you. Let me know anything, anything you can, as soon as you can."

"If cell phones aren't working at the site, I don't know how I can get you any information, but I'll do everything that I can. Don't give up hope. She may have not been anywhere near the Trade Center and Mrs. Callahan?"

"Yes?"

"If you hear anything, anything at all, call me right away. If you can't get through, keep trying. Will you do that?"

"I will of course . . . and Mick," Nora said, "Please . . . be careful."

A thin tremolo started to vibrate inside him. A wave of nausea and fear washed over him. He kept thinking about the cross Dang gave him, the flat tire, and the false sense of security he had always had since a child, and then he had this sudden horrible feeling that maybe there was a God, and if there was, He'd had his number all along.

When he hung up, Buffalo's face had the urgency of a man

trying to defuse a bomb.

"What is it, Buff? What's the matter with you?"

"Mary said that the South Tower just collapsed."

FIFTY-TWO

IN TURNOUT GEAR by noon, Mick hailed a passing ambulance.

"Are you guys heading for the site?"

The driver was a big, barrel-chested man with long, thick, black hair, which curled over his shirt's white lapels. A gold chain creased his thick neck. His partner was small and thin, his teeth long and white, his russet hair wet with sweat.

"Jump in the back, man. We'll get you down there," the driver said. His huge hands blanched on the steering wheel, his knuckles as round as marbles.

Mick bolted to the back of the truck where three other rescue workers sat silently nodding at him. As the ambulance sped to the site, the truck's tires gripped a deserted FDR Drive. Deafening silence permeated both front and back.

Blessing himself, an ironworker had the face of impending doom. A policeman looked as if someone was about to shove him in front of a moving train, and Mick felt as antsy as a skydiver before his first jump. He had been through life and death situations before, but this time it was personal. Fear gnawed at his viscera. He sucked the moisture out of his cheeks and swallowed hard.

If Nora's suspicions were true, and Erin was buried beneath that building, it was because of his pride and stupidity. Guilt strangled him. His thoughts selfishly shifted to how he would live with himself if Erin and his unborn baby were both reduced to a fine gray dust beneath all that rubble.

What would he find when he got down there?

Mick thought long and hard on that interminable ride to the gallows. The list of things he shouldn't have done were long, not gotten drunk, not gone home with Grace, not gambled and drugged, not forced the one unblemished entity in his life to flee. He wondered why he had been cursed with this voracious and visceral Celtic sense that every pleasure must be seized or lost forever, a hedonistic curse that infected so many of his ancestors.

Two long Manhattan blocks from the collapsed towers, the ambulance finally pulled onto a side street, and when the skeleton impersonating a medic opened the van's back door, Mick snapped back to a harsh reality. Even at this distance, he could see rescue vehicles blanketed in residue.

A dust cloud covered nearby streets with a cascade of white ash. The first thing he heard was a dispatcher over a police captain's radio: "Four body bags at West and Broadway immediately." A few seconds later, "Body bag at West and Third," which was followed by one word, "Fireman."

Jogging to the end of the block, he turned the corner, looked up, staggered, and propped his hand against a building. Stopping dead in his tracks, he suddenly felt like his soul had been shoved against an emery board.

In less time than it takes to recover from a sneeze, reality had turned to apocalyptic fiction. Before his bewildered eyes, Mick's mind tried to process the sixteen acres of smoldering destruction before him and the absurd idea that both buildings could have collapsed.

From the metaphorical elephant's tale, it seemed like the entire city had crumpled. Great hills and steep valleys of steel and concrete swallowed the landscape. Jutting above this pitiful, horrific panorama, one burning building after another was pushing black smoke into an already saturated sky.

In what would be estimated later as 1.4 million tons of debris, lower Manhattan was reduced to a mound of rubble, Ground Zero to Armageddon. In FDNY terms, the area was fully involved.

The closer he got to the source, the more devastation, desolation, and destruction shrouded the scene. It felt as though the air had been sucked out from under an enormous dark bowl, and inside this dome of despair, clouds of smoke carrying crushed concrete, asbestos, and glass combined to create a toxic and uninhabitable environment hemming the rescue workers in amid a screaming silence.

The farther he walked, the more the annihilation and haze overwhelmed him. Not a single object was recognizable. Black smoke danced and shifted with the wind and filled his nostrils sporadically with the unmistakable whiff of death. From his turnout-coat pocket, he took a red, cotton bandanna and tied it around his face.

A voice buried under a pile of wreckage whimpered for attention. Mick fell to his knees and clawed away at debris trapping a bewildered, frail old woman. When Mick freed her, she refused to stand, but instead burrowed back inside the pile, her ancient face and scrabbling hands as creased as an old catcher's mitt.

"Help me, please. I was with my son. He may be in this heap. I don't know. I passed out. Please, help me."

Mick plunged back to his knees, furiously scooping, and scouring the swell. He tossed slab after slab of concrete aside, sweeping away the piles of dust before him. After an interminable amount of time, he surrendered and was suddenly jarred by the section's eerie silence, pierced only by the peculiar and unsettling chirping of unanswered cell phones.

"I'm sorry, ma'am. There's no one under here. Hopefully,

your son went for help."

Her face seemed as if she were trying to solve some peculiar puzzle that had no answer, like she had a question mark in the middle of her face and was daring Mick to explain what had happened.

"But you can't stop looking. He was my only son, please."

"Lady, he's not in there. I'm sorry. Just be thankful we didn't find him. That means he could be alive, but I gotta keep moving. So many are suffering . . ."

But she continued to wail from the depths of her soul, and he flashed to the memory of his own mother. Nothing would have ever made her stop searching for him, nothing. Mick picked the woman up and cradled her like a bride before placing her in the arms of a passing EMT.

As he started a slow slog toward the many buildings still chillingly ablaze near the collapsed towers, lower Manhattan looked like it had been attacked from outer space, a bad science fiction film.

FIFTY-THREE

HE PASSED THE abandoned fire trucks that had carried his Brothers to their graves and choked back tears. He reeled past the crumbled rigs and past the grief-stricken, exhausted firefighters. Men sat curbside sucking oxygen, their blue T-shirts stiff with salt, armpits dark with sweat, the backs of their necks oily and glistening beneath their leather helmets.

A confused man covered in white chalk cradled a dead child passed Mick aimlessly.

"She was so tiny, so helpless, just a baby." The man's voice rose from a bass moan and then bellowed into a falsetto wail. "How could God let this happen?"

A Paramedic saw the daze on the man's face and rushed toward him. Mick's nerves were popping, and he reacted by taking longer and faster strides. After a long block, he swore a faint throb like a pulse pounded his ear and stopped a moment to suck in long, deep gulps of air.

If God exists, He has more important things to worry about than that poor dead child. This is Pearl Harbor, Gettysburg, and Guadalcanal all wrapped in one massive package of pain. God has more to do today than worry about one man's suffering.

Death was coming in waves. Nothing was recognizable, not a body or a fragment of clothing, or anything else that would indicate a human presence. Steel, concrete, and rubble, everything was atomized, gone, pulverized. And then his thoughts drifted,

Why do people mistakenly believe that in times of disaster the world is focused on them?

He remembered something that he had read.

In his *Journal of the Plague,* Daniel Defoe wrote that those afflicted by the Black Death wandered the cobblestone streets of London shouting out their sins to anyone who would listen. No one cared. The shutters of every store, house, and cottage were locked tight.

In this more "civilized" era, rescue workers were paid to care, but then Mick's mind replayed the sight of that terrified ironworker in the E.M.S. van, just a volunteer rushing to the chaos. Ground Zero eventually would be teeming with all walks of people eager to help, foreign and domestic, rich and poor, left and right.

Mick had always believed that men were basically good, yet the suicidal zealots who caused this tragedy didn't sport tails, horns, or cloven hooves. They were men, not demons, and New York had held a clear priority for the perverted evil dreamers who had loosed the lightning.

Granted, these were strange thoughts to have on his way to his expected demise, but while jogging, he had trained his mind to drift to places where every muscle in his body didn't ache, and now his brain had to go somewhere, anywhere but here.

Clerics and aesthetics preach that happiness lies in self-denial, self-sacrifice, and self-discipline. He walked that last long block thinking hard about his existence and his atheism, about the dissolute life he had lead and wondered if any of it made any difference now. Since Eileen's death, he had spent his days living life to the fullest, and whether that was right or wrong, his past wasn't flashing in front of him now but unwinding slowly in cadence with each long stride.

Don't think about that. Every man does things that he's proud

of, things he's not so proud of, and hopefully not too many things that he's ashamed of. If God exists, maybe that's how He keeps score. Who knows? One thing's certain. I never deliberately hurt anyone. If I don't get out of here alive, I'll take that as a one-line epithet.

His self-indulgence stopped when he ran into two shell-shocked firefighters fronting a wall of wreckage.

"Anybody in charge?" Both shook their heads no. One extended his hand.

"I'm Michael, and that's Glenn. There are no officers around."

Sweat leaked from under Michael's helmet, creating rivulets in the white dusty mask covering his skin.

"I'm Mick." He shook their hands. "Well, I don't have to be an officer to know that we're gonna need tools and a link to the command center."

Glenn's gray-blue eyes stared at Mick's as if they had no lids, his face frozen, his jaw hooked sideways like some mutated animal. He lit a cigarette, and the match flared upon a freckled young face with a wide nose, pronounced cheekbones, and those two eager eyes awaiting direction. He drew on his smoke. "We came from home, so we have no radios."

"Maybe you could break into a hardware store." Mick said. "Grab anything that's metal. Get shovels, hoes, flashlights, rakes, anything you can find."

Glenn was shorter and broader than Michael, his helmet small on a keg-sized head. His turnout coat barely fastened due to his considerable weight. "I think there's one up toward Vesey Street. I'll jog. You two guys be careful."

"Be as quick as you can," Mick said. "We'll start digging with our hands."

Glenn flicked his cigarette into some crushed concrete, hugged his buddy, Michael, and broke into more of a waddle than a slow jog. The path he followed was like a canyon-carving river, eroding its way through rises of rubble instead of rock.

Then, he slowly disappeared into the great white silence before them and faded like a ghost.

"Your buddy's not in the greatest shape. It might have been better if I had asked you to run for the tools," Mick said.

"He'll get there, alright. He's squat but strong," Michael said. "Let's get to work."

The two began clawing their way up the mountain of wreckage to the background sounds of small arms detonations. They'd find out later that those sounds originated in the Secret Service Bunker, and the punishing smoke was the result of different types of tear-gas bombs.

"Some Brothers are acting individually like vigilantes," Michael said. "I saw dozens of guys milling around piles of debris, unorganized, mostly at loose ends. Many aren't firefighters or even first responders. Some are civilians."

"It's great that everyone wants to help, but it sucks we have no radios." Mick said. "Everywhere you look, people are hurting. We'll have to wing it too. Let's just get to the top of the pile and see if we can do some good."

The two continued to scrape, scratch, and strain their way up stories of stench affianced to slow deaths and sickness. The shifting wreckage spread invisibly beneath the blistering pile, piercing the burnt soles of Mick's boots. With the surface wrinkling treacherously before him, Mick pointed to a dozen re-enforcement beams sitting atop each other.

"Look over there."

"Holy shit. Those reinforcement bars separated more than twelve stories of glass and concrete, yet they're touching each other?" Michael said. "Think about that man. If there are only seven or eight stories of debris spread out around this entire perimeter, the Trade Center was 110 stories tall. Where's the rest of the building?"

Mick looked up. The sun appeared dim, barely visible like an orange-colored piece of shaved ice trying to break through thick smog, which stunk like industrial waste.

"The pulverized concrete, glass, and lead powder have blocked the sun. It's like being trapped under an umbrella of poison. If you have a handkerchief, you might want to tie it around your nose and mouth, like me, otherwise you'd better use your T-shirt."

Michael paused, removed his turnout coat, stripped off his t-shirt, and covered his nose and mouth. He re-donned his gear and continued to climb. Both dodged pieces of hot smoking metal, and avoiding the inevitable crevices, finally crawled, plodded, and lurched to the top.

A mangled body covered by ash awaited them. Mick reached down and removed his glove to feel where he thought the carotid artery should be.

"It's too late for this one."

Michael's face went pale, his eyes almost empty of emotion, but his mouth was twisted in disgust.

"I can't believe you even bothered to check. Maybe we should drag what's left of it down the pile?"

"Are you kidding? Look how long it took us to get up here. Every second counts. If we get lucky and save one life, even just one, it'll be worth it. We have to find survivors. Remember our training, life first, always life."

"You're right, man. It's overwhelming. I can't think straight," Michael said.

"You can't think straight? I just tried to check the pulse of a crushed carcass."

Mick stopped, gasping for breath, his two palms grabbing his knees.

"The only way we'll find survivors is if they landed in a void. We'll dig around the sections where we see smoke escaping. No other places will have oxygen."

Mick and Michael riffed through the rubble surrounding a seeping plume of smoke. The more they dug, the more the smoke billowed in their faces. It was as yellow as rope and laced with a stench that reminded Mick of oily rags or burnt hair. His hand accidentally smacked metal, and he leapt back in pain.

"Aaahhhhhh, Jesus Christ." He removed his glove and kissed the burn.

"Careful man," Michael said. "Even with the gloves, those metal beams are hotter than hell."

"We'll be much better off when your pal gets here with the tools. You know what? Bang your flashlight on the metal. Maybe we'll hear someone banging back or someone yelling. At least we won't waste time. Every second counts."

"We should separate too," Michael said. "We'll be twice as effective."

"Good idea, man, but be careful."

The two patrolled the top of the heap for what seemed like hours. Wherever smoke seeped, both knelt and banged the metal. Mick looked skyward from his knees and saw that when the smoke shifted, it created a pocket of visibility. He watched the sun's slow descent behind the Manhattan skyline.

Suddenly, an ear-splitting air horn.

"Get off the pile, man. Run for your fucken life," Michael screamed.

Mick reacted and raced down the pile. Minutes later, a loud crack preceded a rumble, which gave birth to a bone-chilling roar. As the two huddled inside a store's doorway, Mick's heart thundered in his chest. The sound passed through his bones like the roar of a train in a tunnel. He put his mouth close to Michael's ear and yelled,

"What the fuck is going on?"

"The air horn signals evacuate. After the North Tower collapsed, I heard it loud and clear. I didn't know what it meant then, but I sure as hell do now."

With the crumpling of building seven, the sky turned a blizzard of white blotches. The dust drifted like a foul-smelling cloud over both of them.

"Good God. If all this snow-like shit is dust, concrete and glass, you'd better tighten that T-shirt around your mouth," Mick said.

"You're right, man. This can't be good."

Through the dust cloud, Michael squinted and saw a phantom emerging from the fog.

"Glenn. Is that you? We're over here in the doorway. Bring the tools and lights."

Glenn ran to the sound of Michael's voice. When he spoke, he sounded muffled, like he was underwater.

"Bad news, I have no tools. I ran into a Battalion Chief who swiped everything I had. He said they had possible survivors trapped on the block. He wasn't even going to let me leave until I told him that no one else was working this section."

"Let's get our asses back up there. We'll have to do the best we can," Michael said.

As they wandered from the doorway, a firefighter in a beat-up old turnout coat rushed past them. His hands were liver-spotted, grooved with blue veins, the skin on his bones as thin as toilet paper. A policeman ran toward him.

"Hold up old timer. After the last collapse, that pile won't be safe. Perimeter fires and secondary collapses are rampant. We don't want any more casualties."

The old firefighter's face grimaced and seemed to age decades in seconds.

"With all due respect officer, you'll have to shoot me to stop me. My kid's down here somewhere. I ain't waiting for shit."

Raking through the oatmeal-textured white blotches, the unmasked, ancient firefighter started a slow ascent up the pile with Mick, Michael, and Glenn hot on his heels. The old firefighter's hands trembled uncontrollably, his eyes dilated with shock, his gloved fingers stained in blood, yet he was the first of the four to top the pile and the first on his knees.

DAY TURNED TO night, leaving only a dull green glow over the gigantic graveyard. Corpselike and stark was the pile, the quiet crushing until other rescue workers finally arrived and began dragging corpses down to street level. Police converged on the scene with rescue dogs, E.M.S. and steelworkers began dotting the disaster.

Flashing lights from emergency vehicles cast blue, red, and white nets over the chaos and carnage. In the stark stillness, the searchlights glinted and gleamed, the reflections a bleak ruddiness off the distant skyscrapers, their electric glow turning Ground Zero the cold, dead color of dirty lead.

LABORED TO EXHAUSTION, the four firefighters descended the pile into what had become a grim black hive of activity. Hoses spidered in every direction. An exhausted Mick said to his three comrades, "Nice job, guys. We tried to do a little good, but it's hopeless, nothing but anguish everywhere."

The grizzled old firefighter looked at Mick for a long moment, eyes blinking like an injured insect, his jaws unshaved, his face a confused psychodrama.

"You're not packing it in, are you?"

"Of course not. I'm here for the duration, or until I collapse," Mick said. "But I can't stay here any longer. I need to try and find my company, and I made a promise to a woman that I can't break. I gotta go. Try and stay safe, Brothers."

Toting a shovel, a civilian had handed him, he shuffled through a brilliant square of artificial light, beaming a path to yet another mountain of misery. Mick dug for his cell phone and dialed Mrs. Callahan. All circuits busy . . . then he tried Erin's number, nothing. Despite the hopelessness, he was determined to search until he had news. If nothing came of it, at least he'd find some solace in knowing that he had did all he could.

FIFTY-FOUR

THE DAY AFTER the attacks, the Eastern sun came up clear, yellow, and hot. The heat made Ground Zero's atmosphere smell as if a dome of rotten offal was trapped under saran wrap. With his breath rank in his own nose, Mick felt numb inside and totally disconnected from anything real.

Lion-hearted rescue workers wept openly and unashamedly. Ironworkers cut metal beams allowing desperate, despondent packs to grope on their hands and knees for fragments of hope, an ear, a foot, or a finger with a wedding band. Wrecks of men, with sour smells rising from their clothes, meandered amidst the piles chanting, "Oh my God. Oh my God." Civilians were finding out what firefighters had known all along. Once you've smelled burnt flesh, you can never again believe that man is the highest order on earth.

Mick dug for his cell phone again and dialed Nora's number. All circuits busy, then Erin, again nothing. As time passed, he began to resemble the other rescue workers, weepy, weathered, worn. Looking for small voids, he waded sluggishly through the mountain ranges of rubble, ripples of heat dancing from their piles.

When he glimpsed the sole of a shoe, he riffled the shovel around the ruins and managed to get a purchase on the outer edge of a leg. Mick dropped the tool, fell to his knees, and began to sift with his gloved hands. He dug faster, his heart beating, his throat tingling with anticipation. When he had dug deep enough, the leg fell from the ruins as easily as a leaf off a tree, its skin colored death's gray.

Startled, but immune to shock by now, he laid it reverently atop the pile. Sad lines broke along his brow. Then his battered eyes finally recognized an object not completely pulverized. A small metal wheel from a computer chair had somehow escaped obliteration. He plucked it, holding it inches from his eyes, examining and admiring its resilience.

Propping his foot on the shovel's blade, resting his arm along its shaft, he stood to catch his breath. A thin red wafer of sun reflecting off a hole in the muddy sky blinded him. His squinting eyes suddenly saw a flicker of what appeared to be a shifting shadow hidden behind a crushed dust-encrusted E.M.S. wagon.

It couldn't be a survivor this remote from the rubble, could it, but maybe, just maybe, someone not buried had been overlooked and needed help?

He slid and rumbled down the mountain, running toward the motion. His strides lengthened; his mouth opened. Framed by a distant doorway was an injured firefighter who appeared to have just chiseled his way out of a crypt. As Mick got closer, the blood rushed to his head, and a broad grin broke across his face. He sprinted forward, knelt down, and threw his arms around his Brother.

"Patty. I can't believe it's you."

"Mick, thank God. You can't believe how long I've been screaming for help. I was beginning to think that I was invisible or that everyone had gone deaf."

"Thank, Christ, you're alive. How are the rest of the guys?"

"I don't know, Mick. We never made the site. As soon as we got here, the South Tower came down," Patty's words quickened now, the sides of his mouth caked with a white film, and his sentences without pauses quickly morphed into a rant.

"A tidal wave of girders, and debris lifted me. My muscles collapsed. I felt weightless. When I landed, it slammed me against a car. My ears buzzed, then I slipped in and out of consciousness."

He took the palm of his right hand and swiped sweat and filth off his forehead.

"I awoke a couple of times throughout the night and screamed for hours, but nobody heard me. I watched the sun come up this morning but gave up yelling. I think my legs are broke. I can't move them."

"Hang on, man. I'll be right back."

Mick slogged to a parked ambulance where rescue workers were loading yet another corpse.

"You guys come quick, and bring a stretcher. We have a firefighter hurt. I think both his legs are broken."

The Paramedic turned to his partner.

"Before we move him to the bus, we'll have to stabilize his legs."

His partner grabbed a stretcher and splints, and the three scuttled the distance back to Patty

"CAN YOU WIGGGLE your toes?" The Paramedic asked as he knelt and started to work.

"I can't move my legs at all," Patty said.

"Is there anything you can tell me, Patty?" Mick asked. "Anything at all that you know about the other guys?"

Patty's voice became weaker. The light in his eyes dimmed. His chest swelled, and his breaths slowed.

"I don't even know how long I was unconscious. When I woke up, it was quiet and eerie," he sobbed. "I couldn't think. My heart raced. I felt the veins constricting in my brain as if someone was tightening a machinist's vise into my skull. I think that I fell asleep again or passed out from the pain . . . I don't know . . ."

"Hang on, man," Mick said. "You're gonna be okay. Just hang on."

Patty rambled on, speaking fast, and incoherently with the shocked hollow eyes of a holocaust victim.

"Next thing I know it was pitch black. Everything was covered with white ash. Nothing was moving, not a sound to be heard." His eyes got empty and wide. "For those first few moments. I swear Mick. I thought I woke up on the moon."

"You're going to be all right. You're one of the lucky ones. What about the engine company? Did they make the Trade Center before the second building came down?"

"I don't know what happened to the guys in the engine . . . Wait . . . What . . . The other building came down too? Both buildings collapsed?"

His eyes grew dull and gloomy, the whites specked with blood. Patty bit his lip. Tears rolled down his face.

"Are you fucken kidding? Oh my God, how many Brothers did we lose?"

"Don't worry about what you can't control, man. Take it easy. Pull yourself together. I'll find out where they're taking you, and when I know how everybody is, I'll fill you in. I'm going to try and find the rest of the company. I know this is a stupid question, but I'm desperate. You didn't see Erin Callahan, did you?"

"Erin? Oh man, I'm so sorry. I didn't see shit." Patty was hysterical, repeating himself, "Oh, my God, Oh, my God, I'll say a prayer. That's the only thing that can help any of us now, Mick. Oh, my God."

If Mick would have had the leisure time to reflect, he might have come to the conclusion that enough carnage had already been done in this hellhole by this vengeful God, or Allah, or Yahweh, or whatever myopic, ignorant men were calling him nowadays. Mick didn't have that luxury. Instead, he eyed the caked, black blood on Patty's legs before turning to the Paramedics.

"Do me a favor guys. Treat him like your brother. That's how he'd treat you." He stared at Patty and then at the medics. "Where are you taking him?"

"All the N.Y. hospitals are overflowing. Battery Park is a few blocks away. From there, he'll be ferried to a New Jersey hospital. It's quicker."

Unbeknownst to the medic, the nearest hospital to the disaster, St Vincent's, had plenty of doctors and nurses ready for patients. New York emergency rooms weren't crowded because most first responders were beyond injuries and sadly beyond help.

THROUGHOUT THE DAY, Mick robotically asked other firefighters about his company with the same results, everywhere vacuous stares and misery. Mick tried Nora's phone again, all circuits busy. Then Erin's again, nothing.

Atop yet another pile, firefighters were digging with garden hoes, rakes or hands, anything that could make a difference. They filled five-gallon buckets with debris and dust before passing them hand-to-hand down mounds of wreckage to those below sifting them for body parts. Once thoroughly examined, they dumped the remains into awaiting trucks.

Mick mechanically began to pass buckets at the back of a line. Intermittently, tired workers at the top left the pile while others down the chain relieved them. As he neared the apex, a firefighter shouted, "I've found something. Bring up a police dog."

With his master towing in his wake, a German Sheppard hurtled to the top of the pile. Two hapless victims had desperately hugged before they had dissolved into pillars of dust. The dog sniffed their entwined garments, his speechless handler dumbfounded.

A firefighter carefully wrapped the two coats in twin black-plastic bags, his eyes the color of egg white. From there, grim-faced rescue workers acting as pallbearers reverently shuttled the remains down the pile amid a brief silence as heads were bowed and prayers said. Mick's mind had to shut down a few moments to deny what his eyes were seeing. There were dead people in those bags but no bodies.

The air had turned dark and sour with a blizzard of office paper and white chalky dust. A broad backed firefighter above Mick collapsed to his hands and knees, shaking and hacking, emptying black phlegm from the bowels of his lungs. Pride replaced the red balloon of anger blossoming in Mick's chest as he clawed the few yards toward him.

Alongside the heaving firefighter, an ironworker knelt drained of color or movement, his ridged frame stripped to the waist, his back muscles taut like coiled rope. A bull pin hung from his hand. Beneath his red safety helmet, a leather tool belt hugged his waist, and below it, the contents of his belly finally worked their way up into his throat. He wrenched his head from the wild malignant odor and spewed vomit.

The course stench of fabrics soaked with decay and jet fuel pushing from the pile spread, and then this choking combination of sweet and putrid smells made everything worse, like meat and fruit rotting for days in the same barrel. But the important message Mick would learn that day, and would never forget, was that the real gladiators of the world are humble in origin and demeanor; so unremarkable in appearance that if we bumped into them in a crowd, we would never dream how brightly their souls burn.

These brave men and women fought death to a standstill, long after hope was gone, grinning through their bitter anguish, fighting without let or lease, suffering, stumbling, straining, striving, struggling on, until the night brought with it hours of hopelessness, numb, brutal, and endlessly long.

Losing track of time, Mick soldiered on tirelessly until he finally slid down the steep incline, perspiring, and breathing harder than he cared to admit, continuing his search for Erin and the Brothers. He stumbled into the night, weary, waiting, and fighting back the shadows.

FIFTY-FIVE

NO MATTER WHAT, every person on earth plays a central part in the history of the world, and normally they don't even know it. But here, right in front of him was an opportunity to make a difference and to actually see and feel that difference. After all, that was what his vocation was supposed to be about.

But now was not the time for such grandiose thoughts. He had heard that the emergency workers had set up a temporary morgue near the Century 21 building. His brain buzzed as if his head were a puddle of water with an electrical wire running through it.

Maybe Erin was there?

MORGUES NORMALLY DENY all the colors one's mind associates with death. The surfaces are cool, structured of stainless steel and aluminum, and made even more sterile in appearance by the dull reflection of the fluorescent lighting overhead. The troughs and the drains where autopsies are conducted are spotless.

The makeshift morgue draped by the shadow of the Century 21 building was nothing like that.

It was like walking through a colony of stroke victims, cold, stunned eyes everywhere. Some personnel wore white lab coats while weaving through viscous corpses oozing puss and blood. Unidentified, incinerated carcasses received Extreme Unction from priests walking among the carnage. Mick started to feel that he'd rather Erin stay missing than find her and his unborn child here.

Among the hoards of rescue workers, nurses, and clergy, he spied a familiar face. Father Moriority was administering last rites. The priest kept brushing his runny nose with the back of his wrist as Mick trotted towards him.

"Father, father, have you seen Erin Callahan?"

A plump, redheaded Irish nurse overheard, turned her head, and froze.

"Erin Callahan?" The priest yelled over a din of frantic voices. "I've been here sixteen hours. Body parts are everywhere." His sad, soapy eyes seemed mindless, devoid of reason, and didn't match his efficiency. "No one has any idea who, or where, anyone is. I barely recognized you."

"I've got a terrible story, Father," Mick said.

"Today, they're all terrible," said the priest. "How many are dead? How many more will be brought in? Who knows? It's catastrophic."

Kettledrums pounded inside Mick's head. His spine bowed, his muscles so flaccid that he felt like all his bones had been surgically removed from his body.

"I've been such a fool, such a bloody fool. If only I hadn't acted like a prideful jackass in that hospital, Erin wouldn't have been down here. What the hell have I done?"

"Calm down, my son. Gather yourself together."

Spiritual exhaustion ate like acid through every tissue in Mick's body. He felt enormous remorse and was drowning in a bottomless, irrevocable sense of loss that he had never before experienced, not even after Eileen's or his mother's death.

"You don't understand, Father. The last thing I told Erin was that I couldn't stand the sight of her."

"We all say things in anger that we don't mean."

Regret bent Mick's body.

"I told Mrs. Callahan that I would do all I could. If only I knew Erin was alive, I'd do anything, anything to find her, anything to help her, anything to be forgiven, anything."

The Irish nurse grabbed his shoulder.

"Ya don't mean Erin Callahan the fiddle player? 'Tis that who you're talking about?"

"Oh my God. You know her?" Mick asked.

"I saw her down here this morning. I thought that was who ya were talking about. Ah, sure, she's all right, but I wouldn't say the same for the poor feller that she was combing the morgue for."

"You saw her? You're sure?"

"Erin Callahan, the fiddle player from Yonkers? My parents know her parents, Nora and Brendan," the nurse said. "She was here. I tell ya. Sure, don't I know her well?"

A huge shuddering breath rocked Mick to his knees. He buried his head in his filthy gloves and wept.

FIFTY-SIX

DOCTORS, NURSES, AND medics scurried through the temporary morgue trying desperately to restore order and sanity amid colossal chaos and confusion. Among the corpses, a Jewish Rabbi stood next to Mick, chanting prayers and fighting back tears.

Standing there, Mick's mind flashed to the Twin Tower's structural-steel cross standing tall as a sad, and heartbreaking monument to the sea of hopelessness surrounding it, then his thoughts turned back to the miniature cross that the Mexican mechanic had pulled out of his tire, and then the ceramic cross that Dang had given him as a gift, and then . . . and then he recalled his mother's voice.

"In everyone's life, a time comes when they need God."

In his heart, he knew that if ever there were a time for prayer that time had come. The time for false pride was over. Erin was alive, and no matter what happened next, he wouldn't have to live with the terrible guilt that he was responsible for her death.

Mick dropped to his knees, but despite all his childhood indoctrination, his lips went numb. Nothing came out of his mouth. He lifted his head.

"Rabbi, it's been so long since I prayed, I'm not sure I even remember how. I just want to thank Him . . . to thank the Lord."

"Just say what's in your heart, my son. He'll hear you."

The Rabbi watched the weeping man before him make the sign of the cross, bow his head, and silently mouth a plea for forgiveness. Mick prayed and prayed, and while he did, he thought about his late wife and remembered all the things that a woman could mean to a man.

After Eileen died, he viewed women as legs, breasts, and sexual objects, things to get excited about. Now he realized that Erin had been so much more than that. She had been someone whom he could lean on, someone he could count on, someone unique who eclipsed even his beloved Eileen. Mick shook and started to sob, realizing the magnitude of what he had lost when he lost Erin.

And at that singular moment, his long-held fear of sobriety, indeed of maturity, finally disappeared. Mick closed his eyes in total surrender and rested his hopes and dreams on the tender mercy of whatever higher power would lift him above his fears and foolishness and carry him to a height that he had never been before. A place that was devoid of the confusion, self-indulgence, and chaos that had driven him all his life.

A feeling of euphoria swept over him. A feeling not unlike the one that he had after he rescued that baby, not unlike the charged feeling he got with a morning eye-opener, or a large bet, only stronger, more visceral, as if the universe had shoved a live wire through his chest.

And then, he had an epiphany, an instance of pristine clarity. He knew at last that the gambling, women, drugs, and drinking were just substitutes, just things that he had used to help fill the great emptiness inside him. He realized at that moment that there had to be more to life than self-indulgence. How had Erin put it?

"You must feed your soul."

HE DIDN'T KNOW how long he had knelt there or did he recall rising from his knees. He did know that his skin burned like acid, and that he couldn't draw enough air into his lungs, and that every joint felt as if he were eighty years old. He had never been so totally drained.

And then a strange thing happened.

The horses in his head finally galloped off into the distance and left him spent, empty-headed, and grateful for the peace and for whatever spiritual magic had driven them away. But with that peace came resolution. Mick also knew that somewhere in that massive graveyard of steel and concrete were his Brothers, and he wasn't doing them any good by crying on his knees like a wimp.

AFTER ANOTHER ABOMINABLE night, the sunrise cast its merciful light on an anthill of activity. From cities across the world, volunteer firefighters, emergency workers, frenzied relief organizations, and civilians dotted the site. Even wealthy dowagers swaddled in mink passed out sandwiches.

A battered Mick rambled down an incline of debris and held the back of his wrist to his mouth trying to block the bilious surge from his stomach. He'd finally had enough and could take no more. His limit reached, he just started wandering uptown, zombie-like, dazed. When he reached the site's perimeter, a policeman noticed his blank stare and rolled down his window.

"Hey, pal. Where are you heading? Are you all right?"

"Huh? Me? Oh yeah, I'm fine, just fucking great," Mick said. "Where am I heading? I don't know. I haven't thought about it. I need sleep. The Bronx, I guess."

Mick's face was pallid and one-dimensional, as bland and expressionless as a slice of packaged bread. The cop gave his partner a concerned look and said, "You better jump in the back seat. We'll take you up to the Bronx. What company are you with?"

Mick stumbled into the police car and muttered, "Take me to 46-Truck, I guess. It's right off the Major Deegan."

The policeman fishtailed his car toward the West Side highway and flipped on his siren. As the sedan raced uptown, Mick sat and stared out the window exhausted. With Ground Zero in his rearview mirror, everything gray suddenly died. The sky became as white and finely grained as polished enamel, as though all color had been bled from the air. In Mick's mind's eye, the road seemed bright with light and as shiny as tinfoil.

He sat in the patrol car's back seat, beaten, but alive and full sure that he wouldn't ever want to speak about what he had witnessed the last few days. The sickening memories caused a sensation in the lining of his stomach that was like a flame punching a hole in a sheet of paper and spreading outward, slowly blackening everything it touched.

And then another odd sensation replaced that melancholy, and his face changed to a look of perfect peace. For the first time in his life, he had the queerest feeling that his head was made of gas, and he would have been simply delighted if all his earthly appendages would just leave him and float away.

AFTER DUSK, WHEN all that was left of the sun was an orange smudge, rooftops as far away as Yonkers were flecked with soot and grit. Nora Callahan sat on her front porch and tried her cell phone again. Her husband wiped a smudge of gray ash from her arm as she heard the same endless refrain, all circuits busy.

"No, no matter how many times I try Mullan's cell. It's no good. I never liked him, but fair play to him. In our moment of need, he showed his true colors," Nora said. "I pray that he's safe. Besides, Erin has been through enough. She has been mad with worry about Jamie. Didn't she spent hours down at that hellhole looking for him?"

At the sound of her voice, Brendan turned from where he had been silently mesmerized by the fall leaves scudding across his side yard, his eyes serious, intense.

"She's only alive because she missed that train by a few minutes. All these years, it nearly drove me to drink that she couldn't tell a timepiece from a textbook, but now, I thank God for it."

"Once that sleeping pill wears off, she'll be inconsolable again," Nora said. "If we could find out something definite about Jamie, at least she'd have something. I'm sorry now that I ever told her that I had called that Mullan. It only seemed to make her worse."

Nora set the cell phone beside her on the step and faced her husband.

"I don't think she'll ever get over Jamie's death."

"Sure, what are you talking about, woman? She'll have to get over it. Dying is as much a part of life as living."

'But she's not made of stone, Brendan. Jamie was her soul mate."

"Soul mate, me ass. Did you ever think that maybe you liked Jamie more than she did? The dead are gone. We'll say prayers for them and move on, but it's the survivors we should be praying for. Not everyone who lost their life down there died. A man doesn't have to stop breathing to be a casualty. Life, limbs, and health are not the only things that a man stands to lose. The survivors of this disaster will suffer almost as badly as the casualties. Not everyone who comes back from there will ever leave."

Nora, startled by her husband's insight, looked as if she were seeing him for the first time.

"You're right, Brendan. We must pray for the living. I'm sure that there will be unimaginable sicknesses and deaths to come out of all this before it's over, and we must pray for our adopted country as well. America's not the same nation that we came to. I think America is now part of the world in a way in which it never has been before. As our own Yeats once said, 'everything has changed, changed utterly.'"

FIFTY-SEVEN

THE BLOCKADES CAME quickly with straight-up military checkpoints at 14th Street.

To get to lower Manhattan, you had to pass through National Guardsmen and regular infantry stationed with machine guns at Canal Street and Houston.

Between collecting body parts and the tagging of victims, the weeks passed quickly, the burials so constant that the FDNY ran out of bagpipers to honor their fallen. Any romance Mick had with firefighting fell away like slow cooked pork from a bone, but his respect for the Brothers increased everyday.

IN EARLY OCTOBER, the weather turned cold and bleak. The afternoon wind was so strong that it slapped the firehouse flag's eyehooks, beating a steady patter against the metal pole they hung on. Mick entered the dayroom wearing black, pleated slacks, a button-down blue shirt, and a dark brown leather jacket. Mutt put down his newspaper and fingered a slow staccato on the arm of his chair.

"What are you doing here? I figured you'd be down at the dig."

"I was there three straight days, one day of sleep, and then back again for another three. I have to go out to Nobody's, and take care of a few things. Besides, I won't lie to you. I need a break from the stink of bloated corpses."

Mick plopped into a chair, and Mutt said, "I thought nothing could smell as bad as burnt flesh, but now the decomposed bodies have made even that sickening stench a bargain. Any body parts that weren't crisped smell like rancid, raw chicken. We're scheduled to go back down tomorrow. The dispatchers widened company response districts so guys can work the dig. I'm putting Vicks under my nose. I can't take that fucken stink anymore."

"You can't take it?" Mick said. "The smell's so bad I tried to associate it with anything that I had ever smelled before. Nothing was even close."

"I woke up sweating the last couple of nights. I got insomnia bad. Listen to this shit, Mick. Last night, I had a nightmare where I saw yellow and gray smoke rising from human hair, fingernails curling and snapping, dead eyes popping open in the heat. I'm telling ya, a regular fucken nightmare. I woke up soaking wet."

"I'm the complete opposite, man. I sleep six hours straight but never get a minute's rest. How are the other guys holding up?"

"Pretty good, considering. Most of our guys never made the building. When they heard the roar of the collapse, they dove under an abandoned fire truck. The only one unaccounted for was Patty D, but thank God, he's gonna be alright."

"Did Patty tell you that I was the one who found him?"

"No," Mutt said. "Pete told me."

"I can't believe fucken Thoe is gone, man. You know, I was drinking with Paul in some remote bar up by West Point about a year ago. You know how he was. Everybody fucken knew him," Mick smiled. "Well, we walk in, and there's two guys sitting there. They both say, 'Send Thoe a drink,' like he walks in there every fucken day."

Mick grabbed Mutt's Daily News and turned it to the second page, which was filled with stark pictures of Ground Zero.

"So, I said to Thoe, 'You ever been in this joint before?' He said, 'no.' I said, 'Ya prick, when you die, they're gonna have to bury your ass in Yankee Stadium. Everybody in the world knows ya.'"

Mick closed the paper and stared directly into Mutt's eyes.

"You know what he said, Mutt?"

"What?"

"He said, 'When I die, I hope they bury me in a phone booth. I wanna outlive every one of those sonofabitches,' and then he started laughing. Can you imagine? Who the hell knew that he'd buy the farm less than a year later in lower Manhattan? Ya never fucken know, man. Ya just never fucken know."

Mutt shook his head in sadness.

"Some Manhattan companies lost everybody," Mutt's voice cracked, as if he were swallowing broken glass. "Of course, everybody's sick about Kingsley."

Mick's eyes watered then went blank as if he didn't want the Mutt to read his thoughts. He torched a Marlboro and waited a long time before he spoke.

"That was supposed to be me down there. Kingsley needed a Saturday off, so he was paying me back on 9/11. What a thing to have to live with, and he has kids. I feel so fucken bad, man."

"Luck of the draw, Mick. You can't beat yourself up."

"I know, man, but logic ain't chasing away the guilt."

Mick took a long drag before he spoke again.

"It's surreal down there. Isn't it? It's like a butcher shop in hell. You can order any body part you want."

"But so many good people are there too," Mutt said. "Sometimes, despite it all, for just a few minutes, against all odds, you sorta feel that everything's gonna be okay. But that feeling leaves ya fast when you stumble on another roast, then I start wondering if maybe nothing's ever gonna be okay again."

Mick took another drag, tilted his head, and watched the smoke drift into the fluorescent lights before whispering, "I heard Thoe went back in."

"He was out, Mick. He was safe. He was working with 43 Truck. Paul ran back in to search the stairwells."

"Fucking Thoe was a great dude, man," Mick said. "That really sucks. I loved that fucking guy and Kingsley too. Some guys are ranting about turning the Middle East into a parking lot. I know they're pissed, but they got it wrong. Not all Muslims are bad. Did you know that Kingsley was a Muslim?"

"Kingsley a Muslim, no shit? He never said anything. Ironic that one of the guys who didn't make it was a Muslim." Mutt looked up inquisitively. "I bet you never knew that Thoe was gay."

"What? Fuck you. Who told you that?"

"Pete told me. He knew it all this time."

"He never said shit to me."

Mutt turned the paper around, glancing at it absentmindedly before tossing it aside and raising his head.

"You know Pete. Why would he? Does it really matter?"

"I guess none of it really matters," Mick said. "Who gives a fuck? Thoe was a hero and my friend. I don't think any less of him. No wonder I never saw him with a chick. At least he was single. How are Kingsley's wife and kids taking it?"

"I saw his wife, inconsolable," Mutt's grim eyes glanced downward. He waited a few moments and said, "Hey, I get off in an hour. You want to do something, go somewhere, just talk, hangout?"

"Nah, I can't. I'm glad you're sitting, because, ya ready for this? I have an appointment tonight with Father Moriority."

"Get the fuck out of here," he laughed. "Ain't that the priest you hate?"

"Yeah, just one other thing that I was wrong about. I ran

into him down at the site. He's not a bad dude. The clergy did a lot of good down there dosing out hope and comfort. You heard about how Father Judge died?"

"Yeah, they called it 'blunt force trauma to the head.' Whatta remarkable man and he died doing what he loved."

"Unreal, right? He removed his helmet and was down on one knee administering last rites. Command told him to get out, but he wouldn't leave the lobby." Mick stood and slid the chair under the table. "I always respected him. Atheist or not, only an animal wouldn't love Father Mychal, a selfless, heroic, holy man if there ever was one. But I gotta split, man. I have to meet Moriority at seven. He said he'd give me a general confession."

"He'll get an earful," Mutt smiled but then his lips stiffened. "Hey man, I heard about your friend, Jamie."

"You know how long I knew him, Joe? Since we were kids. We were so small that we weren't even allowed to cross the street to play with each other. I remember asking grownups to cross us. His death will be even tougher on my ex-girlfriend. Those two were getting married."

"It's remarkable, how missing a train saved her life. I'm hearing story after story like that. If it weren't for this, or if it weren't for that, something as simple as a guy deciding to stop to buy bagels, you never know, man . . . Have you spoken to her?"

"No way, I sank that ship but good. She's grieving Jamie's death, and I'm probably the last fucken guy she wants to hear from. Besides, it would take a real lowlife to weasel in after his friend's death. If she wants to reach me, she knows my number."

Mick took the butt from his mouth and squeezed it into a saucer on the table.

"I always said life was short; 9/11 proved that. But I was dead wrong about how we should live our lives. I opted for pure hedonism, no responsibility, laughs galore. I forgot why I joined the department to begin with. Life is about leaving the world a better place. That's a legacy worth striving for."

He turned wistful.

"When I first met Erin, I remember her saying something about how I'd drown my soul. She was right. When we waste time, eternity weeps. I'm done with the drugs and booze. I'm following Kingsley's advice, Lord have mercy on him. I'm gonna make myself a better person one day at a time."

FIFTY-EIGHT

THE INSIDE OF St. Philip's was cool and dark, and smelled of old stone, burning candles, and incense. He sat in a pew under the sixth station of the cross. As a child, he had lined up with other school children in maroon blazers to stop and pray submissively at all fourteen.

Mick lumbered into Father Moriority's confessional and waited for the priest to slide back the small wooden door in the partition. He had known the man over two decades, holding both him and his boss in contempt, yet here he was seeking forgiveness from both.

When the tiny door slid open, he looked through the wire screen and focused on the priest's glasses through the sideways silhouette. Moriority had a small bladed fan in the box with him, his head square, his shoulders wide, his black wavy hair moving slightly to its breeze.

He had asked for a general confession, so the priest went up and down the commandments, and Mick whispered yes to most of them. The priest made it quick and painless, no lectures. He knelt afterwards in a pew near the altar to say penance.

ERIN WAS KNEELING quietly in the back of the church

by the entrance. She watched Mick a few moments, then rose, blessed herself, and walked the few steps to the door. Once outside, she hesitated, thought for one more moment, then turned and re-entered the oak-stained wooden doors. She marched defiantly down the aisle. Her pulse fluttering more in her throat with each torturous step and finally eased into the pew beside him.

"Well, here I am," she said casually. "I'm back." She wore a plain black dress under a long tan cashmere coat. A white kerchief covered her hair.

Mick lifted his head in disbelief.

"You're back? What the fuck does that mean? Just like that?"

"Just like that."

He ignored her, burying his head in his hands, staring through his fingers at the tops of his shoes.

"In my heart . . . I never left," she said hopefully.

Mick lifted his head slowly.

"I got drunk. I fucked up. I'm not making excuses, but I would've told you. You never gave me the chance. You were supposed to be my soul mate. Instead, you dumped me and started screwing one of my best friends. Now, you stroll in here pregnant and act like nothing ever happened. Like, I'm just supposed to just forgive and forget?"

"Yes. I guess so," she hoarsed. "Yes," her eyes wet, round and unblinking.

His throat was as dry and thick as rust. A pain in the pit of his stomach swelled. He shook his head back and forth and finally broke down again. His hand shook when he seized the back of her neck.

"Thank, fucken God."

He rested his forehead on hers and shuttered.

"At the morgue, that was when everything changed. When the Irish nurse told me that she had seen you looking for Jamie,

I dropped to my knees and thanked God."

She rolled her wet green eyes

"LOOKING FOR JAMIE?"

"Yeah, the nurse told me that you were looking for a man."

"God forgive me. I'm in love with a fool," she said softly, shaking her head in disbelief. "Mick, I wasn't looking for Jamie. I was looking for you."

"For me, oh my God? I was wrong about so many things, baby, so, so many things. I gave up on God before I had ever had anything really heavy on my soul, and this confession business . . . well, it was just a pain in the ass. But when I left that booth just now, I felt a comfort that I haven't felt since I was a child."

He lost himself in her eyes.

"I'll handle sobriety. I'll have to. I don't know if I can handle Catholicism, but I guess one conduit is as good as another. What really matters is what's in our hearts. We all have to believe in something. We all need to lean on something, sometime, whether it's God, A.A., cosmic energy, or whatever. Too many things have happened to me to believe in coincidences."

He turned from her eyes and ran his right hand through the center of his hair, fingers curling, touching the heel of his hand. His stomach felt like a stone had dropped into his chest and rustled to the bottom.

"All I ever wanted to do was live life to the fullest. I thought the only person I was hurting was myself. I drank to kill my demons and created more."

He grabbed her hips gently and pulled her body closer, his eyes inches from hers.

"I fell in love with you because I thought I deserved someone special. You fell in love with me for the same reason. If 9/11 taught us anything, it was the value of life. I don't want to waste a minute more of it." He melted into her eyes. "I've quit drinking, and this time for good. That man you thought I could be? Marry me, and I'll try to become the father that I always wanted my father to be. I'll never be a pure man, but with your help, I'll damn sure try to be a good one."

FIFTY-NINE

THAT TUESDAY MORNING was cold, raw, and windy, more like December than October. Pete held a cup of coffee and sat across from Mutt in the firehouse dayroom.

"I'm so happy for those two. Erin's a great girl. I'm glad that they're getting married." Pete sipped from the cup's brim. "So many people end up unhappy because they can't learn to forgive. Of all the deadly sins, pride has to be the worst. Erin's got a lot of it, but Mick has even more. No excuse for pride, totally cerebral."

He reached for a bagel and sliced it. "But those two were destined to be together. The Chinese have a word for it, Yuan fen—a relationship by fate or destiny. Think about it? What the hell were the odds of her being in St. Philip's the same night that Mick was going to confession? Talk about coincidences."

"Hey Pete. How old are you?" Mutt laughed.

"Forty-one. Why?"

As Pete wondered what the Mutt-man was up to, he noticed a spark kindling behind his eyes, and waited for the inevitable punch line. Joe reached for his cell phone, fingered it a few moments, and then held it up for Pete to see. The phone's screen read Erin Callahan, her number clear and blue below it.

"Forty-one-years old and you still believe in coincidences?" Joe grinned. "Sometimes providence needs a little push, even from a Mutt like me."

EPILOGUE

PETE AND MICK didn't know it then, but Mutt would die soon. When the cancer finally strangled his inimitable laugh, his last words to Mick were, "Remember how," face drawn and thin, his voice straining to be heard, "I used to break the Chief's balls?"

Mick told Mutt there might be a book.

"Do you want me to change your name?"

"Don't you dare change my name," he whispered hoarsely, his gaze defiant. "I'm Da Mutt. There was only one Mutt."

Truer words were never spoken.

This book is dedicated to all the victims of 9/11.

To Joe Da Mutt, and the over 1100 rescue workers who have died since, and to the thousands more still battling life threatening illnesses.

I pray that God treats the Brothers in heaven half as well as the Brothers treated me here on earth.

- Billy O'Connor

CPSIA information can be obtained
at www.ICGtesting.com
Printed in the USA
BVHW032153141219
566703BV00001B/39/P